I0567266

Georgina M Donovan books

Reads Like Murder series
READS LIKE MURDER IN HONOLULU

Dragonshire Wizard series
DRAGONSHIRE WIZARDS OF THE WARRIOR
BOND

**

Thanks to my families and friends who have supported my dream of spinning tales and publishing them for others to appreciate. I could not have done it without you! Especially DD, my patron, and BH, who believed in me enough to push me onto the path of novels. Thanks to DM, LM and MM and KDM for your help! Thanks Jan Jenkins for your tireless and talented polishing to make me look my best in print. Thanks TH for your input.

Front cover by Sterling O'Toole
Back cover photo by Devon D Martin

Dedicated to
Walt Disney
My hero
Who understood
the value of imagination
and made our world better
because of his vision

Dragonshire Wizard Universe

Dragonshire – dominant dimension and hub of all other realms, including Earth

Merlin – ancient wizard from the Dragonshire

Majiq – hereditary power held by Sorcerers originating from Dragonshire

Crystal Potency – channeling of Majiq through mystical gemstones

Ayelsborne – Capitol province of Dragonshire

Ameden – province/race of those who have the Majiq of fore-tell or fore-knowledge

Gadion-Obscura – Evil cabal of shadow Sorcerers set on dominating all Realms

Diaboliq – assassin Sorcerers – members of Gadion-Obscura

Dark Majiq – power obtained through elixirs and spells, not heredity

Avelon – mystic island of refuge for Wizards, home to Merlin's Castle. Similar to, but slightly different, than the original island of Avalon

Amulet and touch-stone – tools used by Wizards to channel crystal energy

Wand – can focus Majiq

Priest, Templar, Paladin – Maji of the Merlin Order

Mentor, Tutor – Teachers/partners of young learners

Novitiate, Tyro – New Maji scholars under the schooling of a Tutor

Earth realms
Spania
Britania
Avelon
Ionia
Karpatia

Dragonshire realms
Dragonshire
Ayelsborne
Amed – north of Dragonshire

DRAGONSHIRE

WIZARDS

OF THE

WARRIOR

BOND

by
Georgina M Donovan

PART ONE
THE NEW BEGINNING

The soprano chirping caught Soren Rune's attention. His mind, even quicker than his Majiq skills, analyzed the possibilities before he canted his head in the direction of the interruption.

Yes, there on the marketplace table a few stalls down from him swung a monkey. The tawny, four-legged little creature was scrawny and small, but its long, ringed tail twitched deliberately. His rounded ears were perched above a bug-eyed head and he paused in mid-stride to look directly at Rune. Eye contact briefly established, the monkey warily returned to his business, which was to scamper under the selling tables of the food merchant just down the lane.

Instinctive habit prompted Rune's hand to rub the dragon crystal amulet around his neck. Knowing it was his anticipatory call to action; he dropped his hand and focused on his senses. He did not need his touch-stone of Majiq to determine a threat; he only needed the powers inherent in his role as a Sorcerer.

As an accomplished Wizard, Rune was adept at sensing Majiq in all aspects, including animal awareness. While he could not communicate with many non-sentient creatures, he could perceive their attitudes and emotions; wariness, friendliness, and aggressiveness.

Quickly running down his knowledge of the monkey species, he confirmed what his intuitions alerted him to moments before. The diminutive animals were found in the wild on several temperate climate provinces in the Earth's kingdoms, but in this arid region of Spania, there were no such indigenous primates. The clime was too hot and dry. So, the little scamp was a domestic pet smuggled into the province . . . possibly by some child?

The chirping of the monkey continued as a subtle background noise during Rune's shopping. Sipping his morning brew as he browsed, he slowed at the hut selling clothing and travel bags. His sense of some sinister presence made him stop. Reaching out with his awareness, he tuned into the details of everything around him. It was the monkey that was the crux of this suddenly mysterious aura.

Utilizing the reflective surface of a hanging necklace, Rune watched the monkey scramble up and steal a melon from the food merchant. The proprietor, a big woman who was helping a customer load fruit into a cart, never noticed the theft. The monkey scurried away to a tall man in a purple robe.

Maderia. A lanky, gangly clan, the elongated heads and dark, almost magenta-hued skin covering a towering, wiry skeletal frame made them distinct. Known to be a race of dangerous tribesmen, they drifted between legal and illegal habits in a narrow corridor of questionable ethical practices. Their origins were believed to be rooted somewhere near the exotic isles of the West Indies, in the unexplored seas where some claimed there be dragons. If only the general populous knew the truth about the mystical flying beasts!

Majiq-sage prickled a warning subliminally along the edges of Rune's nerves. His personal alert signal – the light hairs on his arms – swept upright. Rumors spoke of a Wizard being murdered days ago. That ominous news, accompanied by an inexplicable feeling of depressed spirits, confirmed that the grim reports must be true. Not a time to be incautious.

In a flash his right arm snapped out straight. In less than the blink of an eye, blue-mercury metaphysical energy glowed on his dragon crystal amulet, then to a matching gem on the dragon ring on his right fore-finger. As if the energy had suddenly transformed to a sizzling, glittering blade, brilliance ignited along his skin. Summoned through Majiq, the amulet swiveled like a divining rod to sweep the marketplace in search of a target. Tangential, divergent energy sparked the air and set a silvery shine on everything around Rune.

Majiq locked on a direction with instinct rather than thought, shooting out a glowing beam around and behind his body an instant before a lethal, twin-pronged knife sang toward him. Rune then spun, neatly countering the second barrage of two daggers winging straight at his chest. Zing, pop! The deadly weapons vaporized in the aurora of glittering Majiq enchantment.

Before another heartbeat, Rune raced the distance of the dusty marketplace, closing in a Majiq-energized run that was more of a zipping slide/transport. Within another eye-blink he was upon the threatening Maderia. The foreigner stood frozen after wielding the multi-blades. As if to underscore his guilty accomplice, the monkey screamed its soprano cry before flying away from his master to land on the tent top of a fruit seller's stall.

Spinning on his heels at the last possible second, the Maderia dove into an alley. The maneuver fooled Rune and he slowed to make the swerve. He was in no mood for a chase, but the vile attacker could not be allowed to go free! This miscreant had assailed him! No foe was going to get away with that! The ultra-long legs carried the creature quickly toward the end of the marketplace. With too many twists and angles in the alley to use his zip-speed, Rune utilized his enhanced charm/energy on the run to leap onto a water barrel, then a crate, and then dangled atop an awning. Sliding across the stiff material he pushed off with his feet, somersaulted over the edge and landed facing the enemy with few centimeters to spare.

Shocked, the antagonist skidded to a stop, crying out in surprise. His thin arm reached for a weapon under his flowing, striped shirt, but never connected with the object. Rune used his still-energized hand as a blunt instrument and smacked the tribesman on the forehead who, dazed, folded to his knees in the dirt.

Without sympathy, Rune dragged him to a recessed doorway which concealed them from prying eyes and offered protection at his back. Roughly pressing the man's forehead with the palm of his hand, he summoned Majiq power to shock the prone Maderia. On the dark, vaguely iridescent skin, a drop of blood oozed from under the hand of the Maji.

"Why did you attack me?"

The adversary struggled to remain silent, his face contorting as his will battled the Majiq elements. Rune could have used Sorcerer's dust to elicit information from any creature in the realms. Wizards had many tricks enhanced by potions, crystals, Majiqal powders, and elixirs. Used for the betterment of others, of course. No being could resist the righteous Maji touch, and Rune used it now to get what he needed. Only a Maji with pure intent could wield such intense dominance. Majiq worked for those clean vessels that would use it in keeping with Divine purpose. Otherwise, they would drop into the blackness of Diaboliq. The Gadion-Obscura Sorcerers leaned on potions because practitioners of evil were not Maji. Anyone who gave themselves freely to the Dark Arts had a natural inclination for evil. That flaw could include greed or lust or coveting power -- anything that opened up their soul to corruption. To enter into the secret cabal of Diaboliq, members drank a red blood-elixir that caused their eyes to glow crimson. Those who refused to consume the repulsive liquid could still be agents of Diaboliq and used for iniquitous ends against good, but would lack the pure demonic power.

"Confess! Why did you attack me?"

"Noth-th-thingggg personallll," the lankyhumanoid declared slowly, elongating his ending syllables as was the custom of his race when trying to adjust their dialect into the King's English. "Majiiii bountttyyyy. One killingggg whets the appetite for mooooorrrrrre. Maji ammmuletssss going for manyyyy goooooolllddddd coins on the undergroundddd marketttt."

"You could never touch an amulet!" Rune snapped back.

The assailant drew in a deep breath. "Ammmmuletssss can be takkkkennnn."

Disgusted, Rune shoved the man away with another plunk on the head, causing him to fall back and hit the old wood of the thick door. Taking amulets as trophies? It made the Wizard sick. An attacker's hand would be charred to a crisp if they touched a Majiq touch-stone pendant or ring in combat or aggression. Except with the death of the Templar. Then a Maji touch-stone died along with its owner.

Although mighty in their Wizardry, there were still vulnerabilities for Maji. Caught off guard, or ambushed, inexperienced, as well as seasoned veteran Sorcerers could be killed if the assailants were clever enough. They were powerful in a group, but an isolated Maji could be assassinated.

Automatically, Rune placed a hand on the pouch he wore under his shirt. Within it was his most sacred possession, an amulet and ring from the first fallen Maji of this generation. If anyone ever tried to take this treasure away from him it would be over his dead body. And he would never go down easily.

Soren Rune took a moment to calm his anger and clear his head, to back away from the sizzling hatred and rage that distorted every other input. He had to stay focused on the immediate perils, not succumb to the old, yet still raw, emotions.

There was no longer a sense of danger. Reaching into a pocket near his belt, he sprinkled a pinch of iridescent powder that was like fine dust, glittering even in the shadows, onto the combatant's head. When the attacker regained consciousness he would remember nothing of his hostility or his heinous intent. The null-silt sparkles worked against mild transgressions, but Rune used another pinch to make the Maderia's negative impulses latent for a long time. A big chunk of memories might be erased as well, but that was the price nefarious criminals paid for coming up against a Maji.

Instead of leaning too heavily on concoctions, Maji could transform and manipulate air, water, earth, plants, and animals to their will by using the natural elements of their surroundings. Rune could have drawn more power from the province had he chosen, or needed, to do so, but that also depleted the reserves of both the region and the Maji. Such summoning was used only in an extreme emergency.

Drawing the pointed hood of his shimmering traveling cloak over his head, he warily retraced his steps back toward the busier part of the marketplace. He had no desire to draw any more attention to himself. With the recent murder of a Maji there would already be undue attention to anyone in his religious Order. He could have called on the local magistrates to deal with this bounty hunter, but he chose to mete out justice himself. It was more satisfying that way. The monkey slinked in behind as the Maji stalked away in revulsion.

Just as Rune reached the corner of the main marketplace, he stopped abruptly. Spinning, he waited for a clearer picture of the peril. The evil was so palpable it prickled the hairs on his arms. Forcing his hand not to touch his dragon crystal, he extended his arm without summoning any energy. Although unnoticed, he stood ready. Dark Majiq – Diaboliq -- he could feel it like fingernails scratching the back of his neck. There was a Shadow presence close. Very close.

Glancing uneasily at the anonymous faces that perused the venders' wares, he reached into a pouch and surreptitiously threw black dust over his head. As the fine particles of charmed sand settled on his cloak, the pliable material that was as shiny as dragon scales, or stars in the night sky, transformed to a shading that deflected light so the eye could not detect it. Slipping unseen into the deepest gloom of the alley he waited. And watched.

Since the Maderia was still unconscious in the dust at the back of the lane, what Shaded Majiq did Rune feel? It was elusive and dank, like an old malevolence clinging to the rotted dimness, waiting to spring. Like a gust of rancid wind inside his soul. Then, just as abruptly, the Blackness departed.

Rune drew a breath to steady his nerves and refill the lungs that had been slowed in his battle-preparation. Who had that been? The sense was much more malign than a street bounty hunter hoping to collect a prize. Bounty-murder was no easy task, but a crime that was ever increasing in the realm since the re-emergence of the Gadion-Obscura. Stretching his palm flat, concealed by his robe, he scanned around him, but the touch-stone did not glow, the depths of the crystal maintaining a deep and fathomless indigo. No more Dark Majiq around him. Disappointing, when he was so attuned for combat.

Pure evil. Gadion-Obscura. Could that ancient wickedness be what he felt? Here, in this province? Few beings could exude such noticeable Diaboliq without being part of that organized cabal of murder and malice. They were increasing in number every day, growing bolder in their attacks. Executing dukes, earls and knights in the kingdoms, as well as innocent citizens – those supporting the monarchy. So far, they had killed only a few Wizards. Now those valiant-slain numbers were on the rise.

Skin chilling with the possibility that he was facing the nemesis he longed to challenge, he raced back down the alley, dragon ring and amulet glowing as a prelude to the fight, but no foe confronted him; no more Dark feelings lingered. Dejected, he scanned the small, dusty lanes for an extended time, long after he knew the invisible enemy had departed.

Frustrated, he slammed his fist against the nearest wall and stalked back toward the center street. By the time he reached the crowded shops around the civic square, he had mastered his momentary slip into anger and aggravation.

"Dragon's breath!" he cursed.

Patience, he reminded. His time would come. Rune yet would find the Gadion-Obscura who had killed Tor Ion-Gawain -- the first murder victim in centuries for the Templars under Merlin's Order. He would hunt down and destroy that wicked Dark Spirit and avenge the blood of his priest-brother. That, perhaps, would restore some peace to the ghost of his closest friend and, he hoped, a measure of comfort for himself.

Trying to center his mind, he pushed aside speculation of who the latest murdered Maji might have been. Possibly a friend. Someone he knew from Merlin's Castle? Even if it was a complete stranger from among the hundred or so Maji, it was still a colleague and fellow crusader in the Order.

Disturbingly, more and more criminals and weak-willed citizens were embracing the Diaboliq. Their initiation, as they lost their souls to the Black Arts, was to test the strength of the Maji, both collectively and individually. Since the Gadion-Obscura had resurfaced six years ago, times had become more threatening than usual for his Order, with increased attacks and a rising unrest in the kingdom. Unfortunately, there was nothing he could do about it now. The evil cloud was gone, but he would remember that feeling, that impression, for future reference. If he ever felt that rancorous aura again, he would be ready to combat it.

Shaking his head, he sighed, and then whispered to himself, "Merlin's going to be much put out. A battle in a market street!"

With effort, he returned to his original mission: Breakfast, before catching the next ship heading toward Britania. Perusing the luscious and varied fruits before him, Rune chose a bright yellow spear of succulent, sticky-knot melon. Should he follow up with a dessert of melon cream drenched in mead in a bowl? Decadent.

A visit to Spania was a pleasant foray into what Rune envisioned as a wild corner of Earth. Untamed and raw, crawling with nationalities, pirates and ruffians of every kind, it also held a unique beauty. The fresh air of the seacoast was moist and light enough to make the skin feel vibrant, while the scents of tangy fruits and fragrant flowers were neither heavy nor cloying. Evenings were the best; when the hot, orange sun slipped away from the western horizon, reflected off of a nearly transparent, waning moon, creating an idyllic scene. The temperature was hot, but tolerable in the mornings, which dawned mild and pleasant, the glow of light mingling in the sea mists to create a purple sky. It was reminiscent of sunrise in Ayelsborne – the childhood home where he and Tor grew to be as close as brothers.

Instantly, Rune's anger seethed until tactile realization made him aware he had crushed his breakfast in his strong fist. Calm. Breathe deep. Settle the anger behind. It would not help him to be volatile. There was nothing he could fight against now, the Dark Majiq was gone. Save the rage for an edge in battle. One day he would meet the Diaboliq responsible for the death of Tor. Now he needed to concentrate on the basics: food and transportation.

Sticky goo seeped onto his hand and brought his thoughts back to the present. As Rune licked the melon cream from his fingers, he took a moment to center himself. Stepping behind the market stalls he washed his hands and face in a cool stream of blue, bubbling water. Using senses heightened by Majiq, he drew himself deep into the nature around him, marveling at the swaying trees and picturesque smoke-blue sky that made this so ideal as a market port. He appreciated the elemental purity of dirt, rocks, air, water and color.

Rune removed his traveling cloak and crinkled it, tying it around his waist. The robe was too heavy for the rising temperatures. His casual shirt and trousers were light, and he folded down the leather of his soft boots to better deal with the advancing heat of the day. From his belt he drew a wooden baton and, concealing himself in a doorway so no one would observe his Majiq, gripped the knotted wood, instantly extending it to a long staff. Hoping he now looked the role of a casual traveler, his walking stick clicked rhythmically on the dirt as he strolled the bazaar searching for more food to take on his trip. No telling what they would be serving aboard the trader ship and it was to his benefit to have an option available.

Confident there should be no more trouble here, he nonetheless remained vigilant. He detected average problems of petty crime as in any city, but this was a realm of simple people and an easy lifestyle. The Diaboliq had slithered back to its shaded hiding place. Keeping his senses tuned to all around him, wary of further attacks, he made his way to the dock of the seaport on the other side of a rustic square. Here the old brown walls of the ancient city blended with the more modern designs and materials in the newer structures provided for travelers and cargo. His sailing ship was still boarding, he noted, as he entered a cool pub across the street and made his way to the counter.

Two roughly dressed sailors were talking as they sloppily drank their grog. Out at sea for a long time, they treasured each port. They regaled the tavern with the latest news from Britania, culled from recent stops at several harbors along the coast.

Rune's heart dropped when he heard the familiar name of the latest murdered Maji. Jase. Young Maji. Dead from an attack on a road in Devonshire! Not slain in some outer frontier dark alley, but in a well-known path in their home country! How was that possible for a Maji to be murdered so publicly?

Rune sucked in deep breaths, his chest tight. No need to confirm in any other manner – Majiq told him the Gadion-Obscura had struck again. They had so heartlessly, mercilessly started this latest war in the epic battle of good against evil and their first modern casualty had been his closest friend. In that ambush they had killed his old colleague, the greatest Maji he had ever known, aside from Merlin-Maj, of course. Now the death toll of Maji downed in this melee of the Diaboliq – the Gadion-Obscura assassins -- numbered twenty-two. He was keeping count. He would not forget. Well, then, his course was clear. Seek out this Dark Majiq he felt and fight it. Hunt it down like the wretched evil it was and sweep it from the face of this earth and every other realm.

A wave of power struck inside his core, this time not of grief or outrage, but one of Majiq. His dragon talisman, the touch-stone over his heart, was pulsing as was his dragon ring. A summons; Majiq telepathy that connected priests through their crystals. He was to leave this province and go home -- to the foundation of every Maji – the Castle on Avelon.

No! He did not want to go back to the hallowed corridors where every corner, every bright place would hold memories of his fallen compatriots. What reason would he have to return to where he might receive instructions that would hinder him from his primary quest – what his life...what he... had now become – a Gadion-Obscura hunter. Despite what he wanted, Majiq-crystal energy was unmistakable and undeniable: Return to the Castle. Then return he must. But he wasn't going to like it.

**

To Rune, walking the muted, subdued corridors of Merlin's Castle was coming home spiritually as well as physically. His childhood memories -- many years ago -- were of life here in these sequestered rooms and halls where dedicated Maji Tutors intoned and imparted sacred wisdom to the young Novitiates. To a revered Order of Sorcerers regarded throughout the known worlds as the guardians of Divine guidance, Maji Castle was an appropriately grand edifice. The towering designs of turrets and spires reaching toward Heaven offered roomy elegance and encouraged the image of esthetic flow and serenity to the eye. A sense of the mystic majesty of the ancient Order, the architecture was a tribute to the olden times of a monarchy and a chivalrous society. Merlin's red dragon flag fluttered from the highest tower.

In the last six years, Rune returned to this Maji haven only when summoned by the Order's ruling body. Otherwise, he preferred roaming from assignment to assignment, traveling to the far reaches of the known, and sometimes unknown realms, fulfilling his calling as a Wizard and instrument of Majiq to battle the growing Darkness. Anything to keep at bay the memories and ghosts lingering here to haunt him.

Having just completed a mission, Rune could have reported to Merlin through the usual crystal ball or Majiq emanations, using his amulet as a conduit. The gem would have given off a unique energy and he could have translated that through the innate abilities possessed by every Maji. His next assignment, in all probability, then would have been given to him immediately. Instead, Rune returned according to his spiritual duty in following Majiq promptings and Merlin's wisdom.

Notifying the appropriate clerk of his arrival, he knew that soon enough Merlin would be made aware of his presence here and summon him for an audience. No doubt that was when he would be told -- well -- whatever reason it was that he had been re-called. Perhaps the senior Maji did not even know yet. Often Majiq pushed, influenced and guided the Paladins seemingly without reason or logic.

In those times Merlin-Maj, the most powerful Maji ever, would recite the well-known adage, "Listen for the subtle whisperings of Majiq-sage."

This sagacious counsel was one heard often in the formative years of the young student Rune. Now a Wizard, the quote was still something Merlin and other Maji advised him with annoying regularity. Perhaps, if he had adhered more to those teachings, he would understand why Majiq drew him back to his roots here at the Castle. Perhaps his roaming the realm as a hunter of Darkness had been found out. He had tried to be covert, piggybacking his pursuit with routine quests. Maybe he was ordered back as a rebuke for being a maverick, going his own way. Too headstrong, the older Majiqs chided. Independent, Rune liked to think.

Usually adept at tuning into motivations and secrets, Rune was not talented with seeing into the future. Nor was he always good at self-examination. His Majiq instincts could have led him back here to the Castle for the simple reason of mourning with the other Maji at the newest killing. A sharp pang of grief stabbed at his heart. Just the thought of his long-time friend Tor Ion-Gawain, murdered years ago, was enough to burden him with pain. Here in the halls of learning, the practical jokes and endless hours of honing Majiq, Tor had matured from his boyhood companion to become his brother and soul-shield. Everything a best friend should be.

Once released for separate missions as young priests in a big kingdom, they met whenever possible, pulling assignments that kept them in close proximity. They were an amazing team. When the whispered warnings of an emerging Dark Majiq came to their ears, they believed themselves invincible. Nothing could defeat their spirit. But all too suddenly, it was over. The conspiracy of evil was upon them with the first murder of a Maji in longer than anyone could remember. The cold-blooded ambush of a priest had carried to every quarter of the known realms. Rune would never forget that soul-crushing moment when he felt like his heart had been sucked out, his strength sapped. He had actually collapsed on the floor of his manor house in Ayelsborne. Dragging himself to a wall, he had leaned there, sick and unable to move for some time.

In his mind's eye Rune had seen the face of his closest friend writhing in terror and pain. Black cloaked figures surrounded Tor, attacking and murdering the overwhelmed and surprised Wizard.

Maji became soldiers that day as massacres of the wizards as well as other good and innocent people continued. The war was overt and sudden. Over the next six years the Maji learned the Gadion-Obscura had been working in secret for a long time. They were building their resources and quietly recruiting those who worshiped Diaboliq – Cloaked Arts -- rather than Divine; Dark rather than Light. The bulk of the Diaboliq followers were vanquished by the Maji. But evil was not defeated, only driven into hiding. For these long years they had waged an ongoing battle with an elusive enemy. The

Maji stayed vigilant, defending the kingdoms, fighting Diaboliq whenever possible.

As Rune walked down the quiet halls of the Castle, he considered his mixed feelings. Platitudes were fine for beginners, but when a comrade was lost it hurt no matter what your age or experience. The ache still resonated in his soul every time he thought of those now gone. Together they had come to the Castle at young ages and been allies. Tor had been everything Maji should embody. Young Jase and the other lost Maji, too. Irreplaceable, there was a void where such great priests had flourished, then, too soon, were killed.

Perhaps he was here to find solace among his kind. Maybe Majiq led Rune back to learn more about the latest Maji assassination. The public facts of the killing were sketchy and vague, but unlike other Maji he had met in the last few days of travel, he did not doubt a Gadion-Obscura Sorcerer had murdered young Jase. The rising tide of Evil in the kingdom could not be denied.

So it escalates. More Maji murders. Was this how Camelot nearly fell in the olden times? Legend had it Merlin extended all his power to save Arthur and the inspired kingdom of England. Afterwards, his Majiq was so depleted, Merlin returned to the Order's home in this dominion – Avelon.

For the past five centuries Merlin and his bloodline of Maji were not welcome anymore in the home realm of Dragonshire. Their House of Avelon had been replaced by the House of Garraden after the queen's massacre at the hands of Kyre and Maksym, the Diaboliq twins. So Maji Templars traveled through Thresholds between Earth and the other realms, focused on restoring the Order of the Maji and allowing Mankind to progress with limited intervention from Dragonshire Wizards, at least for a time.

Gadion-Obscura had changed that self-imposed retirement. Diaboliq was as old as Majiq, the struggle between the two powers as eternal as the universe. One side for good, for progress. One for subjugation and malevolence. As long as Black Sorcery threatened this world, Dragon Wizards would stay here to combat them alongside Mankind.

Called back to Avelon for a quest. Rune could only hope it meant Merlin had decided it was time to go on the offensive against the Diaboliq. That thought added a determination and optimism to his step as he stalked the old, stone corridors of the ancient citadel.

**

Hundreds of Maji were counted in the ranks throughout the kingdoms and obviously there was not room in the Castle for everyone. Transient Wizards for the most part, Priests, Mentors and Tyros not regularly assigned to Avelon were housed in temporary quarters. Since Maji maintained an austere lifestyle, it was never a problem to survive comfortably in guest housing. Utilitarian, the temporary apartment offered a modest space for meditation or visiting, two bedrooms, storage cupboards, meditation rugs, and a small larder for food.

The highlight was the expansive window looking out at the province hosting the Castle where Merlin's red dragon flag rippled in the hilltop winds. This was one of the core settlements of the Ancients. It was told that eons ago travelers landed here -- pilgrims from Dragonshire and other dimensions. Details were lost in the dusty pages of history, but legend had it that these frontier settlers established the Castle on Avelon.

The Maji knew the misty, supernatural marshes and moors here welcomed Majiq Sorcerers. Led by Merlin-Maj, they founded their Order on the gifts of Wizards, guarding the sacred powers of enchantment, offering their sorcery to the inhabitants of these realms. From Avelon, Maji spread out to distant provinces and regions, myriad off-shoots populating all regions of the worlds. Eventually, that was honed to include Merlin's shining triumph for Humanity – Camelot.

Unpacked and refreshed from his journey, Rune gazed out, observing the city of Avelon. Commerce was sedate, but necessary. Markets thrived, but only those sturdy and hearty enough to live among Sorcerers, Faeries, or Elves came to Avelon. Here it was common to see a Wizard or Elf bartering with sailors. Or young Tyros playing with unicorn colts. The Maji need for tranquility and quiet was constantly at odds with the requirements of a busy city center. In the years since he had been back here, Rune lamented, the congestion was winning. Too much noise and too many people.

This was the center of their society but Rune already longed for the freedom and space offered in less populated spots in the kingdoms. Restlessly, he paced the small quarters; he had been summoned back here for a reason. Solving puzzles was not only part of his vocation, but a skill at which he excelled. Knowing himself very well, he understood he was avoiding the solution because he thought he would probably dislike the answer.

Venturing beyond the closed doors of his quarters might expose him to the knowledge he knew was waiting and he wanted to avoid that fate as long as possible. On the other hand, he could remain here, drive himself to distraction with his grief-laden memories in the small room, and then be summoned at some point by his spiritual leaders. Should he allow that to happen, they would simply inform him of his destiny and he would have backed himself into a corner.

While still a young student in these halls, Rune had accepted, more easily than his Mentors, that he was a free and independent spirit. His schooling had been tests of patience for his Teachers and him. How anxious he was to be through with the learning and get on with the active purpose of a Maji life.

'Live today, not tomorrow, not yesterday.' Merlin-Maj never tired of the admonition.

At times Rune wondered if the quote had been invented just for him. Never one to deny Majiq power, Destiny or good instincts, Rune left the room to ramble the corridors of the Maji refuge. On his occasional visits to the Castle, he had never felt the pressing sense in Majiq that now almost pushed him to whatever the future held for him. As he wandered, he came to believe his instincts would soon be rewarded with an answer.

Sobering, Rune pondered the echoed council with somber grains of regret and grief. His experience in the life-and-death risks of their calling was capped by the loss of his closest friend. He marked his life with that median – the before and after of his world crumbling. After several years of solitary missions and running through the vast provinces in search of solace, Rune could not completely resolve his culpability. He had not been with his friend when Diaboliq ambushed and murdered Tor. He could never forgive himself for that mistake.

Despite the pain at being here, he realized with surprise, he had missed the camaraderie and companionship of the Castle. Respectful nods or quiet smiles greeted him in every hallway. Familiarity and memories of his youth warmed the cold stone walls. Maybe he should have come back sooner. And cut short his mission of revenge? Never, even though his course of covert vengeance against the Gadion-Obscura was ethically against his training as a religious leader. He felt stirrings of guilt about his path now that he was within the hallowed halls of the righteous Order's heart. Here in the Castle there was purity and he defiled that purity by his unapproved and, if known, totally unacceptable, actions. Justified? He thought so. But now, side by side with the most holy of beings, he had second thoughts about his personal quest.

If his motivation for justice was wrong, then Majiq would have deserted him long ago. His darkened heart may not be pure in the greatest sense, but he was still good enough to summon Majiq-sage. If he was truly evil, everyone in the Castle would have known. They would have sensed it before his feet touched the flagstones of the great courtyard.

In these quiet halls filled with spiritual strength, he was still an equal. Never had he desired to sit in audience with the exalted beings that were the supreme authority on Majiq in the realms, but he could handle it if necessary. Certainly that was not the conscience of a guilty wrong-doer. That proved his mission of justice was right.

Was it possible he was summoned back here to work in some administrative post, under the watchful eyes of Merlin? No! His destiny was among Humanity. Working in hot spots all over the kingdoms, doing good by direct action through Maji was his strength.

In response to the political equivalent of the Order's slow and measured opposition to evil, Rune and other Maji had formed a loose association of Paladins. They were not shackled with Tyros. They struck out on their own, continuing to do what was required of them by their Order, but also carrying out covert missions. This small band was dedicated to searching out, finding, and destroying the Gadion-Obscura without the sanction or knowledge of Merlin.

Loosely referred to as the Legion – Rune secretly fancied it a Warrior Legion -- a rebellion within the Castle. They acted against evil, for good. Gadion-Obscura was leading the unwitting populace away from the Majiq principles that their society was founded upon. Many Maji objected to the idea of Templars -- religious soldiers -- but was there really a choice? More and more were joining the enemy. War had been thrust upon them all and it was within the mandate of the Maji to keep the peace. In Rune's opinion, armed back-up was welcome.

Passing other priests and Tutors with their students -- Tyros -- he gave polite nods to those he knew. On a near non-sensory level he could hear the whispered speculations of why Soren Rune was back at the Castle. What brought the mysterious, reclusive, powerful Maji back to home base? As revered and spiritual as Maji were, gossip was still not above them and the Castle always rippled with tales of the latest exploits, and occasional blunders, of the various priests. Not all Paladins were famous or even known at the Castle. Conversely, some were notorious, and he supposed he fit into that category.

His amble brought him to one of the many training rooms available in the student wing of the Castle. Why had he come here? A place of more painful memories. Pausing, rubbing his dragon crystal talisman with a thumb and forefinger, Rune watched through a doorway as four teams of students practiced dueling.

Novitiates received wooden staffs to hone the ancient art of combat. Then, when they reached the age of training away from the Castle, they were given touch-stone amulets and rings to channel Majiq. They would train to use the energy from the heart and mind instead of solely depending on tools. However, forged with powerful spells, mutated, wands enhanced Majiq and gave a boost of energy to the touch-stone enchantment.

True Majiq-sage was more useful than any other weapon, yet, the jewel-powered wands served as a symbolic and sometimes enhanced weapon/extension of their office. The Order had elevated the power of touch-stones and wands to near art objects, using them in well-choreographed stunts and stylish dances that, although meant to be defensive, were often aggressive and sometimes deadly.

Legend had it that King Arthur's fabled sword, Excalibur, was based on the Maji touch-stone principle. Empowered by a Majiq crystal embedded in the hilt, Merlin presented it to Arthur to unite the Britons. Some of the old myths purported that Arthur's mighty and unconquerable blue blade could shoot fire from its tip, and that it was unbeatable and indestructible. Some believed the hilt was encrusted with a piece of Merlin's sky-stone -- a meteorite that had fallen from Heaven and, through Majiq, forged into the handle of Merlin's scepter. The meteorite was the most powerful mineral in any of the kingdoms and drew itself to Merlin, the mightiest Wizard ever known. This piece of sky-stone was rumored to be chipped off the Stone of Destiny. It was a fabled black slab with otherworldly engravings. Possessing this boulder purportedly endowed Majiq to find the rightful king.

Merlin never discussed his days in Camelot, and no Wizard dared ask. So the story remained a rippled reflection of tales and history, distorted, like many mysteries, lost within the vapors of time's sea; the legend becoming more spectacular with each telling. There was no denying the truth underlying the story, though, that Merlin and his scepter were the standard for all things Majiq.

Ion-Gawain's wand had not been among the few possessions of the dead Maji. However, Rune had recovered the dragon amulet and ring crystals, claiming them as the only remembrance of his brother Paladin. Rune pressed a hand to the pouch under his shirt. The habitual tap to Tor's amulet and touch-stone followed the accompanying oath that he would avenge the death of his friend.

The action on the training mat escalated and caught his attention again. Even by callow initiates, the duels were poetry in motion. Rune watched in grudging amusement, then growing appreciation, as the teams executed their prancing and parrying with varying degrees of talent, skill and grace. Touch-stone burning, he placed a palm against the dragon crystal at his heart as, unbidden, came the speculation as to the other reason he might have been prodded to the Castle. To take a Tyro.

Not every priest became a Tutor to a Tyro. Only some Mentors were honored with the ultimate testament of their place in the Maji Order -- to teach and train a young and fresh Novitiate -- a Tyro. Every graduating Novitiate was assigned a Tutor by Merlin.

There was the old story about the Majiq Warrior Bond --where the pure jurisdiction of Majiq mutually drew the priest Templar and a Tyro together -- but no one believed that anymore. When he was a naïve student, Rune had hoped the Warrior Bond was real. Where did that errant thought come from? Thinking of Tor too much? He had not remembered those cob-webbed tales for years! That's what homecomings did for him, forced him to mentally review times, places and emotions he did not want to remember. He had never believed that old myth anyway. Well, perhaps when he was still a Novitiate, when formidable links had been forged between him and his closest friend. Idealism was natural then, in the days before he was hardened and calloused by life. Before loss blunted his soul. After death leveled him, there was no more optimism left inside Rune's pragmatic, wounded heart. He did not believe in myths anymore.

The pang of hurt returned. If only the Warrior Bond was real. Could it have saved Tor? They had been like brothers! If only he had been there, Warrior Bond or not, he could have either saved his friend or died beside him. Could the legendary Bond perhaps be the ultimate weapon against the rising Gadion-Obscura? Aloud, he scoffed. Once he was a dreamer, a disciple of romanticism. That was before death changed everything.

Involuntarily, Rune's lip twitched with admiration as his attention was drawn to two students on the side of the training room -- the team by far the most exciting and skilled in the arena. The acrobatic bounce of the trim student with the longish sandy hair drove all unpleasant memories from Rune. The boy seemed old enough to be ready to leave the Castle and be trained by a Mentor. He moved with a grace foreign to his approximate twelve years and wielded the staff in his hand like a dancing partner. When the shorter, stout, but stronger opponent drove an attack with a low-powered, Majiq-dusted wand, the leaner young man skipped aside with light feet. The shorter one sprinkled Majiq dust in the air then would push and parry. The taller one would flip in a somersault over the foe and, with an easy elegance, tumble back to land gracefully, ready for the next move. He needed no Majiq substitutions.

These girls and boys were mostly ten or eleven, a few older. They might even be the class of Tyros known as the First Orphans. The unfortunate children left parentless in the initial wave of attacks by the revived Gadion-Obscura. A handful of those children had been cared for by families who adopted them. Most however, had been the dependents of Maji. Gadion-Obscura assassins had targeted the Maji Order first. The Maji orphans had been brought here to the Castle to be raised within the Templar system. To Rune's knowledge, all had chosen to remain and develop into full Sorcerers.

The two opponents swirled around the room, seemingly charged with never ending energy. Like trickles of light echoing off a blazing comet, Rune could feel the pulse vibrating from the two boys as they jumped and parried across the mat. Sparkling Majiq powder filtered the air as the stout boy used an entire pouch-full in his battle. There was more than just skill at work here, because the finely attuned Rune could feel the radiance of Majiq-sage working as the youths battled. One or both of them were very strong in innate Majiq. The taller, more athletic student grew impatient, however, and Rune noted with amusement that he was taking more risks, becoming more daring and fancy in his movements.

Pinching his lip with his fingers, Rune smiled, certain the pretentious boy with the flashy style and longish, sandy hair whipping around his face would soon be dealt a mock-fatal blow with his enemy's low charged wand. Novitiates did not yet have the full Majiq of a priest and their weapons were of a tempered, elemental Majiq. Strong enough to sting, but not to wound.

Once the Tyro's were released from the Castle, they were melded with their touch-stone, which blessed them with a higher degree of Majiq. Part of their training under their Mentor was to learn to use this enhanced gift of Majiq-sage in righteous ways. As long as their hearts remained pure, their mystical might developed.

The stout boy had methodically, relentlessly driven his opponent with tenacious vigor, pushing the taller boy back to a corner. As the attacker lunged to what seemed to be a certain hit, the sandy-haired boy flipped up, feet kicking off the side wall, arched over his foe, twisting to land on his feet at the opponent's back. Rune could sense strong Majiq coming from the taller young man. The broad shouldered boy jerked around quickly, tangling his feet in an awkward slant and losing balance. Stumbling, his wand flew back and was about to burn him on the shoulder.

As deftly as a dancer, the tall boy flicked his opponent's wand out of the way to harmlessly land on the floor, automatically retracting to a benign hilt. The shorter boy was now on the ground on his knees. Snickers rippled around the room from the other students who had already completed their battles. With curiosity, Rune wondered how the flashy, over-confident boy would chide the clumsy one. Ego-driven youth could be cruel and unforgiving of others not as talented, dexterous or clever as they. In the ostentatious battle, the lean youth had not only drawn on Majiq, but had also displayed a degree of unnecessary showmanship along with plain, old-fashioned luck.

The taller boy, ignoring the rest of the students, closed down the slight Majiq to his wand and tucked the wand in the pocket of his capacious shirt while reaching out his right hand to his challenger.

"Good fight, Kyton. You really fooled me with that new strategy." It was sarcastic, but easy humor. With an indulgent grace he used Majiq to flip the fallen hilt off the floor, catch it in his free hand and hold it out to its owner. "You won't trick me so easily next time." A dry, casual warning that any future match would be decided more on skill than chance.

From the far side of the practice room came a Wizard instructor Rune did not know, announcing an end to the day's class. All students were reminded to report for training tomorrow at the usual time for final testing. The younger

Novitiates left through a door on the other side of the room. A few of the students congregated, whispering -- obviously gossiping about the two flamboyant fencers -- but the lean fighter gave them no more than a glance of silent and distinct disapproval. Thoughtfully, Rune studied the remarkably generous combatant whose flash and ego seemed inconsistent with a magnanimous nature. Striding confidently out of the room, the youth darted a glance in Rune's direction. So, he knew he had an audience. With a neutral expression the Novitiate disappeared.

"The young are very entertaining." The cryptic comment in a deep voice from behind nearly startled Rune.

It wasn't easy to sneak up on a Maji, but in his defense, Rune reminded, he was in a safe environment and had been absorbed in the fight. Not to mention, the one doing the sneaking was the greatest of Maji. Not realizing he had been holding it all this time, Rune dropped his dragon talisman to his neck and straightened to attention.

"Merlin," he greeted with a nod of his head.

"Impressive skills, wouldn't you say so, Soren?"

Rune studied the stout Merlin-Maj, who stood beside him. If the power and strength of Majiq were determined by outward appearance, the High Wizard of their Holy Order would have been many meters high and wide. Instead, this paragon of supernatural force was barely shorter than Rune, with errant tufts of silver hair erratically curling amid strands that were losing the battle as white overpowered grey/brown. Showing a bit of paunch to the wiry frame, Merlin's straight posture gave the impression of stealth and lithe energy. A short fluff of white beard matted the jaw-line of the narrow face, and perceptive gold eyes focused like sun-power, piercing everything he surveyed.

"Entertaining," Rune agreed, his deep, lyrical voice appreciative but not praising. "Are they the First Orphans?"

"Yes. Our pride."

"They have grown into fine youth." Rune fought down an emotional burning at the back of his eyes. Of course all of the First Orphans would flourish within the Order. Their heritage had been stamped with the blood of their parents. Such a tragic history could only enhance their Majiq.

Over the centuries the Order adopted all orphans who were born as Wizards. It was obvious from birth that their physiognomic heritage included a Maji heart. Sometimes, in babies, the heart glowed even through the translucent skin. These blessed children of the Avelon lineage were taken to the Castle at age ten, and trained until the age of twelve, then given the choice to remain in the Maji Order or take another path. Most foundlings, and all First Orphans, remained.

"I hoped they would all stay. They really have no other place to go."

Everyone in the Order had a sentimental soft spot for the brave children who had been robbed of parents and families by mindless violence. Rune felt a swell of pride for these special ones, but was careful not to display any outward praise. He was subliminally suspicious of Merlin's motives for showing up here and now.

"I am intrigued that you arrive back here now, Soren." Merlin-Maj started a leisurely pace down the corridor. "Unexpected."

The Merlin-Maj was also considered a skilled master of imparting sarcasm in very few words. Rune recognized it immediately from the stout being.

"Really?" He could hold his own in the irony department.

A rattling cackle-laugh proved Merlin-Maj's sense of humor. "No! Not after being summoned." It was a certainty.

The elder ambled away and Rune walked slowly alongside, attracting casual attention from others. Passersby nodded greetings to Merlin-Maj and the other well-known member of the Order. The tallish Rune was fit and muscled but did not stand out in comeliness or height or form. He was aware others considered his tawny, short-cropped hair to be a severe style. An austere fashion accentuated by blue eyes that seared others like slashes of Dragon spit. Soren Rune was known by many, and avoided by most, his demeanor rejecting warmth or welcome.

"We could have communicated through a crystal," Rune tentatively suggested, fishing for information. Without admitting that his touch-stone had indeed guided him here, he redirected with a question. "You have an assignment for me?"

"No mission." Merlin-Maj stopped, his thick, white brows curling down in perplexity. Age indeterminate, he could be considered old, or mature, not too ancient, but not young, either. His right thumb twirled the red, dragon-ensconced crystal on his forefinger. "You expected one?"

Rune would never lie to any Maji, let alone Merlin. Neither did he want his private, intimate dealings with Majiq exposed, even to an old friend such as the robust Wizard. "I did not know."

"Then you must discover your purpose here." Merlin was never one to waste words.

Expression as cloudy as his heart, Rune refused to acknowledge the assertion. From the curled brows of his companion, he knew his obfuscation was useless. Merlin-Maj could see through him. Why did he bother? Innate stubbornness. "I am to be the tip of the spear," he guessed, his voice edged with excitement. "You want me to go after the Gadion-Obscura who killed young Jase."

Merlin's lip curled down. "Revenge?"

"I am looking for justice, not revenge," he corrected, unwilling to concede that he could not yet separate the two in his heart but not caring to bandy semantics over such a sensitive matter. "Gadion-Obscura is out there practicing the Dark Arts, Merlin. With each day they gain power and recruits. They have killed another Wizard! This is war!"

The leader's deep eyes narrowed, veiled with thick lids under the heavy brows. His frown deepened. Without comment the shorter man turned and ambled away. "Are you listening to your instincts or your desire for vengeance?"

Merlin had been Rune's Tutor and nurtured him in so many rich elements of skilled Majiq. The affection between Teacher and Pupil was profound. If Rune was hurting still at losing his best friend, how much greater was Merlin's pain at the murders of numerous Maji since Gadion-Obscura's re-emergence? They were all suffering. All the more reason to find the remaining Gadion-Obscura threat and eradicate them before the war escalated beyond their control.

"Merlin, you know I am best at pursuing the enemy," Rune continued, catching up in a few strides with the older Sorcerer.

Fear drove him. And, yes, revenge. Rune would not admit aloud, especially to Merlin, that he advocated going against his Order. That would be foolhardy – no -- just plain stupid! But he didn't really want to hang around here waiting for – for some unknown that he was beginning to get nervous about. He had a bad feeling about this summons. This was one time he would rather use his head than the spirit of Majiq to rule his actions.

Merlin kept his pace and did not look over at the younger Wizard. "The Gadion-Obscura grows stronger. How do we combat the evil that is all around us?" They were rhetorical questions of course. Any child could respond with answers cherished from centuries of teachings. "After all these years you must put aside your hatred. It blocks you from your destiny. Your thirst for revenge is destructive."

No denying that, Rune sighed. It was always so frustrating trying to out-logic this indomitable Maji. Why did he make the attempt? Like his late friend Tor, he never gave up when he thought his cause was just. "If I could just be given free rein –"

"And you think that is your strength?"

Dragon's breath! Rune really hated it when his former Mentor threw back in his face lessons learned here at the Castle. He already knew the reasons, but he kept on arguing. It was his stubborn streak cursing him to rebel, urged on by his passion to avenge his friend.

"I want to be out there hunting the Gadion-Obscura, Merlin." He needed to come face to face with whoever was in league with Tor's murderer. For six years he had been tracking signs of the Dark presence, but had yet to discover the cultists that killed his friend. Out there in the lands there were Dark Sorcerers leading and recruiting, responsible for murder. They bred their wickedness like a cancer on a law-abiding, society.

Merlin stared at him. There was an old wisdom in the seemingly infinite gold eyes. Dusty tales circulating the Castle claimed Merlin-Maj was around back at the beginning of time when the first Ancients battled for good against evil in Dragonshire. Gadion-Obscura had lost, Maji had won. Was that first Wizard Warrior really Merlin? Reason told Rune no, but when held in the old one's mesmerizing gaze, all kinds of amazing power tingled in the air. Majiq-sage seemed to radiate from every particle of his being. Who knew the truth of the distant past? Anything was possible within Majiq.

"You know the old lessons are always right. Revenge leads to inner destruction," was the wise one's council.

"I have struggled with twisted emotions since Tor's murder," he admitted freely. "The hate returns every time another Maji or innocent is struck down. But I overcome the negatives. Please allow me the freedom to seek out the Evil."

"Sorcerers are already focused on this latest attack. We counter the threat with methodical and relentless vigilance. That is enough for now."

Politics! Rune was a man of action, not considerations and words! He posed his response, respectfully, to the Mentor. "You can feel threats to Maji. The wickedness is growing more powerful. I see it in the disputations and fighting encountered on numerous continents, in many kingdoms! The unrest is just the tip of the spear! The Gadion-Obscura is the organized foundation of violence!" His voice had risen in intensity and volume. He took a breath and concluded, "We cannot remain so – so – complacent about this menace! Eliminate them and the worlds will be stable again."

Merlin sighed, probably in exasperation. "Do you think the Order does nothing while our realms are threatened?" He continued walking.

Rune growled under his breath. That was a verbal trap.

The Gadion-Obscura was the opposite of the Maji in every aspect. The black for the white, the deceptive for the genuine, the greedy and murderous for the altruistic and protective. The Gadion-Obscura was, by nature, ruthless and power-hungry. They destroyed each other for control and supremacy. Theoretically, the Maji should be able to eradicate them quickly because their own greed and self-centered natures corrupted from within. Their cankered souls were unable to trust anyone and eventually their conspiracies should fall apart. However, that cycle of inner destruction was slow. The enticements of greed and lechery attracted more recruits than the Maji could battle. So much death, pain and loss could be spared if just warriors would seek out and end the cabal.

Too impatient to await an official blessing on taking action, Rune and other Maji had formed the League, a loose association of Priests and Paladins – all without Acolytes of course -- who were dedicated to ferreting out, finding, and destroying the Gadion-Obscura regardless of sanction from Merlin. It was a rebellion within the Maji Castle, not of malice, but for good. Rune did not consider him and his League in the wrong for being too eager and impulsive, nor did he consider their motivations to be impelled by revenge. Justice and protection were their goals.

Knowing he was dangerously close to being disrespectful and disobedient, Rune backed off and allowed his emotions to cool. He could not give away the secret pact of his colleagues by losing his temper.

Merlin clicked his tongue and shook his head. He came to a stop on a mezzanine overlooking a great courtyard of the lower Castle. Figures of Paladins and tunic-and-sash attired young people flowed along the quiet corridors. Finally, Merlin-Maj looked at Rune.

"You always aspire to be a detective. The Order tracks the threat of the Gadion-Obscura. There are tasks more important to you, Soren. Such as investigating Majiq troubles."

"Is that why you wanted me back here at Avelon?"

"The reasons will be clear soon enough. Did you examine your heart? Your instincts?"

The man's skin chilled at the Majiq spirituality accompanying that pronouncement. Merlin KNEW why he was here! Were there any mysteries not known to this mystical Wizard? Did he know all? Was his cautionary attitude about the Gadion-Obscura just a deflective device to let Rune know it was none of his business? Maybe this was a little bit of a humbling payback for him. Humility and modesty were never his strong points. He thought of the young Novitiate who was so flashy with the wand and felt uncomfortable at the image that was too mirror-like and too quickly at the forefront of his thoughts.

Merlin continued without waiting for his reaction. "I know two students who will become Tyros this term."

Rune growled under his breath. Where was this line of conversation heading? Novitiate Wizards began their training at age ten when they came to live on Avelon. Then they were tutored for five years under a Mentor. Then they were ready to go out on their own as Wizards serving at a specific fiefdom within the kingdoms until they were deemed mature and experienced enough to travel as solo Templars.

"Make yourself available," was Merlin's command.

"Of course. But not as a Mentor." The rude rebuttal was abrupt, even harsh. Rune's demeanor was as cold as his soul. "I need to seek out the Diaboliq."

Lips curled, eyes narrowed, the oldest, wisest Maji stared at the commanding Rune with a touch of compassion, a degree of knowing patience. "You are too impulsive still, Soren Rune. Tsk. Will you confront the future at such a great risk as to ignore the impulse of Majiq?"

Bristling, Rune's jaw tightened. "The risk is being a Tutor."

Merlin's nose twitched. "You have always been obedient to Majiq-sage. You know well enough to follow it. But you often choose rebellion, Rune." His tone was regretful, but patient. "You have never renounced Majiq-sage. If a Tyro you are meant to have, then you shall comply."

Waves of warm, tingling Majiq rippled over Rune's skin, heating him to the bone. No, he would not resist the spiritual, nor would he knowingly act against the power that guided and directed his life. Majiq was a mixture of the spiritual and the enchanted that enabled those skilled with the gift to wield it for right. It warmed, it consoled, it impressed and guided through the heart and soul. Since his years as a youth here at the Castle he had never denied it. But how could he be meant to advise a Tyro?

When meeting for the first time, Tutor and Tyro sometimes felt an initial, instinctive connection through Majiq. More commonly Merlin screened the students preparing for their Tyro training and chose a Mentor compatible in personality and method. He had served the religion for centuries in this manner. But times were changing. The Gadion-Obscura had reappeared. Were staid, traditional methods going to serve them with the new threat, with the advancing evil?

Some teamings worked so well the Mentor and Tyro became like mother and daughter, or mother and son, father and son or father and daughter. There was no desire for another family. His brother Tor was dead. He wanted to be left alone.

If only the old tale of the Warrior Bond was true -- a Tutor and Tyro unmistakably drawn together by Majiq -- bonding them mentally, spiritually, in a unity of purpose and a future of harmony. A familial closeness said to transcend the usual levels of power and strength and even skill according to the old legends. If only he still believed in flowery Faery tales. If only . . . .

Being a Mentor would be an entrapment. He would no longer be able to follow his quest for justice. He would be committed as a Teacher for five years! That was a long time to be teamed with a teenager! Freedom was what he needed.

"A Tyro I am not ready to take."

Without giving Merlin a chance to debate, Rune turned and strode away, briskly fleeing the field of battle. Disturbed, he stalked through the corridors of the Castle, seeking far reaches of the complex where he would encounter few people. He could not go back to his quarters and meditate -- it would be too easy to hear his Center and the echoes of Majiq whispering to him. Somewhere there must be a place where he could hide from the wisdom of Merlin and the accountability of his Order.

No, he would not deny Majiq, but he was capable of deflecting it if possible. Two students ready to be assigned as Tyros; dangerous for a Paladin trying to avoid commitment. By tomorrow morning he would board a ship off this enchanted island. Far from the Thresholds leading to this, the heart of Sorcery on Earth. He would lose himself in another realm. Escape. There would be no Tyro for him. That would not constitute active rebellion against Merlin or Majiq -- just a diversion.

**

His feet took him to the perfect place; the ancient library. Secluded, remote, few ventured this far into the back rooms of the Castle to study relics. This was the genesis, where the history of the Maji and the rest of the known realms were kept in massive crystal receptacles. But farther back, in the cobwebbed and oft-neglected racks of antiquity, volumes of delicate leather, paper, and papyrus rested. This aged and primitive sanctuary came with earthy smells and time-faded pages of uncountable places and records.

In Rune's youth, this old library had been a refuge for his rebellious and inquisitive nature. On tall shelves were original bound books, ancient and brittle, that one could hold in their hands and smell the mustiness. Here the sense of amassed wisdom and grime of eons was at his fingertips. These were tangible connections to the legends, myths and core beliefs of the ancient Maji. Few understood the treasure within these staid walls, but it was there, and he felt better just opening the huge, tall doors and stepping into the room.

This was his sanctuary now from the hauntings. Outside these doors the best friends had always parted. Here, no ghostly memories intruded. Tor was about rushing headlong into the future – preparing for the destiny that would take him beyond the known worlds. He was impatient to live through the present, and the past was nothing to him. The only interest Tor ever had in this massive section of the Castle was the old lore of demons; the scary tales told when the lights were out and they were supposed to be asleep. Shivering as the ache of loss rippled through him, Rune never thought until now how cavalier and foolish they were as boys. Little did they know the brutal legends of blood-suckers, angry Faeries and demons would be Tor's undoing. Some old stories, all too tragically, came true.

With a sigh he shook off the tendrils of the past and stepped into the comforting aisles of racks and racks of accumulated knowledge. Rune revered the rich history of Majiqs and the mysterious ancestors from the before-times – the eons when the Templars first arrived in this realm, and before, when they came from the ancient lands beyond the Threshold. He yearned to cull secrets and techniques that would enhance his abilities as a Maji.

What information existed in that nebulous history was here in these vaulted rooms? Although there were no recorded annals of the first beings possessing the skill to bend physics and minds to their will, many myths still circulated among the learning classes of Maji-in-training. Legends of Merlin and his Wizards traveling from other dimensions were rife. Rune always liked the yarns telling of Sorcerers guiding the destinies of kings and princes in distant regions before finally coming here. Documented chronicles dated back only a handful of centuries and so anything beyond that dissolved into fantasy.

In the more recent times the Maji home kingdom – Dragonshire – was ruled by a Maji-Queen of the House of Garraden. Matriarchal order had been in place for hundreds of years. Sages were part of the royal bloodline that guided, with authority over, other parallel realms. The Maji's visionary and manipulative abilities made them the natural rulers over various other beings from the other empires. No Elf, Faerie, Ghost, Vampyre or Were-creature was more powerful than those endowed with Majiq. Thus, their worlds were dimensions of a resolute hierarchy.

Controlling the Threshold to keep Majiq-beings to a minimum on the mostly non-Majiq Earth was also the responsibility of the Maji. Marauding pirates, disagreeable Vampyres, errant Faeries, occasionally slipped through, but for the most part the Threshold was impenetrable.

Then came the Diaboliq, five centuries ago. The dreaded demon twins Kyre and Maksym. They seduced followers into the blood-drinking wickedness, and then groomed assassins trained in Dark Arts who, distorted by pride and greed, twisted their vile desires into overtaking the kingdoms. It started with conflict in Dragonshire, the center of the realms. In the Battle Perilous, the Queen of the House of Avelon was murdered, the ruling council killed. The territory polarized into forces on either side of the Line-of-Rebellion. When the horrible civil war was over, all known Diaboliqs were executed. Merlin and his Order became the religious and nationalized authority.

However, the new Queen Garraden felt threatened by the might of Merlin and his Majiqs, so they relocated to Avelon, the enchanted isle serving as the cusp between Dragonshire and Earth. Hard to believe anyone would be so foolish as to alienate the greatest Wizard of all realms and ages – and many ages – Rune thought with a smirk. Hundreds of years old, who would argue with someone as sagacious as Merlin? Well, aside from him, that is. Rune felt justified, though, of course, in countering Merlin's wishes.

Born in Dragonshire, but considering himself and all Majiqs at home on Earth, Rune was comfortable in this sovereignty. And nowhere in the dominion could be found the timeless ambiance that permeated this massive wing of rooms deep in the Castle. With slow, ambling gait, Rune made his way past the low sofas near the front door. Walking down the nearest passageway he studied the towering shelves, noted the alcoves ringing the room, and meandered past titles -- favorably recollected or intriguingly mysterious. Feeling guided, as if pulled by an invisible string, he arrived at the ancient history section. Absorbing Majiq, he stopped short when he realized someone was already in the deep, dark aisle.

A light haired young man rested on the floor. Waving his hand nonchalantly through the air, he was obviously using Majiq to select a book from one of the top shelves. The old tome floated aimlessly, slowly down, as if the instigator was toying with the manipulative power. Awed, Rune remained motionless and mute. Pre-Tyros rarely were gifted enough to use remote power, especially without the channeling amulet and ring, or enchanted powder, that Majiq required!

Eyes closed, the boy delicately fingered the atmosphere, murmuring -- reading the pages of the closed book -- with the power of Majiq! "Dragon kingdom -- Maji crystals -- Maji legends -- ah," he whispered, his smug satisfaction nearly as strong as his power.

In pleasant, subtle waves, Majiq reached Rune, bringing an involuntary smile to his lips. In the presence of such a formidable student, Rune refused to be too impressed. From a long ago past a mischievous and ages-buried Sprite reared its head in Rune's conscience. Without moving a muscle, Rune used his considerable power of Majiq to override the boy's orchestration and the heavy book dropped onto the student's stomach with a thud.

"Ooofff!"

Coughing through the dust, he sat up, brushing grime from his shirt and sash. Picking up the dense volume, he addressed it with a dry twist of his face. "Well, you must have weighty wisdom indeed to be that heavy!"

A laugh sputtered out of Rune.

The sandy haired, red-faced youth -- the flashy sabre fighter from the training room -- jumped up in surprise and turned to the intruder. "Oh! Soren Rune! Uh -- I mean Paladin -- Tutor Rune." After a curt bow he drew in a breath to say something then grimaced and sighed. "I suppose you'll tell me I deserved that for being lazy and not climbing up a ladder."

Trying to judge a Tutor's thoughts? Cheeky, Rune labeled with amusement. And a pawky sense of humor. The Templar didn't want to reward the arrogance, but the boy was naturally engaging and self-effacing. Two charming traits that probably gave him many advantages in the Castle. The innate light-heartedness must make him popular with students and teachers alike.

"Reprimand you for using Majiq instead of physical energy?" All Maji, and particularly youngsters, were supposed to refrain from unnecessary Majiq within the Castle. They needed to remain fit and not allow mental and spiritual abilities to atrophy their bodies. Growth in all areas was required to maintain a balance in Majiq. Rune's eyes narrowed, purposely conveying his most stern expression. "Do you always try to predict the future, student?"

"No." His eyes sparkled. "Just anticipate. Teachers usually tell me what I've done wrong." His lips quirked. "I just thought I'd save you the trouble."

An eyebrow shot up in amusement and he covered his mouth with his hand to hide a quick grin. "You sound a rebellious sort."

Face to face, Rune caught his first good look at the athletic swordsman. Even in the dim lighting there was no mistaking the features. Angular, strong. The lean face harbored vibrant, exotically slanted green eyes that flashed with liveliness. Streaks of gold shimmered in the longish strands of light hair.

Rune concealed his surprise revealing, instead, casual delight at the clever repartee. The boy was an Ameden! So few of them left in the realm! Ameden -- the small province where the native race was driven to near extinction during the original rise of Diaboliq in eons past. A powerful mixture of telepathy and fore-sight made the Amedens feared and prized. Some believed the clan was the beginning of Majiqs, and that the royal House of Garraden usurped power from the tribe of sensitives. Wars against them broke out. Natives were captured, enslaved and controlled. Long before written sagas, Ameds were exiled by the ruling class, ostensibly to bring peace to Dragonshire, but many speculated that the House of Garraden was threatened by Amed power and sought to keep them as far from authority as possible.

Ion-Gawain had traveled to Amed several times on quests to protect the endangered fore-tells. He always had a soft spot in his heart for the plight of these good people. The late Templar would approve of this spunky novice.

Wizards and the kingdom finally arrived to save the Amed province from Diaboliq, but it was too late for the gifted ones. They had been destroyed. Slanted green eyes distinguished Amedens still, long after the holocausts. The strange powers were all gone now, so Amedens were free to travel the realm with only mild suspicion. What a combination -- a fully gifted Ameden as a Maji! Rune wasn't sure the Order could handle such Majiq.

"And how is it you know my name -- ?"

Standing tall the young man approached. "Amestoy Daavv, Mentor."

Sensing deep respect, confidence, Rune was fascinated. "So, a royal Ameden! And a Maji?"

Majiq-sage powers with the heritage of a fore-seer? The gift of visions had died out long ago on Amed. But somewhere in Daavv's family there was a Maji ancestor. In the province it was said the antecedents of the old ruling class – what was left of it – took the name Amestoy. The aristocracy all had the House of Amed in front of the clan name. Then Estoy was the second half of the front name delineating his mother's band. Was Daavv a location or other family name? He wasn't familiar enough with the province to know. What of the gold in the hair? Weren't all Amedens gifted with thick, deep auburn hair? From mixed heritage then. Yes, the eyes were not as slanted as a full blooded Amed.

The boy's countenance seemed to fall and his body slump with regret. He looked away in irritation. "Yes. I am Ameden."

A curse to be instantly branded. Obviously he yearned for an anonymity that his heritage would never allow. Perhaps that explained the flamboyant style of fighting? Striking out to make his own imprint on his life here, where all within the Order were equally judged by Majiq, and not exterior factors.

Rune's tone was harsher than he felt inside, but knew it was the right touch. "Well, you will get no special considerations for your uniqueness, young Novitiate." There was vivid relief in the stark green eyes when they rose back up to meet his. "And you have not answered my question of how you come to know who I am."

In deference Amestoy gave a slight bow of his head. "Every student of history knows one of the greatest Maji of our time!"

The exaggeration was not meant to be flattering, just honest. Rune tried to close down his senses, to stop absorbing so much from Amestoy, and was startled to find he was already tuned low for reception of impressions. What he was getting was the student's strong broadcasting of subconscious praise.

"You're a hero of the realms where you fought with the legendary warrior Tor Ion-Gawain . . . ." His adulation trailed off abruptly.

He sensed, or saw, the shadow pass through Rune's soul, momentarily eclipsing even his deep blue eyes. About his late friend, Rune had few defenses.

"My pardon. His loss is felt by all who honor justice. I know you were friends."

Suddenly cold inside, Rune could not bring himself to respond. He did not take grief well and to share it with someone else – a stranger – a student -- was uncomfortable.

"Uh -- and I know that great Maji don't usually want to talk about battles -- because Maji are warriors second, keepers of the religion first." The quotes rushed out of him in breathless rapidity and at the end he offered a faltering smile.

Flattered at the admiration, disturbed that Amestoy could reach so intimately into his inner feelings, Rune struggled to define an emotion, mask it, and sort out a question among the many puzzles that naturally sprang from the unexpectedly gregarious observations.

"Yes, Tor Ion-Gawain was a great Paladin."

The gasp belonged to the young man, not him, but it should have been Rune's. The pain from the anguish must have registered on his unguarded face. Or were his emotions so clearly felt by anyone in his proximity? Every reminder of the loss of his friend was like a fresh stab in his heart. An inner agony that was repeated time after time on his trips to the Castle the past few years. Here in these halls he had walked and laughed and debated with his strong, mighty friend, Tor.

"My apologies. He was a great Templar, I mean, priest. I beg your pardon at bringing up such a painful memory. His death is a loss to the kingdom. And I'm sure to all those who counted him as a friend."

Not knowing what else to say, but touched at the sympathy and sense of loss emanating from the innocent lad, Rune gave a nod of his head in acceptance. He needed to stop being so sensitive – stop personalizing mourning – and move on. Tor would not have supported his emotionalism. He was with all the great Maji now in the Infinity of Beyond. A place where valiant spirits dwelled after mortal death. A blissful haven of no conflict or pain, where the pure in heart were rewarded for their goodness. Those left behind – Rune -- needed to move on with their missions.

Pushing himself out of the quagmire of grief that was far too obvious, he responded, "Not at all, young Novitiate. It is a deserving honor for a member of the Order to remember Tor Ion-Gawain with such reverence. As his friend, I thank you." He cleared his throat, uncomfortable with – and very unused to – seeking an excuse.

"I beg your forgiveness for allowing my emotions such free rein." He cleared his throat again to quickly move along from this disturbing confession of truth. Rune chose a common battle tactic to swerve attention away from him. A diversion. "What is it you are doing here, student Daavv? This must be a very dull place for someone as energetic as you." It was meant as a mild censure for arrogance. "Is that a book on dragons?"

"One of my favorite subjects. You would know all about them since you are a renowned dragon lord."

Again the unabashed adulation. "It is second nature in my home province." Rune explained.

"Yes, Ayelsborne, the only realm where dragons are indigenous. Isn't it interesting that there are no red dragons. They exist only in the Ancients' realm from where Merlin and the original wizards journeyed. Why do you think that is?"

"That is an old tale I have never questioned," he replied thoughtfully. "You are full of curiosity and dusty myths."

"I enjoy these old books. They have intriguing data in them." The comment was taken as a compliment and, in return, offered a sly, self-assured grin. Befitting his charming personality, his voice was deep and mellow. "I noticed you watching our training. It must be boring for a great Maji to see such amateurs playing with sabres."

Remembering the agile combatant as anything but boring with his flips, summersaults and dashing style, Rune thought back to others he had trained with, taught and known. Khejan's methods surfaced too. The comparison was unfair but it came out unbidden.

"I see arrogance where caution and patience would have been more suited."

If he had slapped Daavv in the face it could not have been more startling. The sharp rebuff whipped his admirer like a rapier strike and he flinched, visibly stung. He dropped his gaze. "My apologies, Mentor. I did not think it inappropriate to be -- creative -- in my training."

Ashamed of his unjust mental comparisons, and with his own impatience, Rune re-directed the conversation. "You do not need to address me so formally. I am not your Mentor."

Daavv glanced up, green eyes uncertain, wavering, and then boldly steeling to take a risk. "No -- I mean yes -- Mentor Rune." He hesitated, tentative only for an instant before plunging ahead, obviously not wanting to waste a golden opportunity in a one-on-one with a hero. "You are one of the greatest Paladins of all, blending warrior skill and spirituality. A true Templar. It is said your understanding of Majiq is vast. And your – unusual -- approach to keeping justice is unequalled."

Now embarrassed, Rune dared to hold the admiring look, feeling an incredible need to not turn away from the uncomfortable praise, to not back off from a student so enchanting. Uncomfortable with responding to the unabashed adulation, again he diverted.

"So, young Daavv, what else do you find so intriguing in these old books besides dragons?"

Amestoy held out the aged volume. "This ancient text on the beginning of the Maji Order." He flashed a grin. "Well, not history, exactly." He searched for a word and delivered it with a wry touch of humor. "Fables or myths, some of my teachers call them."

"The old tales of mysticism?" Rune brightened. Many times he had read those lyrical yarns of the origins of the Maji, Majiq, and the kingdom. It was likely he had held this book in his own hands when he was Daavv's age, thumbing through the timeless territories of Sorcerers and Maji. Disconcertingly, he had been thinking about those, and now Amestoy mentioned them as his focus. "The murder of the queen's court with the rising of the demon twins?"

He nodded in ascent. "That and – uh – others."

"Intriguing. Why do they interest you?"

He could have bit his tongue! Of course this student was interested in legends! Ameden was known as a fabled realm with imaginary powers. The green-eyed, auburn haired people had, for many years, been abducted from their fair province to be scattered across the dimensions. The unprincipled of the kingdoms thought to capture the slant-eyed natives to hold the enchantment of prophesy, of foretelling the future, in their hands. Ameden spells were said to be a talent even more powerful and targeted than the skill of the Order!

What had resulted was the hunting of a people to near extinction! Fortunately, there was no reaction to his latest etiquette blunder.

Daavv's smile was dazzling. "I have taken the Novitiate tests. I will soon be assigned a Tutor." Fleetingly an embarrassed flush wisped across his pale cheeks. He stared at the book instead of at the Mentor's probing eyes. "I know there are legends -- about Tutors and Tyros. Old and forgotten stories."

Rune looked away, concentrating on the once colorful, but now faded cover of the decrepit book. So Amestoy was one of the Novitiates ready to leave the student level and advance to Tyro under the tutelage of a Mentor. As Majiq tingled his skin, Rune fought to ignore the rising anticipation quickening his blood and racing along his spine. He dared not look up to see if there was some kind of reciprocity from the person who, he knew, was watching him intently. Such instant bonds were rare and Rune refused to believe he would be unfortunate enough to be party to one.

Again he deflected, his voice as steady as possible. "And which volume is this?"

Daavv held it out, proffering it to the elder. "It's supposed to contain stories of the Majiq Warrior Bond. Have you heard of it?"

"Old superstitions." His voice was dry and cracked. Warrior Bond. The most elevated level of Majiq to be found between Mentor and Tyro. A joining of spirit, strength and ideals that merged two into a single unit. Uncommon might and hidden reserves of enchantment came with this unique link. A myth. A foolish legend. Such idealistic relationships did not exist between Mentor and student, although he might have believed in the story in his boyish naiveté'. He might have wished it before death brought him to his knees, humbled him to the soul.

"Nothing but old stories." His condemnation was clipped, harsh. "Do not waste your time with such nonsense."

"I always wanted to believe it was true." Amestoy sighed, flinching slightly under the ruthless denunciation. Still persistent, foolishly relentless in his goal, he seemed determined to relay his dreams to the older Maji. "My teachers

-- sometimes even in cursing -- remind that Majiq is a gift in me. Rebellious seems an interchangeable word they use as well." Drollness edged his tone. "They tell me I need a strong Tutor to train me if I am ever to channel my talent and become a skilled Maji." Serious, his voice dropping to intone his sincerity, Daavv stepped closer. "I hoped there would be a Mentor -- someone like me -- someone I could connect with like no one I've ever known before." He drew in a breath. "I would like to believe that could happen."

Deny. Deflect. "It's only a tale." he pronounced, his voice resolute. "Being a good Tyro, or a Paladin, has nothing to do with dreams." He wondered why the young man was staring at him with such an odd expression. Only then did he realize he had been toying with his dragon crystal talisman, and it was hot in his fingers! He dropped it to his chest and looked down, amazed to see the prism glowing green! What? His crystal was blue!

"You wear the dragon crystal!" Amestoy gasped. "The shield symbol of the Warrior Bond!"

"Dragons are the Familiars of my home province," he snapped back.

To disavow any inclinations toward myths, Rune grabbed for the book, intending to fly it back up to its tall shelf, but when he touched it, a shock jolted through his hand and arm and seemed to vibrate to his very core. Gripping the book for an eternal moment, they held each other's eyes, Majiq flowing back and forth between them, confirming profound certainties for both. One received a clear understanding that his wildest imaginings could come true. The other received the confirmation that his worst expectations might come true.

Rune's fingers, numb with cold shock, released the book. Out of amazed surprise Amestoy's grip went limp and the tome fell from his hands with a muted thud. The physical action startled Rune and he stepped back, staring at Daavv, flashes of energy coursing around him. They watched each other, both catching their breath and shaking heads at the experience. One hopeful, one fearful, but neither able to deny the force of the wizardry.

Abruptly Rune spun around, taking quick strides out of the library.

Breathless, awed and confused, Daavv backed against the shelves, staring after the Paladin. When he bent to retrieve the book some time later, he saw that the pages had fallen open to the old, faded drawing of a tall man and a shorter protégé fighting side by side with sabres. Battling in tandem - Tutor and Tyro -- exemplifying the unity and link of the Majiq Warrior Bond. They wielded swords that shimmered green, and shields emblazoned with dragons. With shaking knees he sank to the floor and started re-reading the old, amazing myth, now with a completely new perspective.

**

Long legs marching the halls of the Castle with a quick, strident pace, Rune roamed remote corridors, trying to lose himself in the vastness of the old towers and stone alcoves. No matter how fast he walked, where he tread, there was no escaping his thoughts. He could not run from the memory of Majiq as it whipped through his body and soul with a strength and surety he had not felt in -- that he had never felt before -- he realized with amazement.

Derisively he dismissed Daavv's adoration, but privately admitted to well knowing Majiq. He had felt the comfort of Majiq in times of pain and stress. The might of it as a gift in battle, or the mercy of it when he needed to exhibit compassion and understanding. It had never failed him. Except when he should have been at his brother's side, and when his Tyro fell to inexperience and Rune had been too blind, or prideful, or arrogant to stop the descent.

Even years after that agonizing ordeal, Rune could not think of taking a Tyro again. The pain was still too great. He had invested too much in his pupil, given too much of himself. When Tor died it was as if part of Rune died, too. Now Majiq was telling him there was a new Tyro for him. Not just as a usual pupil, but one with an already formidable connection to him. A Warrior Bond? Rune sneered at the thought even as chills rippled his skin.

How could he deny what he was feeling? What Majiq was telling him? How could he take another trainee into his life, let alone his heart? Shattered and cold emotionally, he had nothing left to offer a Tyro. To succeed, a partnership between Tutor and Tyro needed common respect, trust and faith backing the necessary undercurrent of Majiq. Ideally, the partnership should grow to be as meaningful and close as a parent and child -- or whatever the appropriate relationship – the foundation of trust, love and commitment had to be there or it would never work.

Perhaps because Rune was by nature a loner, an individualist, he had not comfortably fit into the familial role. More likely, since the loss of his brother, Tor, he could not abide the thought of being close to anyone. There were plentiful priests eager to adopt a Tyro. So many here at the Castle right now who longed for the difficult, yet rewarding synergy of a Tutor-Tyro blend. Not him! This time Majiq was wrong. He did not have a heart left to devote to anything but his path of justice!

He stopped at a window to watch the dizzying array of illuminated dots in the crowded hamlets of Avelon. He followed tiny lights that were lanterns on wagons, the slower ones that were probably people on foot, the larger clusters of cargo or passenger ships. In the distance, away from the mystic city, mists shrouded the coastlines, blocking Avelon with Majiq. The center of enchantment, the isle never slept and commerce continued, oblivious to the Diaboliq shadows crowding in from every realm. Around the Castle hilltop, though, there was space, and peace. Everywhere, that is, but in Rune's soul.

Shards of Diaboliq persistently stabbed at the edges of his senses. Even though he was no Seer, he interpreted that to mean a dangerous future was looming. Was this the time to deny what he knew to be true? Should not a Sorcerer pick up the gauntlet now and do all within his power to combat the pressing shades of evil? Was this not the right moment in history to accept a Tyro, despite his own personal misgivings?

In the quiet hours of the pre-dawn he wandered through the corridors, weary and troubled. At last he stopped at a favored spot, a conservatory where the uncovered parapet opened to the night sky. In this high turret of the Castle, he settled next to a fountain at the back of the massive garden. When he realized he was fingering his amulet again, he pushed his hands into deep, velvety pockets and leaned against a wall. Too tired to meditate properly, he hoped he would find a sense of peace in this tranquil setting, absorb enough serenity to cling to, and then return to his quarters and sleep. In the morning he would leave and go somewhere far from the Castle, from the Order, to receive a remote assignment. No meddling Paladins, no engaging students, no threats to his autonomy and isolation.

"Even without Majiq I can tell you are disturbed, Soren."

Remaining still, Rune didn't know what to say in response.

"Have you discovered something unpleasant? Perhaps this is why you are here." Not a question.

Undoubtedly Merlin-Maj knew his inner secrets, too. Should he deny the truth or characteristically meet it bluntly, accepting the worst. What would the worst be in this case? Unable to find the words, he nodded.

"Old lessons could be repeated, but you know them well enough. Sometimes, when your pain is too great, you forget them."

Rune winced, hating his deeply private anguish to be so obvious.

"You were ever perceptive, Soren. You value the past, and live in the present. Never did you dread the future. Because you know to trust in Majiq. Your Majiq. It is one of your many strengths."

It was ridiculous that such trite quotes applied so perfectly to his confusion and doubt. Shouldn't a 'great' Maji Mentor be above these petty fears and hurts? Ruefully, he reasoned he could never be totally free of the many faults that were inherent to his race. Stupidity, however, was not listed among his problems.

Sighing to steady the quavering that threatened his tight throat he admitted. "It is sometimes difficult to adhere to the old training when there has been so much loss." It was not just Tor Ion-Gawain. Many others had fallen in the terrible years since the rise of the Gadion-Obscura. Coming back here to the Castle, on the cusp of a new phase in his life, he hesitated to feel again. Did Majiq demand too much from him, to edge back to an emotional vulnerability in trusting another being with his complete soul? "It is a great deal to ask after the scars of the past."

"Release the blame. It was no fault of yours Tor was murdered."

That truth he could not acknowledge.

"He selected his own path, just as you often do. Impulsive, yes, but deeply rooted in Majiq. Will you not follow your destiny, Paladin Soren?"

His voice was smooth, consistent with the buoyed confidence, but low and deep with lingering grief. "Majiq shows me a path that my heart is not ready to tread, Merlin-Maj."

"Majiq is always clear and true. Do not let doubt divide you. Which path choose you this day?"

Narrowing his eyes, slightly, Rune studied the slightly rotund man. "You felt --" aloud he could not utter the word 'connection', so he stumbled, "uh -- something, didn't you?"

With a nod Merlin-Maj confirmed the suspicion. "I know you two to be magnets. I see the enchantment between you and the student Daavv. You are great conduits of Majiq. Stubborn and strong-willed. A match. The Tutor can teach the novice much." Then, after a split-second pause he added, "But the student can also teach the Mentor. You will be formidable allies. Bonded."

The phrase brought Rune's eyebrows together in a natural glower he hoped would reinforce his position. "There can be no bond."

With a little smile, Merlin's lips twitched. "You are always so certain. And stubborn." He breathed out a soft little hum which turned to a laugh. "I felt it! I need no more proof to know that this myth, at least, is based in truth."

"Myth?"

Rune snorted derisively. He would not even comment on the amazing coincidence that Merlin-Maj mentioned a bond -- a fable. This was not a Warrior Bond! This was not anything! He could not allow that! About to refute the comments, Rune paused. Was Merlin referring to the Warrior Bond or to the Ameden tales? He'd better be sure that they were talking about the same lore before he embarrassed himself.

Deflect. Divert. This had become his mantra. "What is Daavv doing here anyway? Amedens prefer the safety of their isolated province after the purges."

Merlin walked slowly back and forth as though formulating an answer. "Amestoy is unusually gifted in enchantment. You will be one of the very few to know this secret, but he led me to Ameden. He drew me there with Majiq so I could find him and bring him here. One of the First Orphans. No one thought to look for them in Ameden. Daavv was destined to be part of our Order."

Eyebrows hiked in surprise, Rune took a moment to evaluate that statement. Merlin had gone to Ameden -- the forbidden province – himself, to retrieve a young one? Extraordinary indeed, but it did not change his own path. "I am not ready for a Tyro. I don't want --" He looked away, unable to reveal his innermost fears, even though Merlin sensed them already. "I cannot abide another death."

Pursing his lips, Merlin nodded his head, pacing a bit more on the stone paving, then returning to stand by the cross-legged Tutor sitting on the cold cobbles. "If you became his Tutor, would you fail him?"

"No!" The response was instant, sharp and certain.
  With a moment to ponder, he tempered the instinctive response. "Not if I could help it, of course. Once I commit to a task I do not give up, Mentor."

A little chortle of amusement escaped the puffy lips. "I remember that well from your youth. You were stubborn from the first!"

Rune cringed at the reminder.

"Hmmm." Merlin made the sound dubious, as if he did not believe the fervent refute. "Even if he is arrogant -- and he is and --" his brown face crinkled as he searched for a word . . . " – flashy. You would not let him down. It is not in your nature."

The gift of Majiq was hereditary, a spiritual and physiological element blessed to those of the Maji bloodline. Some families were given many Maji children. For others, the enchanted strain skipped a generation or more. There was no predicting it, but religious families throughout the realm prepared for it as part of their culture.

Over the years, the Garraden family emerged as the strongest, most formidable blood connection, and thus they ascended to the throne. In their line women held the mightiest power, and thus, Dragonshire was ruled by a monarchy passed down through the women. Lesser families of Majiq retained the talent and wizardry, and commanded the legions of Dragons in their home realm.

The line of Avelon, once the most resilient of Wizards, then brought their lineage through the Threshold to Earth. Here Merlin and his Sorcerers meddled in the affairs of Mankind. It was a more comfortable realm than serving under the Garraden family back home. Other lesser families chose to reside at Avelon. And after the Battle Perilous, many Majiq and mundane beings sought refuge and freedom in the less structured, but safe haven, of the enchanted isle hidden along the coast of Britania.

Instead of agreeing with the assessments of his personality, and the overt ego of the exhibitionist Daavv, another image came to his mind. This impression was of the myth-book-in-hand young student in the library, solidly locking Rune's gaze; the drawing of the Warriors with the dragon shields. With it came a tingle of enchantment and the memory of the electrifying connection made when they both held the arcane tome together for a Majiqal heartbeat.

"Do you think young Amestoy Daavv will fail you?"

"That's not what I said." Rune snapped out, then kept his silence. Merlin out-waited him. Finally Rune continued. "I can't be sure. I don't want to take the risk."

Merlin chortled, which earned him a sour look from the junior Sorcerer. "Unusual statement when it comes from you, the master of rebellion."

The irony was not lost on the taller man and Rune surrendered a grin. Merlin's thick eyebrows dropped, his face sober. "Diaboliq is gaining strength, Soren. The Gadion-Obscura is thriving.

Our Order is threatened along with all the realms, including this one. Great evil abounds everywhere. Maji are the sentinels of the Threshold. We are called to keep stability and safety for all the dimensions. We will need all the strength possible. Is that not so?"

Rune breathed out a deep sigh. "Yes, I have felt it, too. More evil, more attacks against Maji."

He had lost his friend. Now others were falling to wickedness. The tide of malevolence and targeted, specific threats against the Maji were rising -- even weapons specifically designed to eliminate Maji. There were more and more Novitiates dropping out, failing the rigorous training at the Castle. Disappointment and disillusionment caused them to drift away to the far reaches of the realms, some plying their talent in Majiq to dark pursuits, although a true Maji could not sustain a life of crime or evil. Heredity gave them the physical and spiritual abilities for their talents, but if used against good, their hearts actually shriveled and the Majiq was lost.

More than at any time before, some learners failed their initial tests to advance to Sorcerer. Should Rune include his own stealth group of the secret Templar Legion an act of rebellion to his Order? He didn't think so. He was on the side of right, even if covertly.

His voice lowered, skin growing cold at the remembrance of his own responsibility to this burgeoning dread. "Every day it is more difficult to counter the influence of the Diaboliq."

Merlin patted his shoulder. "When will you believe my lectures, Paladin?"

"I am sorry, Merlin. It takes a great deal of time for the guilt -- the hurt -- to heal."

"Amestoy is your Destiny, within your current of Majiq. Healing will come through helping him, I vow. You will never regret this step." The point was met with silence. "You have always followed Majiq to the exclusion of all else. Sometimes to your own peril. That is folly. Not taking a new Tyro when guided by Majiq, that would be folly as well."

This earned a glare from the younger Sorcerer.

"Again I ask you, Mentor Rune, which path choose you?"

Tangible, feathery tufts of the connection with the young initiate lingered. "I choose the path of Majiq," Rune responded with quiet certainty.

Merlin-Maj gave a nod. "Trust Majiq. A noble destiny is ahead for Tutor and Tyro. Great is your future together. A Warrior Bond it might be."

After Rune struggled to hide his dismayed surprise, the humor of the comment struck him. He fought to hide a smile. "Have you been reading those old Faery tales again, Merlin?"

His eyes twinkled. "I would never tell you, Mentor Rune. I always believe in Majiq."

**

Never one to waste time, Soren Rune appeared outside the training rooms when it was still early morning. He watched while the sabre teacher addressed the students, offering the standard lecture before pupils practiced with swords and rapiers, along with staffs. Lightly-Majiq-dusted, but still formidable wands were next. This exercise in the tactics and skills of face-to-face combat harkened back to the times when the old fashioned blades of ancient, non-Sorcerer knights were the weapons of choice. In a final sparring match, Amestoy Daavv and a wild, black-haired girl named Kenzi -- the two initiates promoting to Tyros -- would take the first set.

With a sense of smugness Rune noted the boy seemed to be tired. A restless night pondering the future? Could he SEE the future? No, Rune was not buying into that myth or ANY myth! Nerves, that's what it was. Amestoy was nervous. It would serve him right, came the ungracious thought. No, he didn't deserve that. He was following the dictates of Majiq in a truer course than Rune. Perhaps even all the way back to his long-standing interest in the Warrior Bond? Could the seasoned Templar apply that stray thought to his own fascination of the old myth? It was something to ponder in the years ahead.

As Daavv took his place on the mat he shot a glance at Rune. The Wizard had deliberately placed himself in easy view of the student. If Majiq wanted him to do something with the boy then Rune had a right to know what mettle his protégé-to-be possessed. Nothing like pressure -- the final match -- the advancement to Tyro. And now the unexpected and possibly unnerving observation by an intimidating and infamous Paladin.

Given the cue to start, both initiates bowed then met in a clash of Majiq and might. They expertly slashed the swords at each other. In inexperienced hands the fight would be dangerous, but their immature skill at using Majiq enabled them to at least react defensively and avoid injury.

Both evenly matched in size and energy, the young people parried and swung around the room, sweat glistening from them both. Neither seemed to gain an advantage. The Master Swordsman halted the match and weapons were changed to rapiers. For the next interlude the skirmish was stylized and orderly, the whipping, thin blades slicing the air and clashing constantly, but neither combatant gaining an advantage.

Then the directive was given to advance to the final level, and they obediently drew their Majiq-dusted wands. Kenzi had speed on her side. Daavv had agility, maneuverability and -- yes -- unmistakable style to aid his endeavor. The battle commenced with several moments of the opponents stalking, assessing and prowling around each other. Amestoy impatiently made several swift, sweeping arcs of the stick and on the last one Kenzi clipped him on the side with the energy of her baton. The sting singed, causing Daavv to wince and twist, just barely avoiding a massive stroke of Kenzi's next swipe.

Most Novitiates had enough Majiq-sage to give low energy to a wand. Customarily, the shortened staffs were dusted with Majiq dust anyway, just to give the trial a realistic tone. At this age, however, any youngster eligible to be a Tyro had some abilities in touch Majiq. Daavv's wand seemed brighter than his opponent's, but that could be the quality of Majiq flowing through the weapons. Each Maji had a unique imprint on elementary telepathic readings of lesser beings, language and fighting skills. It was difficult to attribute the possibility of enhanced Majiq when powders were used to augment the skills during the tests.

As the conflict continued, Rune sensed the emotions of the boy. He pushed aside the thought that the two already had an innate connection and attributed the link to the young man's strong Majiq. It lent, though, to an understanding of the strategy behind his flamboyance. Kenzi was distracted by the fancy skips, jumps and flips, easily giving away her tactics and capabilities. On the weak side of this scheme, Daavv was expending most of his energy, tiring quickly and inflicting no hits at all, while he had been burned by the energy bolts several times.

Then, with a surge of Majiq that Rune sensed nearly as powerfully as if it had been a warrior in the battle, he felt Amestoy feint to the left. Knowing it was a ruse, he watched with glowing appreciation as the boy flipped to the right, slashing the enchanted wand across the neck of Kenzi on the exposed right side of her body.

The nip was enough to penetrate the skin and she cried out, falling to her knees in decisive defeat. Exhausted, panting, Daavv returned to face his foe, releasing the energy to return it to a benign short staff. Daavv gave his opponent a quick nod and a few words, making sure Kenzi was only stung, not seriously injured. He then went to the stone bench at the side of the room to sit with the other Novitiates. Casting a glance at Rune, the Mentor could sense a feeling of contentment and curiosity in the boy. Amestoy was pleased -- not arrogant -- with his performance and wondered what Rune thought about it.

Walking away with a straight face, Rune ambled down the corridor to a battlement alcove to think. There was a great deal to consider. Whoever became Amestoy's Tutor would need a strong hand and firm resolve to countermand the willful confidence, pretentiousness and -- his lips twitched in an amused smile -- spirit. Amestoy seemed to possess that in abundance.

With a resigned sigh, he stopped the silent pretense. His instincts – Majiq -- demanded he take this boy as his Tyro. This was no subtle inspiration; this was a subconscious shout to his soul. He could not deny being virtually commanded back to the Castle, lead to Amestoy on three separate occasions, and unmistakably feeling the connection between them.

Rune sat in the corner of the niche, not easily noticed by passersby. The students would come past here at the end of their training session. As a final test, Rune wanted to examine the enchantment of Majiq one more time. If they really were connected, Amestoy would find him. Not that he felt there was a -- link -- a bond -- but just in case, this little ploy would serve as a game.

Before long the low murmurs of conversation filled the quiet corridor. One was high-pitched, excited and taunting. Boys! They could be so rude! And selfish! It was a strident condemnation rising above the rest. There was an uncomfortable wave of contention emanating from the source that was palpable to a Paladin attuned to such subtle and non-subtle disturbances.

"You always have to show off, Amestoy. It was even worse with a Mentor watching."

"And he was watching you." A lower, less irritated voice chimed in. "You don't really think he'd pick you as a Tyro, do you? He's one of the most famous Wizards in the Order!"

"'A mysterious recluse' is how they describe him." The strident-toned student continued. "You're too much of a show-off for him, even if he ever takes a Tyro, and I've heard he never will because he can't be bothered."

The young people stopped in the corridor and Rune could see their silhouettes. Several crowded around the taller, trim, stiff form of Daavv. Not so long ago in history, Rune was an Initiate. Most fellow students were decent and likable. Some were harsher personalities. He had endured his own periods of persecution from those who did not appreciate his quirky, but studious nature or his sometimes rebellious individualism.

Now, even though the barbs were aimed at Daavv, they managed to sting the not-so-thick skin of the Paladin in question. Wishing he could see Amestoy's face, he realized he didn't need visual proximity. Through their tenuous-but-very-real connection, he could feel ripples of defiant, defensive umbrage at the invectives. Not that they were hurtful to Daavv, but that they were insulting Rune.

"Thank you for that piece of old gossip, Brisbane. Fortunately," Amestoy stated clearly, slowly, deeply, in his driest tone, "he will not be coming to you for advice. If Mentor Rune is looking for a Novitiate, I would bet he will stop well before he gets to your door."

The instinctive defense made the Mentor smile. He certainly couldn't fault the boy for loyalty. Not that he expected allegiance from this stranger, but it was nice to know he had an ally. At least one being within the Castle would defend his honor.

"You'll see," the high-pitched Brisbane assured, then left with his little clan.

When the others were out of sight Daavv kicked the wall and flung himself into the nearest stone edging. A moment passed and he slammed a fist on the rock wall. Placing his face in his hands he rubbed fingers through his long, shimmering-gold streaked hair. Even without Majiq, Rune could have sensed the frustration, the irritation, the -- uncertainty? So, this skilled, seemingly superbly confident boy had deeper insecurities that he let slip to no one. Complex, but strong, Rune labeled with appreciation.

Daavv's head snapped up and he peered into the darkness, directly stabbing Rune with a stare. Instantly he came to his feet. "Mentor."

Rune tried not to be annoyed that even in small things he would not be given an out from this unexpected -- unwanted -- turn of events. "I am not your Tutor, student Daavv." The nod was civil and neutral as he stepped into the light.

The boy flinched and bowed his head. "No, you are not, Mentor – uh – I mean Paladin Rune. My apologies."

Rune was deservedly known as an aloof, stern Maji. He had never considered himself cruel, but his situation seemed to be bringing out the worst in him. That was no defense for incivility, yet to apologize would seem to encourage the possibility of a shared future for them -- which there should not be -- but which he could no longer deny. Rebuff? Accept gracefully? No. He could not bring himself to like the direction Majiq wanted his life to take. So he chose to not respond.

"May I ask you something, Mentor Rune?"

"Yes."

Glancing up, the resolve overcame his uncertainties. "What was your opinion of my duels?"

A spark of Majiq flowed between them. Rune didn't even attempt to tune it out this time. Neither would he acknowledge it openly, or give any praise.

Some thought Maji needed to remain pure, faultless and always within a perfect light to keep their Majiq. Not so. Maji were not monks! They were mortal and given all the imperfections of any being in the realms. Maji bloodlines and hearts gave them a spiritual advantage. But Maji on the side of right and skilled in Majiq could still be less than sterling people. Not Daavv. He was a dazzling light that was almost too brilliant for this jaded, cynical Tutor to like.

"It is more important what your sabre Mentor thought."

Daavv smiled, eyes sparkling. "At the top of my class, Mentor. Although I did get points marked down for the overly dramatic slash across the neck." Gingerly he rubbed his tender, singed side. "Not to mention some other marks I was sloppy about receiving."

The Majiq tingled him, nearly propelling his amusement out. Despite all his best efforts, Rune could not remain disappointed or even disapproving, of the student. After relinquishing a grin, he admitted, "Caution seems to be a lesson you should remember."

Daavv slightly inclined his head. "As you say, Mentor," but there was little humility, only a lilt in the tone.

The Majiq was too strong! All right! I give up! I accept what Fate has decreed! In keeping with his unconventional nature, Rune characteristically approached this matter head-on. Most Initiates were introduced to their Mentors when the senior Maji felt it was time to adopt a Tyro. Merlin was then informed, and the new partnership began the trials of learning to work and live together while helping the peoples of the various kingdoms. In these dark times those would be warrior duties rather than friendly patrols assisting the myriad beings in the realms.

There was no denying the boy's stubbornness. Or was it persistence? Or an understanding and acceptance of something Rune was unable to admit to himself? "And I am not your Mentor," he reminded again in his own show of willfulness.

"Sorry, Tutor Rune."

Lips tight with disapproval, he gave a nod of acceptance. "There is something I would like to ask you if I may?"

"Anything, Mentor Rune." Daavv stood back and waited. Not in anxiety or contrition, but in a steady, forthright look of anticipation. As if he was ready for anything, but already knew the answer.

That brash self-confidence was challenging to Rune -- too reminiscent of himself -- and he decided to try a little one-upmanship. "Do you believe in the Warrior Bond, young Daavv?"

Accepting the question with glittering eyes, Amestoy considered for a brief moment. "I believe in Merlin's Order, Mentor Rune. If I ever find myself lucky enough to be Tyro to a noble and wise Mentor then I will try my best to establish that Warrior Bond."

The answer was nothing more than a tease. Betrayed by Majiq, Rune knew the minute the words were spoken they both felt a confirmation through Majiq. The connection was there. Tentative, slight, but unmistakable. With this power between them how would Rune ever control the headstrong boy? He had a rueful feeling it would be a wild adventure to find out.

Older, wiser, stronger in Majiq and infinitely more experienced with cheeky students, Rune chose to use maximum weapons now to knock the youth off balance. He had to end this on his terms.

"We shall see." His face was stern, his voice neutral. "You are coming with me."

"Mentor?"

Rune gestured to the corridor. "We are going to tell Merlin your future has been decided." Rune's skin prickled and Daavv shivered from another shared blast of Majiq. Soberly, Rune studied the clear, almond-shaped green eyes.

"I believe you are right." The smile on Amestoy's face presented only a fraction of the joy exhibited in the trembling Majiq emanating from him. "I mean, yes, Mentor."

Feeling a flicker of breathless expectation and a smidgen of anxiety shoot out from Amestoy, Rune offered him a thin smile of support. This was not going to be easy for either of them for vastly different reasons. Poised on the brink of a life-changing moment -- on the edge of eternity -- they exchanged knowing glances. For once the expectant Tutor and Tyro were on equal footing, uncertain of the future, but convinced they must face it side by side.

They found Merlin at the top of a circular turret room, in one of the front gables of the Castle. Filtered sunlight shone through square windows. This tower was warmer than most areas in the old bastion, and the leader of the Order and a few other Maji present had removed the glittery robes and pointed caps that helped protect them from the chill in other regions of the old citadel.

Amestoy should have been nervous surrounded by these mighty legends. Instead, Rune felt from him a calming hush. He stood straight, centered and relaxed. This was where he belonged; standing before these great Mentors, taking the next step in his life in the Order.

Outside the tower windows the moon beyond the mist cast a yellow light on the quiet city of Avelon. The advent of province twilight radiated vibrant shades of amber and purple across the horizon. Lights from buildings stretching across the landscape, noises of conversations, singing and music in the distant pubs gave the atmosphere in the room the feeling of detached peace. Out there was the everyday, common life. Inside here was the binding enchantment of Majiq.

"Soren Rune," Merlin greeted.

Slightly bowing his head, Rune wondered at the picture this must present to the others. A disenchanted, disillusioned Sorcerer/Paladin -- old and worn by harsh experience. Next to him the fresh-faced, eager, idealistic Daavv, whose eyes shone with awe and heart raced with excitement and anticipation.

"Merlin," he greeted and gave a nod to the others. "I --" he stopped and glanced at the waiting Pupil, giving an inclusive bow of his head. "We have come to inform you it is time for me to take on student Amestoy Daavv as my Tyro."

With dismay he realized he had reached a point of reluctant acceptance and he almost wanted a Novitiate. No, he almost wanted Amestoy -- sidekick, student and constant companion for the few years of their lives -- as his Tyro.

Merlin's lips held the hint of a smile. He gave a fractional bow to Rune, and then faced the young man. "What say you to this request student Amestoy Daavv?"

Levelly staring back at the great Maji, Amestoy's deep, pleasant voice was more serious than Rune had ever heard.
"I am honored to become the Tyro of the noble Maji Mentor Soren Rune."

Merlin's eyebrows lifted slightly at the unconventional and excessive reply.

Flattered, certainly, Rune was nonetheless a bit annoyed at Amestoy's shower of praise. Instantly, that negative was replaced with something profound. In his soul, Rune suddenly felt a stab of an emotion he had never felt before: Uncertainty in his qualifications. Did he have what it took to be the proper Tutor to this incredible young man? What would he do with this trusting, optimistic boy?

The other Maji were murmuring in subdued tones of approval or amusement, or both. They were an odd lot, Rune considered as he observed them silently studying Amestoy.

The oldest Maji, aside from Merlin, was Robert of Ecktor. A white, closely-shorn beard dusted his face and the cropped white hair under the peaked hat made him look like he was bald. Maybe he was wearing the warm cap because he was losing his hair? His piercing brown eyes were almost a match for the Lodalite-Shaman dream crystal, clutched in the talons of a bird of prey amulet, which hung suspended from his neck by a finely braided gold cord. The wavering, aurora-like patterns in the dark amber crystal induced visions for meditation.

Wizard Joan Izelt was striking. The diminutive woman with raven black hair wore an impressive Staurolite grounding and healing stone at the end of a woven, horse-hair strand. An unusual touch-stone that could connect a wizard with other realms, including animal and Faery dominions, through visions.

Almost a polar opposite to the woman beside her, Mead Cardok was a head taller, her flaxen hair almost colorless in the gold-tinged room. The healing touch-stone around her neck, a blue aventurine, was nearly the same shade as her sky-blue eyes. The multi-faceted gem contained within the silver grip of a gryffin was a powerful mental healing crystal. It accentuated the inner strength of this Sorceress who was said to be Merlin's closest advisor.

Uther Agravain was the youngest of this group of veterans. His head was brushed with thin hair that never seemed to remain in place on his cranium. His attire shimmered with a regal shade of purple, reminiscent of the amethyst enchantment and protection crystal that was stylishly embedded within a castle talisman at his neck. In his years at Castle Avelon, Rune had worked with Agravain and found him confident and solid in opinions, knowledge and dealings. Someone good to have at your back.

Most impressive of all was the stout Merlin. The short, white beard and hair and sparkly robe made him look like an eccentric old spellbinder. His presence, though, was as arresting as the spectacular red, rutilated quartz captured by a red dragon talisman that hung over his heart. The crystal, known for healing and balance, was the epitome of Merlin-Maj. He was the equilibrium of their Order, of the Majiq within this realm. His strong aura was the backbone of everything they stood for as Paladins. When Merlin and his Wizards entered this dimension it kindled the dormant Maji heart in all sense-beings and changed the future of this earth.

This formidable gathering should intimidate a young man, but Amestoy seemed completely controlled and confident. Amazing. Rune was more on edge than his protégé! Merlin motioned for silence. Amestoy and Rune both held their breath, the older man realized with some irony. Again, for vastly differing reasons, they were sharing a common emotion.

"My valiant Templars, I wholeheartedly approve of this teaming!"

Amestoy smiled wider and more enthusiastically than Rune, but their shared glances confirmed their mutual relief and pleasure.

Patting both of them on the arms, Merlin canted his head toward the door stairwell. "Come with me. I have something special for this occasion."

They followed the great Sage down the spiraling stone steps, winding their way to the next level of the Castle. After traversing two hallways and the open-air of an upper courtyard/observation deck, they found themselves back inside. Two flights of stairs later they entered a crypt-like chamber with no windows. A torch was brought in from the corridor and Merlin snapped his fingers at it. A shower of sparks, then a glowing, cold, incandescent radiance hovered from the wick.

"Soren, you have always been one of my favorites," he admitted with a little chuckle. "But if you ever say that to anyone outside these walls," he glared and pointed a finger at them both," I will deny it!"

Swirling around, he pressed his hand against a plain wall of bricks. Out popped a long drawer. Amestoy gasped. Rune's eyebrows hiked up. Merlin turned and gave them a smile worthy of a carnival conjurer who had just pulled off an amazing trick before the astonished crowd. Set inside the red velvet lining, were ornate boxes, crystal baskets, glass bowls and more than one object that looked like a treasure chest.

"This is quite a fun Castle," Merlin muttered as he poked around through the various items.

Finally, he opened the lid of a small chest and pulled out a gem ring. In the changing rainbow hue of the torch, the Amethyst crystal shown dark cerulean/purple. Both Rune and Amestoy gasped slightly when they saw the design clutching the stone was a silver dragon setting. It was presented to Rune, who then placed it on Amestoy. When he tried to fit the ring onto Amestoy's right hand, it would not slip past the knuckle. When he tried the left hand it slid on perfectly. Rune looked into Amestoy's eyes, glad his Pupil grasped the unusual nature of this event. There were only a handful of left-handed, supremely powerful Maji in the Order! One of them had been Tor Ion-Gawain! Both Mentor and Tyro gulped when the stone clutched in the talons of the beast glowed a bright blue-silver, then gradually faded to a dull indigo. The same shade as Rune's iolite crystals!

Merlin stared at one, then the other, his eyebrows raised up toward to his snowy hairline!

Rune had never heard of a crystal changing its nature from one gem to another when touched by its owner! Amazing Majiq indeed! What did it mean? He didn't speculate and had no time to ponder it now. He rubbed fingers through his russet hair in nervousness.

"You both must understand this bond between you. It will not be immediate. It will take time. To learn from each other, to grow into a family." The authoritative voice crackled in the silent, sepulchral room. Closing his eyes, Merlin-Maj seemed to see beyond the moment, beyond this time and place. "Bright and difficult your future might be, but I am certain you will see wonderful accomplishments. Hardships and danger are also ahead, my friends. You will face a great deal in these vast realms. Trust in Majiq. Trust in your bond. Then your joy will be unending."

Opening his eyes, Merlin-Maj nodded at the two men and grinned. "You are both suited for each other. Rebellion within a match." More seriously, he continued. "Tutor and Tyro you are from this day forward until your learning is complete in five years time. Training will begin with your first assignment tomorrow. Go in strength of Majiq and the blessings of the Order." Merlin leaned back and beamed a huge grin from one to the other. "Now go. You have much to do. You should get started!"

Tutor and Tyro bowed and exited. As they walked down the hallway and descended the staircase, neither spoke, both sensing the emotions of the other, both sharing the anticipation of excitement of the unknown ahead. Rune was awed by the blessing Merlin bestowed on them. He wondered if Amestoy had any idea of how special it was to receive a blessing from the greatest Maji of their time. And a dragon ring that metamorphed from an Amethyst – native to Ameden – to match Rune's Iolite! Unheard of!

Maji were encouraged to walk within the Castle. Vast distances between turrets and levels, however, occasionally demanded a quicker mode of transport. Using Majiq, Rune and Amestoy skate-slid with lightning speed to the nearest spiral staircase. They slid down thick, stone banisters three flights – moving at the blink of an eye without moving their feet, as if the floor itself was in motion. In reality, the two were hovering slightly above the ground. They did this along a few turns to zoom down the last hall before coming to a stop at the Novitiate dorms.

Rune took the lead. He was the Mentor now and it was time to act like one. Giving Amestoy instructions, he told the boy to gather his belongings and join him in his guest quarters. In mute obedience, Amestoy nodded as they parted.

**

Rune took the long way around the Castle to his small room, walking instead of skimming the hall. He paused at several slit-windows between the stones along the way, stood at an alcove for a time and almost missing his quarters in his preoccupied wanderings. His mind was crowded with thoughts bouncing from the future, to the past, to the trivial. Growing interest in an evening meal, however, was starting to take precedence over the life-changing events of the day. Emotions still bubbling and troubled, he arrived at his rooms and stared out the window. Pacing the small living area, Rune's nerves were unsettled until the boy arrived with a single bag of belongings.

Taking comfort in nominal, ordinary tasks, Rune ordered the gear stowed in the small bedroom next to his. Amestoy then joined him as they studied a scroll sent by Merlin, detailing their first mission. It was at a province a few days sail from Avelon and he advised they would take that time to train and join in a working pattern; studies and informal instruction at all times from Tutor to Tyro, interspersed with assignments from Merlin. It was a big, busy kingdom and there was much to do for every Maji.

With a sigh, Amestoy leaned back in his chair. "It's exciting and breathtaking, Mentor." The subliminal current of Majiq confirmed his pleased, eager feelings, even while his placid, nonchalant exterior strove for mature acceptance. "But I was wondering something."

Rune formed the title carefully, testing it out again. It had been so long since he had addressed someone in the possessive, intimate label. "Yes, Tyro?" Rune almost held his breath, waiting for the first Inquiry, the first request for knowledge now that they were officially Tyro and Mentor. "What is your question?"

"When can we eat, Mentor? I'm starving." The green eyes were alight.

Rune smirked, caught cold -- again -- by the precocious young man. "Ah, we already share some things in common. I love to eat!"

"So do I."

"And I am starving!"

"So am I!"

"We shall give you your first test then, Tyro. We'll see if your skills in the kitchen are any match for your flamboyance in duels."

With mock deference, Amestoy blandly retorted, "No question, Mentor, you are bound to be disappointed now."

The evening meal was simple -- bread and fruit -- standard stock for the guest rooms. They ate in silence, cleaned up quickly, and were soon standing by the table, at a loss as to what to do next. Neither seemed comfortable with this team angle of a relationship. Well, someone had to get things organized and it was his job as Mentor to set the example. At least he had the advantage of having been a Mentor before.

Rune made a show of examining the gold-streaked hair. "I think we shall need to give you a trim. Such a style might work here at the Castle, but the realm expects Maji to look presentable."

There was no real uniform for the Sorcerers, but simple shirts, trousers and boots were considered acceptable in any company and in most provinces. Men and women Maji dressed similarly and were never without their staffs or pocket bags which were filled with the standard collections of potions, powders and crystals. The shimmering cloaks with the pointed hoods were their most distinctive apparel. Through Sorcery dust, these very useful articles could be almost nulled to the eye, thus enabling the Maji to disappear in plain sight when necessary.

As a matter of ceremony, one of the first acts of service to his Tyro was the Mentor's duty of bestowing a staff. The other was to assure the novice was presentable in every way to represent the Order.

With a wave of his hand, Rune ruffled the longish locks of sandy hair on the side of Amestoy's head. Slicing his palm flat through the air in a sudden flourish, the fine strands were blown around in a swirl, and then knotted into a pony tail!

The boy seemed uncomfortable. "Is something amiss, Mentor?"

How could he diplomatically get out of that question? "I believe a shorter hair style would suit you better, Tyro."

The shot of a skeptical glance was enough to let the elder know his prevarication had not been accepted. And was there a bit of vanity in the young man who was undoubtedly proud of his attractive hair?

Amestoy seemed a little nervous and disappointed, but as he often did, opted for humor to ease the moment. "As long as you do not shear it with a sabre, Mentor."

The dare was too much for his confrontational nature. To serve the cheeky boy his just desserts, Rune deliberately took his hilt from his belt and activated the singing, emerald blade. "Do you doubt my skills are as good as yours with a sabre?" The tone held no hint of mercy.

Amestoy's expression was nothing but sincere. "Never, Mentor. I am completely in your hands."

With an adroit flex of his wrist the wand shot out a sizzling, silver blade. Then Rune killed the energy and placed the instrument on the table, denying the dare. Holding his right hand out at arm's length, enchantment sizzled from his touch-stone talisman, through his ring, past the end of his fingers and cleanly carved through the ponytail, leaving hardly enough hair to cover Amestoy's ears. In a stroke of flamboyant expertise, Rune then slashed along the top of Amestoy's head, sheering off the fine locks to fractional fuzz on the top, the stinging energy slicing close to the boy's head and neck! It could have been a dangerous stunt in less skilled hands, but Rune's talent was legendary for good reason.

As the hair wafted down in shimmery tufts, Amestoy spun around, his eyes wide with astonishment. "I never even felt a sting!" He drew in a breath. "You truly are a great Mentor!" The voice and face were filled with awe.

Rune nearly blushed. Now who was the show off?

Whether his face or Majiq betrayed his ironic thought, he did not know. Amestoy, however, grinned. "A very flashy display of skill, Mentor. I shall have to remember the technique."

"You better not!"

They both chuckled, Majiq rippling through them in a mirrored charge of delight.

Rune then gave him leave to prepare for bed. After cleaning up, Rune sat on the edge of his bed, comfortable in the silent solitude. Staring out of the window, he wondered at the incredible transformation that had swept through his here-to-for solitary existence in just two days time. He marveled at his emotional upheavals and incredible reactions of mirth, annoyance and humility in the few hours he had known this boy. And at the fantastic, reverent enchantment of Majiq, he was astonished -- that it had wrought such a change -- so instantly -- in his life.

Wandering around the quiet quarters, Rune paused at the door of the second bedroom, watching the obviously-not-sleeping form on the cot. Aware of his presence, Amestoy sat up in alert readiness. Thinking back to the first time they spoke, Rune covered a smile with a cough, remembering the dexterous and flamboyant use of Majiq, the idealism of the student quietly committing to memory the ancient myths. Despite himself, a compliment was on his lips before he could recall it.

"I commend you for the clever use of Majiq in the library, Tyro. You are indeed strong in spirit."

"Some of my teachers would probably be impressed that I was using it at all for studying." His face sobered. "I promise to use it wisely, Mentor, as you direct."

For years Rune had rejected the thought of tutoring a Novitiate because of his own independence, his single-minded focus on avenging Tor. Now the responsibility gave him pause for an entirely different reason. This young man was full of promise and dynamism. Was Rune ready for the enormous responsibility of guiding and helping him to become a great Sorcerer?

"A question, Mentor."

"One more only, Tyro, then it is time to sleep." He would have to be firm with the boy.

"Do you believe in the Warrior Bond, Mentor?"

Rune ignored the hope and anticipation in the words, the face bright with faith. He COULD NOT believe! It was not true and he did not want it to be any more than a worn out fable. "I believe in Majiq, Tyro. That is enough. Good night."

Neutral, expression closed, Amestoy gave a nod. "Good night, Mentor."

In his own sleep chamber Rune laid on his cot, staring up into the faint shadows cast through the slats of the window. Avelon's port never slept and the busy traffic away from the city was faintly detectable in the Castle. The activity reflected the Mentor's restless mind. The memory of Amestoy's vivid eyes -- full of faith and trust in him -- burned in his mind. Rune would not deny this challenge. With Majiq, and Amestoy on his side, he could hardly fail. And one day, he hoped, he would learn to trust with even a slight element of the certainty his Tyro showed from his side of this incredible bond.

**

The first Mentor-prepared meal was a simple one. Rune was accustomed to grabbing anything handy on the run and realized that would not do now. He needed to set an example, assure that his growing lad had enough nutrition to carry him through energetic trials and natural metabolism. Rummaging through the cupboards, Rune sensed the arrival of his Tyro before Amestoy had a chance to speak.

"What do you like for breakfast?" There should not have been a choice. He hated this diplomatic stuff. He just needed to take charge and his Pupil would have to like it. "I think I'll fix grains."

Decision made, he gathered bowls, pouring assorted dry bran mixtures. Then, from a cold box set into the stone wall that was kept near freezing by a charmed crystal, he scooped out lumpy mush. It was standard fare in the Castle and to mix in a little flavor, Rune added sweet berries to the gruel. They could have joined the other Wizards in the dining hall near the kitchens, but Rune wished to begin their partnership with no distractions.

Amestoy hesitated after he was handed his bowl.

"Something wrong?"

"Just waiting for you, Mentor."

It was not a cheeky dig but a respectful gesture.

"No need to stand on ceremony, Tyro. Eat when you like."

"Thank you, Mentor."

Amestoy dished his porridge out double-time of what Rune managed and after asking for, and receiving permission, for a second bowl, he repeated the process. Amused, Rune ate at a more leisurely pace, and it occurred to him that the young man was probably starving. Rune had a healthy appetite himself, needing to munch and snack frequently. There was a hazy memory of always being hungry in his youth and he knew he had more than a few adjustments ahead in his responsibilities for another person.

"I believe we will have to go shopping for more stores," was his wry comment as Amestoy refilled his bowl for the third time.

"Yes, there was very little here last night."

Surprised at the odd comment, Rune checked a few of the shelves, realizing that the lean supplies stocked in the room were already depleted.

"We had such a light dinner," Amestoy explained sheepishly.

Snack runs. Yes, shopping must be a high priority.

He took another bite. "The kitchen is an option, but they restrict access." His eyes were hopeful over the rim of the bowl. "Perhaps you could influence the staff? They do anything for Wizards."

"I never ask for special favors," he informed. "Finish up, then, Tyro. We have training first." He turned, startled at the grin on the boy's face. His silent question was given with a raised brow.

"A wonderful feeling to be called a Tyro, Mentor. It is the greatest achievement of my life."

It was not so very long ago for him that Rune would forget his own anticipation and excitement at advancing from

Initiate to Tyro. What great thrill came with the expectation! Then the choosing! To become the Tyro of the great Merlin had been beyond his wildest dreams! He was honored that Amestoy was so enthusiastic at this teaming. He vowed again to do his best for this lad who so revered him.

Patting his shoulder, Rune allowed his growing regard for the youth to show. There was always a fine line between the familial closeness of Mentor and Tyro, and the necessary discipline and distance of teacher and pupil. Thrown together through expediency, through convenience, and through Majiq, there was always a period of adjustment when the guide and student learned to live and work with each other. He liked Amestoy, even though he guarded against exposing his emotions. He could not welcome that full closeness into his life yet. With time, he hoped to care for Amestoy as he should.

"Clean up, Tyro. Then we spend our first day together."

**

The Castle corridor was crowded with residents beginning their morning routines. Many Paladins, Mentors and Tyros walked the halls in purposeful strides. On one of the lower levels Amestoy and Rune passed a class of youngsters on their way to instructions. Both smiled, appreciating the blissful childhood enjoyed in the sequestered and hallowed protection of the Castle.

The training rooms were mostly filled. For their first sparring match, Rune did not want to mingle with other teams or group testing. He led his charge to the upper gardens near the top of the spires of the Castle. The open battlements were clustered with plants and trees blocking most of the township and sea port. There were no threats or wars here on the enchanted isle, and the fortress was now a defensive seat of power instead of a center of battle readiness.

Rune chose a shrubbery-enclosed spot within sight of a waterfall cascading from the nearby mountains. Flowering bushes nestled around a close-cropped, matted lawn. Sitting cross-legged, he invited Amestoy to follow his lead. Across from each other, separated by a few meters, Rune drew in a deep breath. He had given much thought to the physical training necessary in his new role but, before the corporeal, came this vital part of teaching. Centering was something he wished to forestall until later, but it seemed Fate had other ideas.

"I prefer to engage in battle techniques first thing in the morning," he told his pupil. "Then I feel my mind is cleared for tuning in to inner Majiq. However, since the training rooms are too crowded today, we will work on meditation."

"I wondered about the tour of the Castle." The remark was delivered with a quirk of a grin. "As you wish, Mentor. What is your method of meditation?"

"Silence," he shot back.

Amestoy pressed his lips together. Was it to keep from laughing? Or an exaggerated example of obedience? Either way, the slanted green eyes glittered with joy, the usual cant giving the impression of exaggerated mirth.

How was he going to handle this mischievousness? "The key is to connect with Majiq, Amestoy. I don't think it has much of a sense of humor."

The boy sputtered out with a laugh at the stern response before pressing his lips momentarily closed again. "I beg to differ with you so early in our relationship, Mentor," he countered after a beat. "But I think Majiq has a strong sense of humor. It has partnered us together, has it not?"

The emerald orbs shined. Was the boy ever serious? Yes, he was. Yesterday, this morning, odd splinters of reverence and honor alternately shot out from his inherently cheerful nature. Jocular amusement was not something Rune was used to in dealings with Mentors or Tyros. Life and death had rooted him in a sober foundation. Amestoy, though, had his moments of varying traits. It must be this rising generation. Then he amended that thought. Tor also had the driest humor. Surprisingly, the memory did not come as it usually did with a lance of pain at his heart. Recalling his fallen friend's wit was pleasant. Silently he thanked Amestoy for providing that moment of insight.

"Then we will accept the droll side of Majiq and move on," he countered, knowing there was no point in arguing. "Meditation. Lesson one. Our goal is to listen for our Majiq balance. We will sense the presence of the other while keeping our own sense of self."

"Excuse me, Mentor. We have already achieved this level, have we not? When we first met in the library –"

"It was a fluke, Tyro."

Amestoy longed to say more – it was clear on his face and in the rebellion that surged from his being. Reading Rune's expression, feeling his command, he obeyed. "Yes, Mentor."

"Lesson one. The Mentor is always right."

"Understood."

"Lesson two. Silence."

"Yes, Mentor."

There was no hint of sarcasm. The expression was completely placid. Why did he get the impression his pupil was laughing at him again? After clearing his throat and mind he continued. "Since your days as a Novitiate you have learned the Maji methods of meditation. Steps to inner calm. Connection with Majiq. Strength for your abilities to complete duties."

"Yes, Mentor."

Rune closed his eyes. The blandness of Amestoy was too contradictory with what had to be going on in the adroit mind. It was distracting. It made Rune question his methods as a Mentor. Had he always sounded so pompous? Was every point to turn into a lecture? He strove for a conversational quality.

"Obviously we are not here to fine tune meditation, student. You have mastered that many years before. We are here to draw together as one within Majiq and each other."

"Like a Warrior Bond?"

Eyes snapping open, Rune scrutinized the boy. The plain mask was in place, even reaching the colorful eyes. A condemnation? A taunt? A prompt? A challenge? It was impossible to tell what Amestoy had meant since he had skillfully blocked any projection of emotions. His Majiq barriers were formidable when he wanted to conceal his inner thoughts and feelings. Rune would have to learn to read the nuances of his character; the voice inflections, the flick of an eyelid or the twitch of a lip. It would come with time. Frustratingly, now there was no way to tell what the cryptic comment really meant. If it held any hidden message aside from the blatantly obvious one, or not.

"Yes. Like a Warrior Bond," Rune responded carefully. "If such a thing existed."

If the denial dashed any hopes or dreams it did not show in the younger face. Amestoy merely closed his eyes and appeared to be concentrating on the lesson.

Rune closed his eyes again and blew out a soft exhalation of frustrated tension. This was going to be a very long ordeal, this partnership. Clearing his mind, he methodically pushed aside the errant concerns and one by one drew on the might of Majiq to create an open field, a blank slate that would leave him open to the Majiq energy surrounding him.

There came to mind a foreign landscape of lime-tinted hills and a soft, pastel-rose sky. A dark river snaked to the right, flowing down to a deep-toned sea. The shore was lined with shadowy, emerald trees that blossomed with some kind of fruit. A sense of foreboding misted over the scene like a thick cloud shading and obscuring the light. A black silhouette emerged from beyond the curve in the narrow walking path. A sinister shape. The aura reeked of the Darkness Rune had felt in Spania! It was a cloaked figure with glowing red eyes! He approached . . . . peril close . . . death . . . sacrifice . . . danger --

Rune's eyes snapped open as he tore away from the connection! His chest tight, his breathing sharp and short. He stared into the frightened eyes of his Tyro, who was sweating and pale. Fear. It had entered into his senses when the dreaded shape arrived. It had not been him – it had been Amestoy who feared the looming intruder. What had happened? What had they seen? A moment from Amestoy's past? How could that be? Since arriving here at the Castle as a child, Amestoy had never left the sequestered halls of this sanctuary except on closely supervised excursions!

"How?" Rune asked, not able to articulate a coherent question or comment. He was completely off-guard. A condition he had not experienced for a long time. "What was that?"

"I – uh – that was Ameden."

His home province in the wild north country of Dragonshire. "You dream of home? But that was more than a moment from your past."

Shaking his head he responded, "I have no real memory of my homeland."

Some Maji did not. The First Orphans had been of varied ages. A few were removed from their homes before the age of separation, which was ten years old. Sometimes, when their Majiq signature was sufficient to be a hindrance in the outside realms, the children were given over to local Maji. If their inherent enchantment was strong enough they were raised here at the Castle. When children were only mildly attuned to Majiq they were trained while living with their own families. They knew nothing else until they were released into the kingdom as Tyros. As one of the First Orphans, Amestoy should have remembered nothing of his home realm.

The vision had been so real, though. Rune was certain he could smell the scented trees and feel the freshness of the sea breeze. And who was the approaching threat that so frightened his pupil? There was no doubt real dread emanated from Amestoy. It was not imagined, it was absolute and tangible to both of them.

Could it have been Diaboliq raiders plundering Ameden? Had Amestoy witnessed the destruction of his home, his family, as a baby? Such a strong, latent memory was possible. Subdued for years perhaps until this training – this connection with an experienced Maji – could tempt it into the light.

The cloaked figure with red eyes was unmistakable. A Gadion-Obscura warrior. Diaboliq was not inherent like Majiq. To practice the Dark Arts, a black wizard needed powerful potions that cankered the soul, elixirs that shriveled the heart and conscience of any being foolish enough to trade free will for temporary potency. The corrupt formulas needed in dark practices also exacted a lasting toll on the body. It wrinkled and mottled the skin, the eyes turned red, and the fingernails were tinted crimson. Once surrendering to the wickedness there was no going back, the effects were irreversible. Diaboliq forever marked it's followers. It was said the demon twins had red skin, eyes, and hair! Fact or fiction? It was hard to believe any living thing, even one living on evil, could be branded in such a way, but they did drink blood.

So, was that horrible vision from Rune's experience or Amestoy's? Although he refused to accept the Warrior Bond, he did not find it difficult to acknowledge the foresight said to be a gift of the Ameden people. It was commonly recognized that precognitive powers did exist in the past for the nearly extinct race. Could they still exist today?

"I request that we try to find a training room now, Mentor. I think I can no longer concentrate on meditation."

Without seeking permission, Amestoy bounced to his feet and scurried away. The Mentor was left to slowly rise and wipe away the sweat from his face. What had just happened? What had they seen? He was certain they had shared that fearsome vision. And he was also convinced of something else. It had not been Amestoy who had pulled away, it had been him! Not from fear, but from the raw, profound emotions assaulting him. He could not stand up to the battering that was so personal to his soul.

Disgusted with what that might mean, and what deficiencies that might show about him, he hurried after his Tyro. The kid had the right idea. Let's go expend our energy through wand sparring and hope it drives away the haunting images and disturbing questions lingering in the wake of the psychic encounter.

**

Expecting to find a tattered and unsettled Tyro, Rune was surprised when he caught up with his charge, to find a completely different attitude. Amestoy stood to the side of a small training area, arms crossed, his staff clutched in his left hand.

Rune paused in the arched entryway of the expansive room and studied his new Tyro. There was no Majiq connection, no reading at all from the young man. No trace of a mental or emotional barrier exuded from him, either.

Amestoy was still. In mind, in body, in presence. Like a placid mountain lake that was so large no ripples affected the center. That was exactly the tone surrounding him. Gone were the physical remnants of distress.

Control. Self-assured mastery worthy of an older, more experienced Sorcerer was now portrayed. Impressed, willing to go along with this detached aura, Rune entered the arena. Removing his wand with a single swipe of his right hand, he settled into a relaxed stance and offered a shallow, courteous bow. Making eye contact, but betraying no emotion, the traditional prelude to battle was returned by giving a respectful bow of the head.

Rune pushed Majiq through his wand and blue-silver energy leaped from the wood, singing with the quiet buzz of power and vibrant light. With it came the always present jump in heightened awareness; in nerve-excitement, in mental preparation for the clashing of Majiq. Whether in practice or in real combat, every Sorcerer felt the surge of enchantment when the symbolic weapon sizzled to life. Without the use of charmed golden powder, Amestoy responded by pushing his own supernatural enchantment into the weapon. Blue fire-blade danced in his hand in an impressive show of energy.

Amestoy sucked in a breath of involuntary surprise just as his Mentor did the same. They exchanged incredulous looks. Tyros should not have any ability to cull colored sparks from their wands! Not until after they received their touch-stone and weeks of preparation and control over the new Majiq they wielded! Then their personal energy stamp would be whatever combined from within and through the touch-stone. Both looked at the glowing weapons, amazed that the sparking fires were almost the same hue. This was not supposed to happen!

Taking the first step was expected in the Tutor/Pupil relationship, but Rune was completely off guard. Amestoy, recovering first, stepped forward to start the attack. As Rune worked to ward off the aggressive blows of his opponent, he realized he was unable to anticipate many of the hard swipes because Amestoy was sending out no signals. Unlike the other battles he had witnessed of the young man, there was no flair or excessive showmanship now. Also, his control of steady Majiq was extraordinary. This was straight-out fighting with strong, decisive lashes to attack him. While Rune's skill and experience outdistanced any tactic Amestoy could throw at him, the older Wizard had to work at every parry, every counter ploy as they wheeled and danced around the circular room.

Frustrated that he could not break through the closed barrier projected by his new Tyro, Rune increased his speed and might as he tried a few of his own dashing maneuvers. Once he clipped Amestoy's shoulder with a Majiq touch, but the minor pain from the powered-down energy hardly registered on his opponent. With an instant shift, Amestoy ducked and spun, nicking Rune on the top of the knee.

To keep the game edgy and full of surprises, Rune extinguished the energized wand and used only his touch-stone ring's spark. Amestoy maintained his stride and focus without pause or waver as he changed weapons also. His control was complete and level.

Sweating, Rune nearly upped the ante with a higher notch of energy. Nearly. A Majiq impression stayed his hand. As he defensively parried and returned the hammering blows from his pupil, he analyzed the fight. Aloof. Amestoy was disconnected from any passion. Aberrant behavior indeed for the usually flamboyant student. Ever since the disconcerting experience of the strange, shared vision, Amestoy was not himself.

Disliking the stonewalling, taking it personally even though he knew better, Rune wondered what he could do to resolve the situation. With a swell of abrupt command, he drove for the Tyro, swinging his wand like a slicing axe. The young man countered every blow, seeming to anticipate the moves with uncanny brilliance. When the aggression did not work, Rune retreated to more fanciful jumps and leaps, not quite so flashy as the boy, but good enough to wipe out almost any opponent, Majiq or not. While Amestoy was caught off guard a few times, it was not enough for a victory. They were now drenched in sweat, gradually wearing down, their technique degrading with sloppiness and fatigue.

Irritated with himself, Rune realized he had managed to do almost everything wrong this morning. This was no training exercise; this was one-up-man-ship. Not what a Mentor was supposed to do in teaching his pupil! Ramping down on his attack he backed away, holding up a hand in surrender. He gave a bow and placed the sabre on a rack, his student mirroring the actions. Together they turned toward the archway to leave, and both stopped abruptly when they saw Merlin observing them.

The stout leader inclined his head to the side so far his pointed cap nearly toppled off. He contemplated them with a neutral expression. "Grave matters, my friends. Your original assignment is cancelled. You will be leaving Avelon later today for a new assignment. Come to my tower after you have made preparations and I will give you all the details."

Tyro and Mentor exchanged surprised looks.

They shot their eyes back to the Wizard when Merlin stopped, turned and gave them a level stare stating candidly, "I have seen better training."

"Guess he told us." Amestoy observed, his dry wit returning.

Whatever had caused the Tyro to close down was past now. Rune still didn't know exactly what had happened, either in the meditation garden or since. Boys! How was he ever going to handle one? He tried to tell Merlin this was a bad idea!

**

The rush of water streamed over the craggy waterfall and filtered through glistening crystals before being channeled into the smooth, river-rock wash rooms just off the training arena. Eyes closed, Amestoy cleansed, relishing the coolness of the pure mountain liquid. He rubbed fingers through his not-yet-accustomed short-cropped hair, glad of the pause in training. The duel had been a chance to purge the raw emotions of his jumbled heart and thoughts. He had tried unsuccessfully to drive out the dread and uncertainty. Now he had to face Merlin with the exposed confusion still nestled within.

The vision – what did it mean? Another vision wavered into his mind. Ameden again. The black figure with the glowing red eyes. Between Amestoy and the Diaboliq assassin – Majiq assured that was what this murderous person was. There also was a Templar, shield imprinted with the Warrior Bond crest. This was vision symbolic, was it not? Maybe, he felt, but he also believed it was literal. Amestoy was being protected from death by a Majiq shield! Then the image faded, leaving him weak.

Was this another fore-vision? Did Rune think fore-tell skill was wrong? Did he believe in the fore-sight Majiq of the Ameden people? No more than he believed in the Warrior Bond, Amestoy scoffed. He can believe it a myth. Amestoy would let him keep thinking that.

Would Merlin reveal the truth to either of them? Only Merlin would know what was inside their hearts. He was the Sorcerer who brought Amestoy to the Castle, knew his parents before they died. Was there a hidden secret? Were his parents Ameden fore-tellers? Should Rune know? Who was the sinister, red-eyed figure coming for them in the vision-scape? If it was a threat to Rune, Amestoy would demand Merlin divulge all. And what if all it revealed was of Ameden, and Amestoy's past? Was it so wrong to see the future? Merlin had the Majiq-gift of seer-sight. In the wrong hands, however, it corrupted the weak and greedy. That was how his province had been decimated, his people nearly exterminated and now living in self-imposed exile. The debased and mercenary beings of other kingdoms had tried to destroy the Ameds.

Black distress instantly swept over Amestoy, erasing the elation of moments before. The reason why his kind was hunted down was to capture the treacherous talent of seeing the future. But few really wanted to know their fate. It was one reason why Amestoy had no close friends – who would want a companion who could tell you when you would fail, when you would die? Even if few believed the tales that Amedens could fore-tell, the spectre of the threat was enough to warn most away. Was that why Rune was so reluctant to take him on as a Tyro?

And if Rune believed their shared vision was a fore-sight? Then the Mentor might reject him! And that would end his chance of being a Sorcerer! At establishing a Warrior Bond with Rune!

Amestoy leaned against the wall and rubbed his face with both hands. He moaned aloud at the remembrance of the illusion and how Rune had yanked away in disgust at the fore-tell. His new Mentor rebuffed the hint of fore-sight! What was Amestoy going to do? There was no way to control the fore-tell gift. In his childhood he had vivid dreams and strong premonitions. Through careful study he grew to understand it was more than Majiq, it was some kind of latent heritage of his Ameden people. Never one with any close friends, he kept this dangerous knowledge to himself, studying, and learning of the old legends of his province. The search for wisdom had guided him to the ancient texts on the Warrior Bond and the strong impression that he would be part of such a select, elite team. Those were child's dreams, though. Now, as a neo Tyro he had to face reality. He might believe in the Warrior Bond, and in fore-tell talent, but his Mentor did not.

There was much to be uncertain about, but his natural enthusiasm punched through the doubts. His emotions soared as he thought how far he had come. He had waited for this time all his known life – leaving the Castle as a Tyro to a Maji Mentor! What would the first assignment be? How would he measure up? What was it really like outside these hallowed chambers and away from Avelon?

Awe, excitement – his lifelong wish fulfilled! The Majiq, and his hereditary skills of fore-gift, told him this would be the first of many successful highlights in his career! There were shadows, too. He didn't dwell on those, though. No Ameden citizen could clearly read his own destiny. The power of fore-sight was a gift to serve others. Or had been, until it was abused by the more ruthless and greedy of the realms. No mention of this was ever spoken by the Ameden people – he had researched it as extensively as he had the Warrior Bond.

Amestoy held his dragon ring in one hand. Did this talisman, so like his Mentor's, give him an extra connection to Rune? And a dragon – Rune's home realm familiar! What did it all mean? That they were connected beyond what either anticipated? It seemed like they were moving as one, thinking as one all day! It was more than he had ever hoped!

He cleared his mind of the torments and questions, reaching inside to summon his instinctive talents at Majiq centering, while stretching outward to connect with ritual disciplines. Calm prevailed. Innate courage and optimism returned.

'The Warrior Bond WILL happen. I have seen it in the dream-scapes. Whatever else we experience, my Mentor, the Bond will be ours.'

Dressing in clothes brushed with crystal powder for cleansing, Amestoy cleared his mind. He pushed away the negative and reveled in the positive. Bubbling with barely subdued laughter, he could hardly contain the thrills of glee at the great good fortune he had experienced in the last few days. Chosen as the Tyro to Soren Rune! Already given a mission for his Order! Life could not be better!

**

Pacing on the large balcony overlooking the port of Avelon, Rune watched a heavy transport barge lumber across the bay. Below, the small figures of people at the docks, merchants in the market, shoppers in the streets showed the Majiq village bustling with work-a-day activity. A fleeting smile pulled at his lips. Some priests were leaving, others returning. Goods and people, comings-and-goings. The constant flux of motion in a busy realm. His Tyro and he would soon be among them. They had an assignment. Something that sounded important! The anticipation of adventure, of using his Majiq for a mission, sent a thrill throughout his body.

Even the hints at what might come to pass were broad strokes of a fuzzy possibility. Not certainty. Not Destiny or Fate. Merlin always said there were too many strands of options flowing through time and space to be able to predict anything with certainty. Merlin, through his crystal ball, could detect patterns and probable outcomes. He could not pull out full-fledged visions of what was yet to happen because there were too many variables. Rune understood those talents better than most, he had been tormented by those cryptic commentaries his entire career as a Tyro under the great Mentor Merlin. It had been a growing, but humbling tutorial.

The new Mentor was still pacing when his Tyro joined him on the balcony. They walked in silence down the circular stone steps of the outside parapet until they reached the common room of their quarters. Small, but functional, the living area boasted cushioned chairs and stuffed pillows to insulate against the cold stone of the floor. Inset on rock shelves in the walls were growing plants and formed crystal-falls that emanated soothing hues and subliminal currents of energy exuding peace and a tranquil ambience. The mood was accentuated by the pleasing tones of elegant, scenic tapestries on the curved walls of the tower.

Everything smelled fresh. Aromatic buds from the flowers induced a relaxing atmosphere. Far different from the four-person dorm room Novitiates shared when they entered the Castle. Before that, quarters consisted of a small room with four bunk beds where Amestoy grew up with various other orphans his age.

Rune turned and offered a pleased grin. "You are completely presentable, Tyro." Funny how the title flowed so easily off his tongue! As if he had known his new charge forever. That was Majiq working, settling him into a situation he was still not sure he was qualified for, or that he even wanted. "Ready to prepare for our first assignment?"

"Yes, Mentor."

He did not seem nervous at all. Calm and relaxed. Amazing. On his first journey out of the Castle, Rune had been a bundle of nerves! Curiosity and a low rush of excitement was all that could be detected from his Tyro. Good. That made things easier on both of them. Majiq was helping them adjust to this new arrangement.

"Excellent. If there is time afterwards, we will return here and you can fix us lunch."

That order visibly knocked the confidence out of Amestoy. "But Mentor, I have never fixed a meal before."

Of course. Initiates lived in dorm conditions and took all nourishment in the common dining hall.

"And we have no food!"

Frowning, Rune paused at the door and observed the boy. "I was sure there were bread flats and cheese in the pantry."

The pale cheeks flushed. "There was, Mentor. Before we left for meditation."

When had Amestoy managed to get into the cupboards and grab food in the few moments before they left this morning? What a sneak! What an appetite! He remembered his own early years and an undercurrent of suspicion that Merlin was trying to starve him. There never seemed to be enough food! Trying not to see too much of himself in Amestoy, he dismissed it with a shake of his head.

"We will eat with the others later."

"What about lunch?" He was desperate. "What if we are late and the kitchen closes?"

"I promise to feed you, Tyro."

"We will need more stores –"

"We will get them! You are about to embark on your first mission as a Tyro and you're worried about food!"

The impish grin was delivered just before the punch line. "First things first, Mentor."

**

As they walked to Merlin's chamber, Rune felt a ripple of pride in his new Pupil. So little experience and yet so controlled, as if he had received a multitude of missions in his short life. Rune and Amestoy bowed slightly, coming to a stop as Merlin and his closest Maji allies came around the corner. They were acknowledged with subtle nods from Merlin, Sorcerers Joan Izelt, Mead Cardok, Uther Agravain and Robert of Ecktor.

"We have need for your service, Mentor Rune and Tyro Daavv," Merlin introduced.

Ecktor explained in a grave, deep voice, his expression dark. "There is trouble on the Briton coast."

Merlin instructed they were to take the first ship out of Avelon. Debarking at the first port, they would transfer to a ship that would take them the rest of the way to Ionia. Mentor and Tyro looked to Merlin, who remained impassive. Ionia was the legendary isle where the Stone of Scone was found. The massive meteorite from which Merlin derived his touch-stone -- his staff gem and, it was said, much of his Majiq power. The island was rife with Majiq.

"The isle is in turmoil and mercenaries are enflaming the unrest. It is rumored that Faeries have infiltrated from Dragonshire. Your mission is to help end the interference by Majiq-kind, possibly stop the rabble and make sure the mercenaries have no more Majiq aid there."

A tall order! Halt a conflict involving renegade enchanters. And run off dangerous thugs! "Yes, Merlin," Rune agreed.

It was illegal for Majiq beings to interfere with Earth-kind. And unusual for Faeries to bother with the puny affairs of Humans on such a scale. Distrustful of any other species, Faeries played tricks for gain or mischief. They were shifty, tricky and full of tomfoolery, but he had never heard of them entering into violence on the side of hooligan Humans. Still, his was not to question, his was to obey. He and his charge would travel to the isle of Ionia and discover what troubles were brewing in the turbulent land.

"Go in safety." Merlin blessed as he bowed his head.

A shimmering surrounded them, and the walls seemed to melt into nothingness. Amazingly, they had been transported, it seemed, onto a misty heath, complete with the scent of musty earth, the dampness of a soft rain, and the cold of winter in the country. Wide-eyed, Amestoy gazed around, taking in a quick breath as he immediately recognized the stone monoliths around them. Stonehenge! Had they been transported? No one else seemed as stunned. All the senior Maji were reverent, intent. Merlin displayed somber respect. Rune's demeanor was silent and serious.

"Go with the power of Maji to guide and protect you," Merlin incanted. "You have with you this ancient power as you work for the good of the people of this land."

Lowering his hands, he placed them on Amestoy's shoulders, giving the novice Magi a kind smile and a nod. The room reappeared just as it had been before. As if the scene of Stonehenge was a dream, or a vision. Shivering at the astounding display of Majiq, Amestoy rubbed his arms. His shirtsleeves were damp!

Rune led the way to the door, apparently unfazed by what they had just experienced.

They were hardly more than a few steps from the closed doors of the chamber when Amestoy released a long breath. "Amazing!"

"Now you've seen a glimpse of the power in Majiq that is wielded by Merlin."

Still coming to terms with what he had just seemed to have experienced, "Yes, Mentor," was all Amestoy could muster at the moment.

Rune patted him lightly on the back, aware of the myriad feelings swirling within his Tyro.

"Now we should prepare for the trek." Maji retained few possessions. Packing would take no time at all. Greater familiarization with the history of the province, the unrest, etc. would come before they left.

"There is one thing we still need to do, Mentor."

"Eat?"

"That, too. I meant my touch-stone."

The final mark of a Novitiate graduating to Tyro. It was a wonder the exuberant Amestoy had resisted this long before requesting it.

"I didn't forget. As soon as we return from the markets we will seek your touch-stone."

"Markets? You're taking me to the Avelon markets?"

"Certainly. I don't want you to faint from lack of food."

**

Shopping!

Amestoy had never been outside the Castle except on controlled field trips. His Initiate groups were occasionally taken on explorations to the myriad educational and cultural locations of Avelon and other nearby regions. Such excursions were always delightful for the curious and intelligent Amestoy. But shopping! Wow!

Rune and Amestoy walked the crowded, colorful, noisy, dusty marketplace which lay within view of Castle hill. Close to the harbor, the stalls were hung with flags and tarps to shade the goods and merchants from the mid-day sun that, even though muted by the constant mists surrounding the enchanted isle, was still intense.

Amestoy did his best to control his exhilaration, but it was impossible amid the plethora of fabulous food! Purplish fruits from the tropics, grapes from the Mediterranean, and passion fruit from lands down under! He could feel the mirth of his Mentor as they strolled along the stalls, but Amestoy didn't care who was laughing at him. This was heaven!

"How do we buy things, Mentor? I've never handled coins!"

"Select what you wish, my Tyro, and I shall pay. In future, I will issue you an allowance wherever we go. Then you can bargain on your own."

"Bargain?"

"Mmhuh. That is how these street merchants conduct business. As well as vendors in most parts of the realms. Outside of Avelon it can get a little – risky. Anyway, you pick what you want and I will demonstrate."

Amestoy plucked various fruits and candies from numerous merchants. When his arms were full he sought out his Mentor, who had stopped at a belt display. There were so many things to buy; the young man had to focus on his mission of food alone. He could have wandered for days browsing clothing, boots, cloaks, hats and all manner of goods. When he spotted a table piled with old, bound books he forced himself to turn away. The merchant would be there another day. Then he would search for ancient treasures without a prickly Mentor looking over his shoulder.

On cue, Rune turned to him. Chuckling heartily, he shook his head. "Amestoy, we are leaving this afternoon! You have enough food –"he studied the armload of treats. "For at least another day," he finished teasingly.

"Sarcasm does not always suit you," the boy replied with chagrin. "It all looks so good! How could I contain myself! Besides, we'll be traveling for days! You don't want me to starve do you?"

"Never. Come, we will pay. Did you know you can use a basket for multi purchases?"

"Baskets. Dragon's breath! I could fill a basket?"

"Where did you get all this?" he queried as they retraced steps along the seller's alley. "How did you get away from the stalls without giving them coins? Must be your innocent face."

Both stopped suddenly. Chills running along Rune's spine, his hand slipped to place a finger on his touch-stone dragon pendant. Glancing at his charge, he was pleased to note the Tyro did not panic. Good lad. He felt it too, though! Their eyes met and each confirmed the ripple of danger brushing at their Majiq alerts like a gusting, icy wind to the soul.

"What is it?" Amestoy barely whispered.

"Diaboliq," Rune grated back in disgust.

The boy, though unarmed, was prepared for action, but did nothing melodramatic like dropping his merchandize or calling attention to the alert. Even though Maji were common fixtures to the streets of Avelon, fighting here was unusual. And, due to their presence, it was rare to feel the chill of Diaboliq at the heart of the kingdom, the home of the Maji. The unseen apparition that had passed near them was not just a deep, Dark influence or the criminal intent that was present anywhere in the realm. No, this was Dark Majiq.

Rune cursed himself for not arming his Tyro before leaving the Castle, but it seemed a moot point here on Avelon. Rune promised to never take any safety measure for granted in the future. Not where his Pupil was concerned.

Then as suddenly as it appeared, the Darkness left. Rune stretched out with all his instincts and felt Amestoy do the same. No, it was gone. Whatever it was, it had vanished without making its presence known through anything more specific than a shadowy malevolence. The Mentor felt like racing through the streets in search of the wickedness, but there was no reason for such futility. The mystical trace had vanished.

Practically throwing coins at the merchants, Rune rushed them out of the alley and back to the main road leading to the castle. They maintained a tense silence until they were back within the safety of their rooms, but as soon as they reached the paving stones of their quarters, the questions began.

"What do you mean Diaboliq? The Gadion-Obscura?
Here at Avelon?"

"No." Their voices were low, but their manner intense.
Rune had not expected to have this conversation until some
distant, future mission. Events had provoked him into too
many irritations lately. "It was Dark. Not Diaboliq, but I think
Gadion-Obscura."

Sober, aware of the gravity of the moment, Amestoy
studied his Mentor. "I don't understand the difference. You
have encountered both?"

"Yes, in varying degrees." He paced, sorting his
thoughts until he had clear and concise words to explain. "I felt
the rankness of Diaboliq before I returned to the Castle, but I
didn't have time to investigate. I will warn you, it is a presence
that is dank and seems to suck your soul away with Darkness.
It is different than the standard vileness of criminals. It is
malicious evil. A pure and collective evil. It is a focused
violence to the core. Those with Diaboliq are assassins.
Gadion-Obscura are minions for Diaboliq. They are cretins
who profit off misery and violence, disorder, chaos and greed.
Thugs." Amestoy's face was still a picture of perplexity.

"I know it doesn't sound like a clear distinction, but
trust me, when you have the unfortunate circumstance of
feeling both, you will understand."

Amestoy stood still, having hardly moved from his post
just inside the doorway of the cabin. Thoughtful, as if
cataloging and imprinting the experience in his memory and
under his skin, he gave a slow nod. "One of those life
experiences that must be felt, it cannot be learned any other
way."

"Exactly."

"I have many of those ahead of me."

"Yes, you do."

"I have never felt that Darkness, Mentor." At least not
in reality, only in vision, he silently corrected. "It is – nasty."

Some of the old cocky attitude returned and Rune
breathed easier. He wouldn't remind the boy that they had
both felt that kind of wicked stench on a psychic level in their
meditations this morning. Nor would he tell his new student of
the secret legion within the Maji – the guardians of Majiq

seeking the trail of the Gadion-Obscura to destroy the Diaboliq.

He matched the Tyro's lighter tone. It was time to move on. "It is nasty. I don't think you will have trouble discerning it in the future."

**

Since the inception of the Maji, the touch-stone was the companion of the Sorcerers of the Merlin Order. It was part of the physics of history that a strong defense was a deterrent to aggression. That principle had to be repeated time and again for those who did not understand or respect the might of the religion.

For eons the touch-stone and ring were the focal point of strength, an ancient, elegant weapon symbolic of policing the imbalance between lawlessness and stability, between Light-Majiq and Diaboliq. Hidden in the mists of time were the specific histories of the weapon, but it was as legendary as the great Paladins of justice. The first Maji and the enchanted amulet/ring sets traveled originally from Dragonshire. They first came to Earth, or brought their Majiq through kingdoms, chasing the Diaboliq. Details of those early battles were buried in the forgotten pages of the Ancients. Among the legends, however, were the tales of the Warrior Bond.

Deep in the heart of the Castle, Rune brought Amestoy to the carved stone vault where powerful crystals, metals and woods were stored. In other vaults nearby were enchanted elixirs, potions, dusts and plants from thousands of provinces across the realms. These were the tools used by Maji to enhance their abilities. Each Tyro, when beginning life under a Mentor, was brought here to choose the personal items that would become extensions of his individuality.

First, they started with a staff. Standing in the center of an octagonal foyer, they bowed their heads and entered into a centered calm. In quiet meditation, Amestoy connected to Majiq as he studied the designs, shapes and qualities of woods in his mind. Eyes still closed, he drifted beside the racks of displayed branches carved into walking sticks.

Opening his eyes, taking a few samples, he held them in his hand, balancing and gripping them, flipping them in the air in his customary, showy fashion. As he perused the selection, he gravitated toward a smooth silver-toned wood with ridges hued in a shiny blue. The stick was from a branch of an Ayelsborne fir! Amestoy twirled it several times, weighing it, getting the feel of the handle. Once again, that feeling of connectedness. This was the one, and he knew in the back of his mind that his Mentor was surprised and happy with his selection. Pleased with the results, Amestoy was ready for the most important part of the process.

"Now for the heart of our religion."

"The touch-stone pendant to match the ring."

"Yes."

Moving to the crystal vault, they studied the myriad mineral pieces that rested in individual casings. Every Majiqal rock was unique to the province and region where it originated. Every color and jeweled aspect of the angles and prisms were as exclusive as the Maji who came here to assemble their own weapons.

When Maji first crossed the Threshold from Dragonshire to Earth, they discovered the natural elements were most powerful within this realm. From then on, Maji chose tools indigenous to this dimension to aid them in keeping Majiq order for Mankind. Interestingly, the Wizards found when they returned to their home of Dragonshire, their talismans worked there just as well. Some theorized it was because the crystals, woods and various essentials had grown so intrinsic with their owner that they would work in any kingdom. Whatever the reason, Wizards kept their trappings close no matter where they roamed.

"What do you think?" he quietly asked the studious young man.

Each Initiate knew the theory of touch-stone selection by heart. Being here and doing it was different than studying about it from lectures or books. The history of the province and the color and allure of each stone made a difference. Majiq guided a Novitiate to choose the right crystal, the perfect metal substance and design. Rune knew Amestoy was tuning in to formidable inner Majiq to choose the charm-crystal that was waiting for him.

To prove the point, Amestoy's left hand delicately hovered over several possibilities. His palm stopped over an indigo-faceted Iolite gem from Ayelsborne! Crystals Rune had chosen as his own, just as Amestoy had picked wood from the forests of the dragon-cliffs of Ayelsborne! Uncanny! Amestoy's palm seemed to tremble over the blue, six-sided, crookedly etched raw stone that actually pulsated its color when his fingers touched the rock. Rune had never seen that happen!

"I believe I have located my crystal, Mentor. Ayelsborne Iolite. The soul stone. It is a match for my ring."

Rune responded in an equally dry tone. "I believe you have."

Iolite opened a path deep inside to the true core treasures within a soul. The gem could be used for psi visions and oneness of the third eye. Uniquely compatible with an Amed citizen.

The indigo crystal levitated from the case into Amestoy's hand. His whole arm shook as the gem took on an aura of glowing-silver. The first real test for a Tyro. His hand, clutching the crystal, guided him forward to shelves lined with elements and designs. The Tyro would find the attuned material of metal and mineral that would serve as his core of power for the rest of his life. What natural elements from different places in the realm would be harmonious? Would it make a powerful instrument for the Maji? Could an inexperienced Tyro handle such power?

Rune held his breath as Amestoy's hand – his left hand – the only left-handed Maji he had seen besides Tor! -- hovered around the Qarlylium. A rare metal of a silver hue mined from the mountains of Ayelsborne – Ion-Gawain and Rune's home province! Rune held his breath as Amestoy placed a block of the mineral atop the crystal in his hand. In the blink of an eye the talisman and ring were formed, the gem and metal separated and reformed into two matching, morphed, connected power conductors.

Rune gasped. The shape of the amulet matching the ring was a clawed dragon! Just like Rune's! It took a moment for the Mentor to recover his equilibrium and composure. The Tyro had not noticed the reaction; he was too busy admiring his touch-stone and ring.

With shaking hands, Rune placed the amulet around Amestoy's neck. A left-handed Maji. A Qarlylium dragon ring and talisman with an Ayelsborne Iolite crystal! Rune stopped trying to analyze and speculate and guess what it all could mean. Tor, himself, and Amestoy. Was there actually a mystic connection? Or was it all just coincidence?

"This will be your best friend, Tyro –"

"Except for you, Mentor."

"Er, uh, yes, Tyro. I am your Mentor. Your teacher. Not your friend."

"Yes, Mentor."

Was that a smirk? "Anyway, never allow this touch-stone and ring out of your possession. This is your personal connection to your heritage as a Maji. It is the badge of your office and responsibility. These crystals are the focal power for channeling, controlling and mastering your Majiq. They will save your life and the lives of countless others as the balance and conduit of enchantment. They will command respect and authority in places where you will receive neither without it." His voice deepened, saddened, recalling his recent encounter with the bounty hunter. "Unfortunately, they will also make you a target of those who wish to destroy us along with law and justice. You must honor the touch-stones as you do your oath as a Maji."

"Always, Mentor." He looked down at the touch stone and his demeanor suddenly transformed from serious to gleeful. Laughing, still filled with amazement and pride he exclaimed, "Dragon's breath! That was amazing!"

"Just so." Rune chuckled, recalling his own feelings when he had constructed his touch-stone. "Now for the rest of your gear."

In the clothing room, Amestoy received all the accoutrements entitled to his office. A glittering, translucent robe which was sprinkled with material-shrinking powder to give a better fit to the skinny Amestoy. Utility belt, various pouches with numerous pockets for general potions, dusts and herbs. There were more extras Rune did not allow him to examine with any detail, but assured they would come in handy. There would be plenty of time when they were aboard ship. The several days journey to Ionia would allow much time to play with the new toys.

Outfitted for almost anything, Rune felt more at ease as they hurried to their quarters to collect their kits. He had done all he could to physically prepare Amestoy for the big world they were entering into today. Hopefully, with time, training and experience, it would be enough to keep Amestoy safe and alive for many years. The Darkness was growing and the young man would need every bit of skill and Majiq to survive in an increasingly dangerous universe.

**

Amestoy had never been to the port of Avelon. Standing on the dock waiting for the sailors to complete loading cargo, Amestoy was a little awed. He was leaving on his first mission! And here with him were famous elder priests! He was part of the real realm now, not a kid anymore!

The recognizable Mead Cardok stood in silent contemplation of the seemingly infinite sea. Wiry and tall, the woman was covered in a tight, bronze cloak. Her skin was mottled and stretched, as if it had too much sun. With her was a short, stout, Celtic girl-priest named Morgan, several classes ahead of Amestoy. The teens exchanged acknowledging nods. A flowing, rust-colored mantle made her even more impressive. And her matching crystal-embedded ear lobes glistened in the reflection of the high sun. It cast an elegant hue on her youthful features.

Another looming personage, much taller than Rune or himself, was Bryne, from the province of Cumbrish, one of two Maji Paladins. It was the other Sorcerer, however, that caught Amestoy's attention the most. The slight, blond haired, blue-eyed, wiry, Sorceress with pale skin and a mysterious air. Amestoy discreetly studied her as Rune gave the necessary documents to the captain.

After they boarded the ship, the blond Templar hoisted a bulging rucksack and tossed it with negligible ease into an overhead bin in the common bunk cabin. Adroit and thin, the lack of strain the action took made her seem like a walking contradiction. When she turned and grinned at Amestoy, the Tyro drew back, startled that she was comfortable with him staring at her.

Taking a place at the rail next to Rune as they weighed anchor, Amestoy felt the eyes of the blond woman on him. It was thrilling to watch the dock, town, and castle fade from view, swallowed by the ever-present mists that surrounded Avelon. From the keep, he had seen the grey of the bay and the foggy sky, his cloistered circumstances making him feel as though he were trapped away from the rest of the world. Now, from the opposite perspective, Amestoy felt like he was leaving his childhood and past behind. Within this swirling vapor, he was embracing his future.

Eventually the ship broke free of the mists, and the blue ocean and vast sky took Amestoy's breath away. He stayed on deck for hours, even forgetting to eat the evensong meal and Rune had to bring it up to him. The two then stood and watched as, with the approach of twilight, Amestoy had his first glimpse of a foreign shore.

Alongside a rough and rugged coastline they dropped anchor. A long boat was lowered into the churning water. Cardok, and Morgan, along with Bryne, debarked at this first port. There was no pier; no lights of a town, no dock, no discernible civilization.

"Where are they going?" Amestoy asked.

"I could tell you, but it would mean nothing to you. Sometimes Wizards are needed in remote places. Their entry is required under the guise of stealth. Our responsibility is not to get too curious. We have our own mission.

The youth nodded in reluctant acceptance.

"Let's go down below and study. You have learned much of the various realms and provinces in lessons. We need to go into a little more detail now. Ionia is like no place you have ever seen."

"I have seen only Avelon, Master."

"Exactly."

Apparently the blond Sorcerer was traveling to the farther reaches of the realm, along with them, Amestoy reasoned when they came down to the bunk cabin. Glowing crystals hung suspended in mid-air, providing light for the below-deck regions. As they sat cross-legged on upper beds, they were joined on a top bunk by the woman.

"Artemis Pellinor." She held out a hand for Amestoy to shake.

Most Mentors did not bother to notice Tyros much. And Pellinor! Such an illustrious name! A family from the deep origins of Merlin and the original Maji who migrated to this realm centuries ago. It was not his place to express curiosity about personal matters with a senior Maji, but he so wanted to question her about – everything!

"Pleased to meet you, Mentor. Amestoy Daavv."

Her light eyebrows rose. "Ameden royalty!

"The decimation of your race was an atrocity."

Rune gave a glare to the Sorcerer who seemed young and frail in comparison to him. "You know there are no longer such things as fore-tellers."

It was a defense offered in protection against bigotry. Rune seemed sensitive to such possibilities, while Amestoy hadn't given them a thought. His life sequestered within the Maji Castle sheltered him from severe prejudice. While other students were sometimes suspicious, they were rarely rude. He understood that Rune was trying to ease him into the harshness of the realm. There might be some who would recognize him as Amed. What would they do? For the first time he was worried, and wondered if Rune's reaction was a precursor of trouble to come. Some would want to attack and kill them for their status as Maji. There would also be those who would shun, or even try to harm Amestoy, because of his clan. While he didn't feel he needed protection, Amestoy was grateful for the thoughtfulness and caring of his Mentor.

Artemis gave a slow nod. Her blue eyes darted for a brief, but incisive look to Amestoy, and then she leaned back in bland indifference. "Amed. Quite. And for future reference, I am not a Mentor."

"Yes, Ment – uh – Sorcerer Artemis."

There was no outward sign, no verbal comment, but Amestoy knew Artemis believed the denials Rune so cavalierly flung out about Amed. The blanket objections were accepted in muteness that seemed to repel the ideas without effort.

So, the Sorcerer accompanying them was a slender being of deceptive physical strength and sharp wit. Amestoy received it as his first lesson outside the Castle: never judge by appearances.

PART TWO
LESSON ONE: NOTHING IS AS IT SEEMS

The world was amazing. Even in the dark. Stars filled the sky like a diamond-studded blanket. The ship was better than he expected considering some of the Maji accounts he had overheard at the Castle. It could be a rowdy realm and members of Merlin's Order had to take what they could get to accomplish their missions. Things thus far had been pretty civilized. Cramped quarters were tolerable since Maji traveled without many possessions. The food was below average, but Amestoy had made friends with the cook and was able to snack as much as he wanted as long as he chatted with the gregarious man.

During the first day and night of the journey, Amestoy studied the details of the mission. It was a policing excursion. Ionia's various tribes were being plagued by meddling Seelie – or Faeries. As practitioners of the strongest enchantment known – Majiq – the Templars were expected to balance out the Human and supernatural conflicts.

Daily meditation and wand practice kept Mentor and Tyro on alert and fit. They were learning to synchronize their rhythms and pacing, reading each other's nuances and Majiq surges. While Amestoy felt he was naturally open and accepting, he found in Rune a formidable defensive shield. The Mentor was tight and controlling in his methods and emotions. There was no opening up. No real sharing. Was that the way it was supposed to be? Amestoy had hoped otherwise.

There was another sense that Amestoy liked even less. Rune was hiding something. Artemis and Rune DID seem to spend a lot of time together. They acted – covert. Secretive was perhaps too strong of a definition. What were they concealing? They were not romantically involved, he thought, but had to admit he would not know too many of those signs if he saw them. No experience with that at the Castle, although there had been some teasingly flirtatious encounters between him and the opposite sex. That pretty Ema who was two years his junior had given him the eye more than once. She was distracting enough to make him lose concentration in a few classes.

Amestoy did not pick up those sparks between Artemis and Rune, and since they were Maji, they lived for concealing weakness. Maji were not celibate, but they were, out of necessity, careful about liaisons. Partiality, loyalty, affection could not be allowed to cloud their missions, or their judgment.

As Amestoy munched on his fruit, ambling back to his cabin, he pondered the nature of his Mentor. What was Rune doing and why wasn't he including his Tyro? What was Rune's passion? That was easy. Everyone at the Castle knew he was a rebel when it came to Merlin's attitude about hunting down the Gadion-Obscura . . . . Gadion-Obscura. Could Artemis and Rune be plotting on tracking the Gadion-Obscura? Amestoy worked at calming his excitement. He did not want the Mentors aboard to feel his spike in anticipation. Were they really going after the Dark cabal? Wow! This was a first mission to remember! But he was being left out of battle plots! Was it because of his inexperience, his naiveté?

He stopped, slowing his heartbeat and his wild theories. He would collect evidence first, figure out what was going on, and then ingratiate himself into the action. No matter how new he was and how experienced they were, he was not letting arrogant Mentors keep him out of a juicy fight!

The wooden deck boards shuddered beneath his feet and Amestoy used Majiq to keep his balance as the old vessel hit stormy seas. He was not showing off – there were no witnesses to observe his prowess. It was difficult, however, to deny the gentle rise of pride cresting in his thoughts as he watched the others around him grapple for any nearby handhold, while he barely levitated above the shuddering deck.

He felt the sense of a rebuke wash into his mind from his Mentor. To the credit of the venerable Maji Soren Rune, the twelve-year-old's new teacher diligently reinforced the principles of humility to the energetic and confident young man. A practice the elder Sorcerer constantly vowed would be his lifelong trial. Teachings that sometimes seemed futile.

Becoming a Tyro was an amazing experience so far. Through meditation and physical training, Amestoy had grown closer to his Mentor. They shared a spiritual bond through Majiq, and were growing to understand how each other thought and moved and reacted. Any hint of a deeper, Warrior Bond, was rejected still by Rune, although Amestoy worked at subtle hints to keep the subject alive. The sense of disapproval from his Mentor was, in a way, amusing. Rune might deny a Bond, but was not above using Majiq across several decks of a ship to display his chiding.

Amestoy smiled as he made his way toward the cabin. The old and creaky ship had been the best vessel -- the only vessel -- available to them. Living space was uncomfortable, but they didn't need much. Food was rationed, but his friendship with the cook kept him from starving. The lack of exercise rooms made daily practice sessions difficult, but still, they managed. On the bright side, they would only be aboard another two days.

When he reached the cabin he was not surprised to find Artemis just leaving. With a tight nod the Sorcerer slipped away. The atmosphere was tense. Definitely not romantic. This really was more like a council of war.

"Amestoy, a Maji is supposed to be patient, modest and humble in his powers."

"Yes, Mentor." The internal sigh was irritated. "Is that your favorite quote?"

"I'm beginning to think it is yours, Tyro."

"Funny." He ignored Rune's glare. "I know you don't believe in the Warrior Bond, Mentor, but it would be so much more convenient to share a true telepathic link. Then you wouldn't have to waste so much breath scolding me."

It was a daring bit of sarcasm, a subtle challenge that hit too close to the mark when he instantly felt his Tutor's displeasure. Maji mental links were very limited – impressions, strong feelings, nudges. Nothing like the Ameden powers of telepathy. Amestoy thought they were comfortable enough to make light of the mythical talents, but apparently not. He must guard himself against too much revelation, even to Rune. No one must suspect he understood more than anyone knew about his race's hidden aptitudes.

Rune gruffed under his breath. "You picked up my displeasure well enough to return here. I doubt we need anything as arcane as a Warrior Bond." A trickle of unease from the Mentor swept into the young man's mind. "There is something -- not right."

Sobriety replaced the sarcasm. "What is it, Mentor?"

"Trouble," he snapped.

The ship shuddered again and Amestoy instinctively reached over to catch his Mentor's shoulder pouch that flew off a shelf. A misty landscape surged into his mind, and the flush of danger creeping around him and his Mentor. Amestoy fought to hold the fleeting image, but it escaped before a breath could be taken. He saw that Rune was watching him closely, carefully, for just a heartbeat. During which time he instinctively, successfully, shielded his flash of fore-gift.

Rune, then his Tyro, scrambled out the hatch. Before Amestoy reached the passenger deck, Rune's prophetic words came to pass when the vessel violently quaked under their feet. That was more than rough seas! He caught himself on the bulkhead and focused his Majiq. Tapped into the constant, subliminal link with his Mentor, he had no trouble perceiving Rune's concern and disturbance over the unnatural incident with the ship.

Sifting past Rune's wave of perceptions, Amestoy pushed deep within himself to center on his Majiq ability. Through those powerful senses he could discern the disquiet of the crew as they searched for damage from the sudden lurching of the ship. His insight picked up the anxiety of the passengers. It was all vague feelings which he pieced together, using deductive skills, to determine the cause of the problems. Rune's expression indicated he was doing the same thing and they both seemed to reach the identical conclusion simultaneously.

"Breach —

" — starboard cargo hold!"

"How did you detect it, Mentor?"

"Maji have yet to achieve a singleness of thought with inanimate objects."

Amestoy coughed on a laugh -- his Mentor's dry sarcasm was rare, but when delivered so perfectly it was highly amusing. "Yes, Mentor."

As they raced up the narrow, steep gangway, then up another set of stairs, avoiding terrified passengers and rushing crewmen, Rune tossed back a slight smile. "Impressive acuity, my Tyro. How did you determine that? You can't read my mind, right?" It was almost an accusation.

"Mind-read, Mentor?"

"Did you pick up on my sense of danger?"

"Uh - that and other indicators. The listing of the ship. General – feelings – from the crew allowed me to – uh – guess – the nature of the crisis."

"Good job."

Panicked passengers were emerging from their cabins, nearly stampeding up and down the corridor. The Maji pressed themselves against the bulkhead to keep from being trampled. Rune grabbed hold of Amestoy's shirtsleeve and pushed him against the gnarled wooded hull.

Amazed that Rune could read him so easily, Amestoy tried to brush off the probing questions.

Rune's eyes narrowed, then gave a slight shake of his head, as if uncertain what to say next. "I know you are not used to such emergencies. Coping will come with time and experience. Just – just remember not to interfere unless it is completely necessary."

"I will use caution when we make landfall, Mentor."

"Landfall?"

"The breach . . . ." Stupid! He should have never said anything! Rune was going to suspect him even more! How was he going to share quarters and years with a Mentor and not tell him the Amed mind talents were real? "Do you not think the ship will need repairs?" He held his breath hoping the lame recovery would not be found suspicious. His teacher could not know about his gift!

Rune seemed to concentrate for a moment, and then slowly nodded his head. "Yes, I believe we will be landing for repairs, Tyro. Good reasoning."

When the older man clapped a strong hand on his shoulder, Amestoy did not allow any thought, any unguarded emotion to stray from his tight control. That was close. He had to train himself to keep better domination of vision-scapes and not share them with his skeptical partner.

**

The crew managed to temporarily patch-up the breach. Then the sails shifted, the ship drifting into a rocky harbor off the Cumbrish coast. The damage would require repairs and they awaited the announcement from the captain as to details of the delay. Artemis tossed her bag to the cabin door as if there was nothing inside the kit. She was debarking on one of the first row boats ashore. Awaiting there were the few available coaches to take travelers south to the nearest tavern where they would either arrange for horses or walk to a busier port. Word had it passengers heading north or inland would have to make their way on foot. She bid Rune a cheerful farewell. Then the blond Maji leaned close to the Tyro.

"Do take care of the old man." A smile gave the bland comment a sardonic edge. "He is a fine Maji, but not very imaginative, is he?"

Momentarily startled at the comment, but bound to defend Rune no matter what, the boy responded, "He is a great Mentor."

Chuckling, Artemis finally agreed, ending with, "Well said loyal pupil. Despite his dubious opinions, though, young Tyro, watch for his tendency to be skeptical. Maybe you should lean on your heritage for some creative thinking."

With a nod of her head, her blond hair fluffing in his eyes, she turned and sprinted down the rocking hallway.

What was all that cryptic stuff supposed to mean? Two days from Avelon and he was clouded within a mystery! His Mentor was calling him and he hastened along, wondering what his next adventure would bring.

As he packed his few belongings into a kit bag, Rune explained that Cumbrish was a small, rural province along the trade route between Avelon and greater ports in Britania and

Europa. With no more horses or coaches available to hire, Rune decided they would walk to the nearest village and find transport from there to Ionia.

"It is impossible to know what to expect from any province," Rune lectured as he threw his bag over his shoulder. "This coast has been of interest to smugglers and other undesirables." He waved a hand over his cloak, then over Amestoy's. The shimmering material dulled to give the appearance of rough cloth, a common, inexpensive traveling garment. Then he tucked his dragon talisman under his shirt and nodded for Amestoy to do the same. "Let's not advertise our presence as Maji. We don't want to attract attention."

Criminal activity in this backward, rocky province? Amestoy thought it, but not strongly enough to cause even a ripple of sarcasm or dissent to register on his Mentor's senses. His afterthought-shielding must not have worked because Rune gave him a canted glare.

"Remember, Amestoy, these people are bucolic by nature. Please control your impressive mind skills."

This time it was gentle humor and Amestoy responded with an easy smile. "Yes, Mentor." One of the nicest things about his Tutor was that Rune could be strict and exacting, but he was never harsh, nor lingering in his censures. And he did have a sense of humor.

**

As they walked, Rune suggested they investigate the countryside and local inhabitants -- using this as an opportunity for education and broadening their experiences. It could be one of many tests for his protégé. Amestoy knew he had to get used to life as a constant training session, but once in a while he would like to give it a rest and just enjoy himself in this huge universe! Here they were in a new realm and it was going to turn into lessons!

"There is much to be learned even in the most unsophisticated offerings, Tyro."

"Of course, Mentor," he automatically agreed.

He left unsaid that he had heard THAT lecture more than once or twice the last few days. He was not so foolish as to speak -- or even think too loudly -- the opinion. For during these early Majiqal experiences he had received incredible, life-altering wisdom from Rune. Always he strove to be a student to make his Mentor proud. That meant keeping the sarcastic predilections to himself when he thought things were about to get boring, or tedious. Occasionally, he had voiced his naïve opinion only to be proven wrong by his sagacious elder.

Amestoy absorbed all he could in the initial impression of the province. It was nice, he decided. Slow, maybe, but that lent to the rustic appeal. There were lush hills buried in the shadows of the evening, and sunset-rose-shaded dusty roads. His first province-fall as a Tyro was not very exciting, but it was – scenic. Trying not to be sarcastic or too jaded from his upbringing at the spiritual center/holy core of Avelon, he took in a deep breath. The air was fresh, scented lightly with sweet, floral smells and something more earthy, like livestock. The trees were tall and swayed gently in a low breeze.

The village was small and primitive as viewed from the top of the road coming up from the beach. Walking straight, they peeled off from the few other passengers who turned inland at the crossroads. Silently, the Maji entered a clearing not far from a quiet town, with numerous rows of neat, but weathered, wood buildings. Because of the temperate conditions the main street marketplace sported stalls for sellers. They were shaded from the dying rays of sun by straw awnings lining the street. Torches along the small dirt main lane were lit, and Rune managed to buy a last loaf of bread and four chunks of cheese from a merchant before the shops closed with the advent of night.

Amestoy bit into the sandwiched items. "Thank you so much, Mentor. Ah waasoh worried –"

"Amestoy, please do not talk when your mouth is stuffed beyond reason with food. Slow down, enjoy your meal. Besides, your gratitude at eating is so obvious it takes no Maji to interpret it."

Swallowing the barely chewed chunks of food in his mouth, he responded. "Yes, Mentor."

Gazing around the rural region, Amestoy breathed a controlled sigh of relief. This was not anything like his frightening vision-scape during meditation at the Castle. They were safe. No danger here that he could see. He was entering a new phase of life, though. This region was a match for the brief fore-vision he had received aboard ship. The confirmation of his hereditary skills was exciting, but he was careful not to allow that thrill to surface.

It was also extremely small and sparsely populated. The region must be filled with farms. There was no commerce from the sea or main highways. Then he remembered Rune mentioning the area being rife with smugglers. Yes, he could imagine many an unfortunate ship smashing to bits on the rough rocks below. And quick brigands rushing down the hills to scavenge cargo to sell in the larger villages.

"I hope that meager meal suits you for a time, Amestoy," Rune broke into his thoughts. "There is no tavern here. No place to spend the night. We will have to press on."

"Yes, Mentor. But I thought Wizard Artemis said she was going to the nearest tavern."

"She did. Apparently that was not in this little mud spot."

Rune directed them along the footpath into the hills. He watched as his charge gazed around in amazement at the new province. Good. The boy was absorbing all the new input flooding into his mind. He wondered what amazing traits would surface in their career. And would the Ameden heritage have any bearing on his Maji path?

Rune's birthright legacy instead offered powers over large beasts – dragons specifically. His were the Wizarding gifts of controlling the simple, but formidable natures of dragons. It had been too long since he had returned to Ayelsborne, or had the pleasure of riding the great winged creatures of home.

Origin provinces were important. Thoughts returned to Ameden. There were times when Amestoy seemed to possess second-sight, the fore-tell talent of his inheritance. Was it just an extension of his unique imprint of Majiq? Or could Majiq endow with skills Merlin-Maj would have never guessed? Was there a bigger destiny for Amestoy than the life of a simple Maji? There could be danger in the enchantments of Ameden surfacing again. Merlin-Maj must have been aware of that when he brought the baby, Amestoy, back to the Castle.

A tall, thick-set local dressed in simple clothes approached on the country lane. In the dying evening light little was discernible except he was a big man carrying a load of logs across his shoulders.

"Fair visitors," he addressed with a guttural growl.

"Good evening to you, sir," Rune greeted.

"Do you need our help?" Amestoy asked.

The man scoffed. "For this load of branches? More like you need help! My protection if you roam the hills," he glared at Rune. "The bandits prey on the weak."

"And you're going to save us?" Amestoy almost scoffed, but managed just in time to color the words in a neutral tone. From Rune's glower he knew he had not entirely succeeded.

Without changing facial expression, Rune replied, "Thank you, friend, but we are careful travelers. We will find shelter in the nearest town. We are making our way to the coach stop on the other side of the mountain."

"There are dragons that attack without warning. I can protect you! For a fee, of course."

"Dragons?" Amestoy repeated. "I have never seen a drag –" His declaration was interrupted by Rune's elbow jabbing him sharply in the stomach.

Eyebrows raised, Rune gave no hint of outward delight at such a warning. "You mean smugglers. Pirates, of course."

"Any Faeries?" Amestoy asked.

The stranger seemed angry. "No Faeries! No such things as Faeries."

Rune cleared his throat. "Well thank you, but we can take care of ourselves."

"Take care of yourselves," he mocked in a low, threatening tone before adding "You have been warned." He shrugged, the big shoulders shifting like grassy mountains in a quake. "Beware. For a few credits you could have eluded the lurking dragons."

He lingered for a moment, giving the Maji a chance to change his mind. Rune offered a benign smile and bowed. "Thank you. We will not need your assistance."

The man gave a low, grunt of a snort, then shuffled away to accost other sojourners.

As they walked away, Amestoy asked quietly, "Why didn't we ride dragons to Ionia? It would have saved us a lot of trouble."

"You know that dragons are used rarely in this age of disbelief. You must go to Ayelsborne to see them now."

"I would like that."

Rune shot him a stern look. "Lesson one, Tyro. Nothing is as it seems."

"The old man is a warrior in disguise?" Amestoy couldn't resist a bit more teasing. "Well, apparently we need a guard to take us into the country. I thought you said these people were bucolic and peaceful? Dragons! Little did he know you are a dragon master! Do you think we can handle them?"

Rune ruffled the short, spiky hair. "Enough of your cheek, Tyro."

Not bothering to conceal his triumphant, mischievous, grin he wondered, "What about these bandit dragons?"

"Maybe some of Ionia's troubles have reached here. We will use caution, and arrive at the next village before sundown." He threw a lopsided grin at his shorter companion. "We will use this unexpected opportunity to expand your knowledge. Where is your sense of adventure?"

"Apparently up ahead, Mentor." The green eyes scanned the surrounding hills. "Did he mean brigands controlling beasts? Real dragons? With fire? And teeth?"

"Why, Tyro, are you afraid of big teeth?"

"Not with your advanced skills to keep me safe, Mentor."

Of course there would be no dragons in these regions. Mankind was coming to the day of confidence in their own skills and departing from the realms of Majiq, dragons and Wizards. It was a sad realization to Rune, who had come of age at a time when the order of Merlin was bound with tales of chivalry and heroic deeds. Now such gifts were looked upon with suspicion and dragons were considered dangerous beasts. They could be, of course, but handled by a Dragon Master, they were domesticated and excellent companions.

The province was certainly rustic, Amestoy admitted to himself, but pleasant in its own way. Convinced these simple farmers living on the outskirts of the realm could teach him little, Amestoy took this as an unexpected holiday. Strolling along a country road with the good company of his Mentor, he promised to enjoy the humble offerings of Cumbri. So far, at least, there was no sign of any robbers, or vicious dragons-pirates. Considering Rune's legendary proclivity for finding danger, he remained on guard, but only slightly. What could country peasants possibly do to intimidate two Maji priests?

Cumbri was physically much like a few of the small realms Amestoy had visited as a Novitiate on training expeditions close to Avelon. He had never seen any place so quiet and rural, though, and accepted that there were many backward, pastoral provinces in the world and he should not make comparisons.

Entering the village not long after sunset, they encountered shops open under the bright moon and moderate summer evening. Stalls sold the usual grocery and supply necessities for an agricultural community. A blacksmith, an herbalist, and two pubs rounded out the main section of commerce. In the middle of the hamlet was a central square. On this day it was filled with the colorful banners and booths of a festival. There were entertainment stalls, food vendors and talented street performers in the large, torch-lit park.

Amestoy was the first to stop at the several food kiosks, spending a liberal amount of his allotted coins on strong smelling morsels that were quickly consumed. Rune bought a few cups of local cider and the second round of tasty meat pies as they strolled the common. The buzz of conversation seemed to focus mainly on accounts of the vicious bandits roaming the hills.

"Perhaps we should find shelter for the night, Mentor?" He chewed a wad of green crunchies. "This seems a satisfactory place."

Rune helped himself to several goodies from the soft, flat bread Amestoy was using as a plate. "With plenty of good food, you mean?"

"Well you can't argue with that."

Rune grinned. "I have known you only a handful of days, Tyro, but have already learned that if you ever lose your way I simply find the closest food vendor."

In the middle of a mouthful of food, Rune froze, and then abruptly swallowed. Instantaneously, Amestoy picked up on the wave of -- Majiq -- that rippled through his Mentor and into him. Through meditation and training sessions they had learned much of each other in this first week as Teacher and Pupil. Accustomed to Rune's distinct Sorcerer signature and the unique trademark enchantment of what Amestoy insisted was their Warrior Bond, he knew Rune was reacting to an external wave of Majiq. Amestoy was reacting to it as well, along with the Bond. And the Majiq they were detecting was not along the positive light associated with Maji. It was a much heavier, darker energy.

"What is it?" Wary, Amestoy kept his communications close and personal. Whispers only his Mentor could receive enhanced through Majiq.

"Someone very Dark, very close."

Amestoy resisted an involuntary shiver. In his limited time as a Tyro he had, of course, never encountered real Dark Majiq. He knew it on an instinctive level from the vision he had shared with Rune and that brief brush of something sinister on Avelon. Now he felt it for real and would never forget its indelible mark upon his psyche.

Turning slowly, Rune shrugged his broad shoulders toward the edge of the village square. Some entertainers were singing comical songs, others acting out scenes of plays. Three glaringly, garishly dressed harlequins were juggling food items before a small group of amused spectators. Nearby, an elderly woman performer was shooting darts from a small crossbow. Then she threw blades, axes and other deadly objects toward a slender, blindfolded young man with orange dragons tattooed on his forearms. The performer seemed in mortal danger but, amazingly, remained unscathed! Without sight he was slicing the lethal projectiles with the singing blade of a smoke-grey sword that sizzled with incandescent Majiq!

"Using Majiq for carnival tricks!" Amestoy audibly gasped. "How is that possible?"

The elder Maji's mouth was set in a thin line of grim disgust. His blue eyes were hard, icy crystals of denunciation. "There is only one way." The condemnation in his thoughts rang with harsh gravity. "You know that."

"Diaboliq?"

Rune gave a subdued, single negative shift of his head. "No. I know the signature of the Gadion-Obscura, and Diaboliq, the specific imprint of the assassins and mercenaries. This does not belong to either group. They are using Dark Art potions and powders with an above average level of skill."

Amestoy was baffled. "Diaboliq and Gadion-Obscura. I'm still confused about the difference. Aren't they the same?"

"With a subtle difference. Gadion-Obscura is the secret society of Dark Arts. Diaboliq is the evil side of Majiq-assassins, the Sinisters who are the Gadion-Obscura cultish killers who are trained to seek out specific targets and murder them. Two prongs of the same dagger. Both groups have used corrupt potions for their ends. Elixirs that canker the body and soul, they operate as a substitute for Majiq. It is as deadly as any force in the universe, but it is temporary. Soon the artificial enchantment destroys them from within."

"A true allegory of wickedness."

Rune gripped his Tyro's shoulder. "Very astute, Amestoy. This is Dark and wicked nonetheless."

Amestoy bit his lip, quelling the shudder of repulsive certainty. Edges of dread rippled into his senses. For the first time he was facing true evil. Deep down, Amestoy felt a tremor of apprehension for his Mentor's safety; his mortality. In the advancing Darkness of the Gadion-Obscura and the sweep of evil Diaboliq, these were dangerous times. He had been so sheltered within the Castle. He was in the real world now, and this would be his first, and probably not last, encounter with the direct opposite of what he and his Mentor represented.

Rune's hand squeezed his shoulder again and kept the pressure on for a moment. "No need to worry, Tyro," The warm reassurance whispered into his ears filtered into his senses as well, consoling the anxiety with a blanket of serenity. "There is an evil here, but it is no match for us, my young warrior. Nevertheless, we will be cautious. We will control our Majiq and investigate this miscreant who flaunts Darkness. Then we will act."

"I am at your command, Mentor."

"I know."

There was no point in shielding his eagerness to bring justice to such blatant threats to the Order. His Mentor could feel the emotions Amestoy did not bother to conceal. Being the exemplary teacher that he was, Rune did not comment on such vibrantly charged feelings. Instead, he patted Amestoy's shoulder a final time, and then led the way toward the performer with the smoke-grey blade.

Dressed in simple tunics covered in cloaks, the two Maji blended nicely with the rural crowd of the village. Studying the team of entertainers, Rune quickly assessed the situation. The slight Majiq skill and the sword attracted a big crowd. This larcenous team probably traveled to remote, backwater provinces to avoid Maji and other sophisticated beings that might turn them in to authorities. A rough-clothed Gypsy-type young woman roamed among the spellbound spectators, expertly picking the pockets of the rapt bystanders. So that was one angle of their game. What else? Three criminals would not waste the value and flash of a charmed blade just for pocket change.

The young stage performer was exhibiting a limited, semi-skilled ability to slice the various objects hurled toward him. The painted dragons on his arms seemed to come alive under the flickering torch light. The exercise was elementary -- something Maji learned before the age of eight. What caught Rune's attention, and concern, was the accomplice. From the older woman throwing the lethal daggers and blades at the young man, Rune sensed a powerful Darkness.

A commotion at the far end of the common distracted Rune. It was a political gathering apparently, with one boisterous Cumbri female, in red robes, the center of attention. The Maji gave the rally little thought until he noticed the entertainment troupe had started to close down their acts. Performers -- including the sword wielder and his handler -- drifted over to the outskirts of the assembly.

The Cumbri Praetor -- the proclaimed leader of the community -- started an oratory on the dangers of the local bandits, nicknamed dragons, who preyed on the innocent. This commander of the village was a short, muscled woman who exuded an innate strength of body and soul. She saw it as her mission to rid the local hills of the robbers plaguing and murdering within her territory. Her bold speech was met with enthusiastic applause. Apparently this rallying of public support was the reason for the festivities.

With interest, the Maji moved closer to the Praetor's dais, edging nearer to the suspect performers. The Praetor asked for, and received, pledges of volunteers to combat the dragons while the crowd rippled with community spirit. Eager, altruistic men and women stepped forward to serve their district and leader.

"Do you think they have a chance of winning against the brigands?" Amestoy wondered skeptically. "These people are farmers. The robbers are armed, organized and vicious."

"I believe good will prevail if good is clever enough," he quietly considered. "These are people defending their families, homes, their way of life. Powerful motivations against outlaws who only fight for gain, Amestoy."

Nodding in agreement, the youth stilled abruptly. "Do you --" Amestoy whispered, then caught his breath.

"Sense a Dark purpose? Yes." Rune quietly finished the thought. "We must be on alert."

"Agreed."

As he rushed through the square, Rune watched the foe, and the possible target, while in the back of his mind, cursed himself. Amestoy had no real training in the touch-stone Majiq! There was so much to learn, but as yet there had been no time! And the Mentor was leading the Tyro into danger on their first province fall!

"Use whatever means necessary to safeguard yourself and others, Amestoy."

"You, too, Mentor."

Rune smiled at the bravado. *I think you can take care of yourself. But I'll be watching out for you anyway.* Amestoy knew how to handle himself, but this was his first battle and in the back of Rune's mind there was concern.

Ever mindful of danger, the alert, older Maji nearly missed the subtly cunning maneuver of the actors. The three brightly dressed, clownish jugglers were overtly blundering through the townspeople to reach the politician's platform. The crowd started to murmur their objections to the performers and all attention seemed focused on the flashy intruders. Except for two sets of trained eyes, led by Majiq, to watch the Cumbri Praetor.

Slipping around to the side of the crowd, Rune and Amestoy briskly approached the stand. They mutually felt a surge in Dark Power before they saw the old woman entertainer and the young man who un-sheathed his shimmery weapon. The two Maji slipped around behind the dais. When the young man held the sword in his hand, it seemed an extended blade shooting from the orange dragon tattoo, powered by whatever Dark potion was used to energize it. The Maji picked up their speed and the forces of good and evil, Light and Dark converged at the foot of the speaker's stand.

Intending to stop the sword wielder, Rune nearly missed the last-instant-warning sense of danger from the old woman. She turned to attack him! From the periphery of his sense he tracked Amestoy as the Tyro moved on to confront the brigand with the enchanted sword. Ha! Amestoy pitted against someone with a blade? He almost felt sorry for the fool opposing his expert Tyro!

Rune turned in time to stretch out his right arm and fire out a wall of energy to deflect a bolt from the old woman's crossbow. The weapon surprised the Maji. Not exactly taken off guard -- still he had not expected a modern weapon. He had been lulled into thinking the bandits were unsophisticated; because of the rural settings and banal tactics of these crude dragons, he considered them nothing more than thugs. An old lesson he would have to remind -- and admit to -- his Tyro: looks can be deceiving.

In the next moments of personal combat, Rune appraised his adversary as she fired blast shots and he deflected them with twists, turns and parries worthy of his Mentor status. He shot out surges of non-lethal, silver-blue flame to shock her into retreat. Frustrated, she backed off, circling him. The momentary lull allowed him to reach out with Majiq to reassure that his new Tyro was all right. Amestoy had decided to engage with his staff weapon instead of his touch-stone. A shrewd option. It revealed the Tyro's sense of fair play with one who didn't deserve it and his certain confidence in his own skills with such a weapon. Amestoy was brilliant in Majiq sword fighting in training sessions, but was he a match for a malevolent enemy using an energy bladed weapon to kill him?

Amestoy used second-nature skills to evaluate his opponent as the other teen raced up to confront him. When they were approaching the bandits, mentally, Rune had assigned himself to the younger one with the sabre and conferred back-up protection to Amestoy. The verbal command had never been issued. As happened in combat situations, the plans were unexpectedly altered and the Maji team forced to improvise. Because of their strong connection, tactical regrouping was simple and instantaneous. They moved smoothly as a unit -- positioning themselves according to requirements of the battle.

The stranger's smoke-grey Black-Majiq sword slashed into the air millimeters from Amestoy's arm as he plunged into an attack. Tactically it lacked finesse and under training conditions would have earned him a sharp reprimand from Rune. It still might if Rune was aware of the stratagem, but in Amestoy's impatient passion, he wanted the battle to be joined! Somehow, his opponent possessed an enchanted sword! He must have ambushed a Maji to get it! A more heinous offense Amestoy could not imagine. He would assure justice for such a crime.

His opponent was good, he admitted as they closed; the smoke-grey and silver-blue sword-beams slashing the air as the combatants swirled into a whirlpool of movement and light. Peripherally aware that the people had scattered, Amestoy appreciated the open space. Knowing that any innocents were no longer in danger allowed him to focus completely on his foe.

The pirate's burning eyes stared into his; bold, set in an expression that the Tyro's Majiq interpreted as committed hatred. Confident, driven by his own motivations of right and justice, Amestoy plunged forward, intense and determined. What he didn't expect was the level of proficiency offered by his enemy. The orange-dragon challenger lacked subtlety, but his ability with the sabre was impressive and more than enough to keep Amestoy occupied. Several near misses and a few slices in his tunic attested to the serious confrontation as they pranced in their duet of death.

When the old woman's blast gun sputtered out, Rune moved in for the kill. Hers was not a controlled Majiq owned by the Dark side -- he had felt that and was able to discern between Diaboliq, Dark Power, and Gadion-Obscura. Three very different, but equally dangerous and evil energies, but only the Dark Power was pitted against him today. Its aura swirled in the very air. The woman with grey hair and a wrinkled face was someone who dabbled with Majiq-enchantment and used it for criminal intent. That undoubtedly included murder. Probably the murder of a Maji for the enchanted sword. Malevolent energy manipulated against the charms of Good and Light. What they had stumbled upon here were talented outlaws. Whatever the label, his Tyro and he would take care of the problem. Not only for the sake of those as yet unaffected by the villains, but also for whatever Maji formerly owned the smoke-grey sword.

He was nearly close enough to render a fatal blow to her when she sidestepped, whipping out something from under the folds of her robe. Adept with the Dark Majiq, she adroitly feigned away and nearly caught the Maji off guard on his right. Just in time his touch-stone wave deflected flying objects shooting from a slender weapon attached to her wrist. A few darts sang close to his face and he deftly seared them into ash. The ploy gave her what she needed -- enough space to get out of Rune's reach. In a spurt of vigor she dashed over to join her collaborator, blasting her darts at the tenacious combatant.

"Amestoy!"

The warning came barely in time. The Tyro didn't question, just rolled into a dive, and then leaped to his feet as he twirled around to face their opponents from an angle close to his Mentor. Side by side, as they so often trained, the Maji moved with practiced synchronization against their enemies.

During the intense battle, several of the townspeople had quickly rallied. Armed with what appeared to be small daggers and various blades, the people turned on the attackers and managed to defend themselves by wounding or killing the carnival bandits. Using the mayhem to their advantage, the old woman and her accomplice turned and ran, the darts flying into the crowd of spectators. As one, Rune and Amestoy swept their hands toward the darts, touch-stone Majiq igniting the deadly weapons to flames.

Rune warned everyone to get out of the way, but confusion and panic aided the flight of the criminals. By the time the crowds cleared the woman, the teen and the surviving harlequins were gone, fading into the thickening night.

"Shall we pursue, Mentor?"

Slowly shaking his head, Rune felt it folly to run after the offenders who had fled to the safety of the deep woods beyond the town. Such a hiding place would be a trap, spelling doom for anything less than an army.

He turned to his anxious, still prepared Tyro. "It is too dangerous to meet them on their own ground." He seized the youth on the shoulder in a strong grasp. "You did very well, Amestoy. Your first battle and you performed brilliantly."

The pale face flushed at the compliment. A modest grin flashed before he responded. "Not my first battle, Mentor. I have been fighting with you for days."

"Cheeky," Rune muttered. This young Maji had more courage than was probably prudent for one so new to the raw side of the realm.

Disappointed at the criminal's escape, the people began the aftermath of any skirmish -- the clean-up. The Praetor organized a quick response, with people treating the wounded and tidying the park with a practiced efficiency. Before the Maji could blend into the proceedings, the Praetor joined them, greeting both with a slight bow.

"You are Maji. I am Praetor Qarta. As protector and leader of our fair community I thank you for your skill in defending our village."

The men bowed respectfully. Rune introduced them and offered more assistance, but the woman insisted the task was nearly complete. Impressed with the effectiveness of the civilians, Rune observed that the common was already nearly back to being an empty town center.

"Join me, please, Templars," she requested with the forcefulness of one accustomed to being obeyed.

Rune agreed and they followed her to a humble but comfortable dwelling at the far edge of the park. Praetor Qarta poured some liquid refreshment that stung the atmosphere with a tangy odor and tasted heavy, sweet and tart all at once. Out of politeness, Rune took a few tentative sips, guarding against the unknown stout. The local brew was heady and he shot a warning glare at his Novitiate. Amestoy, thirsty and fatigued from the battle gulped down the grog without caution. Choking, he sputtered out a cough.

"Be prudent, Tyro. Exotic brews can be dangerous. Especially for one just away of the Castle."

He had just fought his first battle! He had helped save a town! Instead of praise Rune was treating him like a child! Amestoy cleared his throat, trying to mask his irritation. "You encouraged education and adventure on this trip, Mentor."

"Tyro!"

"Yes, Mentor," he promised. Then sipped moderately at the grog.

Rune turned his attention to Qarta and asked her to give them a brief history of the bandits known as dragons. The Praetor explained that the thugs on the shire had organized themselves into effective bands of outlaws. Most stayed in the hills, preying on the nearest villages or single travelers. Some communities were more skilled at deflecting the invaders than others. This village had organized and fought back. Now the dragons intensified their fight, as if to teach the simple folk a lesson. But they were not going to give in, she promised fervently.

"Why did you not pursue the criminals?" Amestoy asked, his words thick, his voice deep.

Frowning, Rune pushed the goblet of drink out of the young man's reach.

"Too dangerous." the Praetor supplied simply. "They own the wilderness of the woods with the night as their ally."

"Do you think they will return tonight?"

"Unlikely. We have hurt them badly thanks to you. Stay until morning and allow us to offer protection. Daylight hours provide security on the busy roads. There are many travelers who are armed. The dragons respect the safety of numbers."

For quarters, the Maji were offered a small storeroom at the back of the house. Sacks of grain and flour provided adequate bedding and soon the Maji and the rest of the village settled down to quiet slumber. Roaming guards with trained attack animals patrolled the housing areas. Torches at every doorway gave the added aid of light.

Amestoy snuggled against the rough sacks, cuddling under a comforting blanket. He was very sleepy -- surprisingly tired after the brief but intense battle. Eyes barely open, he watched Rune sitting near the darkened window, surveying the quiet town.

"You expect trouble, Mentor?" He yawned, unable to keep his eyes open any longer. "Are you going to stay up?"

"For a time, Tyro."

"Mmm. Mentor?" he slurred tiredly. "Have you ever seen criminals like these with Black-Majiq?"

"A few. It is uncommon." After a moment of silence he continued. "Diaboliq assassins, known as Sinister, have burning eyes, from a red elixir. They can hypnotize, then strike for a kill. Their power is limited, but formidable to overcome."

Was he thinking about the vision they had shared? Amestoy would never forget the cloying feel of evil, or the fear, from seeing the red eyes in that dream.

"Those who give themselves freely to the Dark Arts have a natural inclination for evil. This flaw can include greed or lust or coveting for supremacy or anything else. Their soul is left open to being seduced by Darkness."

"Hmmm. Impressive," Amestoy slurred. "How do you know so much, Mentor? What else?"

Rune shook his head. It had come through a terrible price. Knowledge through experience. "Any criminal who practices Dark Majiq for long in the kingdom will be found out by our order. In some shires, though, they are more plentiful. This old one and young man -- they have a wicked strength in their Majiq. Cunning is their chief ally. They imitate Maji tricks but can never understand them, never really beat a Maji. But they are dangerous." He fondly studied the fatigued youth. "Don't worry, Amestoy, we are more than a match for them."

"They overpowered one Maji," he admitted in a mumble. "Mentor, did you know a Maji with a smoke-grey sword?"

"Only Mentor Gwen and she was alive and well last I heard. I don't know whom they murdered. But we shall find out."

"So what are we doing for our next amazing feat?" Amestoy wondered around a yawn."

Frowning at the drunken condition of his Tyro he quipped back, "When you have learned lesson one we will move on to the next."

"What?"

"What is lesson one, Tyro?"

"Uh – that – uh – you're always right?"

"Very good. And what did I tell you about the grog?"

"Not to drink so much?"

"Correct. So apparently we need more lessons on obedience."

"Oh, joy."

"And one more thing."

The answer was a soft snore. Rune shook his head, but an amused grin refused to be dampened. "So much for adventures for you tonight."

**

Turning back to scan the village common, Rune absorbed the view while tapping deep into his core senses. The men and women walking in volunteer patrols crossed in front of the window. Soft voices of 'all's well' rippled through the community.

This was his first opportunity for solitude and he used it to ruminate over the battle and their enemies. He reviewed the fighting techniques and skills of the opponents. More than that, he kept returning to the abilities of his Student. Mentor and Tyro had moved with uncommon talent. As if they had worked together for years, not days. They were synced, as if on a subliminal level far deeper than common Maji duos. Amestoy knew how to fight as if he was born to it.

Perhaps, though, it was not the battle mechanics, but the inner maturity that was telling here. Was there something to the knowledge Amestoy had culled on the ship? Did Amestoy have telepathic skills? If so, why wouldn't he admit it? Because there was a price on the head of any Ameden who might exhibit the inherited, supernatural fore-tell traits? Because he did not know his Mentor well enough to trust him with such a secret? Why, when Rune knew the boy trusted him with his very life! They were well bonded.

Warrior Bond? He denied it even as the idea leaped into his mind. He would continue to reject that fanciful notion. But Amestoy believed in it still. Could that be enough – his blind faith – to push such a myth into reality? Did he have enough latent talent of his heritage to make the Bond come true by sheer force of will? The mind of a Maji was powerful. He should not deny anything and yet he refused to believe in the Bond. Was that just stubbornness or practicality? He kept telling himself it was the latter, but grudgingly admitted it could well be the former.

A subtle, instinctive warning filtered through his ponderings, hovering around his consciousness. The hairs on the back of his hands were standing straight. What was wrong? Would there be another attack tonight? Were they safe here? He had sensed no duplicity from the Praetor. From someone in the town? The faint suspicion, although elusive, was powerful enough to keep him awake. Folding a blanket around his shoulders he leaned against the window frame and watched, listened, and stretched out Majiq instinct.

With the passage of time, in a thoughtful, yet guarded state, Rune at last solidified his suspicions and was able to define the mystery of his unsettled feelings. The Dark Majiq he had felt before was back. The old woman's evil was like a shadow on the moon, a shimmering blackness around the stars. It was close and elusive -- an insidious malevolence that lurked just beyond his detection, just out of reach. There was a camouflaged purpose within the dragon-woman. Dragons. He wished it was the old, scaly beasts from his home realm. Wicked bandits were much more dangerous.

Slowly removing the blanket from his shoulders, Rune straightened. Attentively, soundlessly coming to his feet he drew his wand, keeping the wood solid in his hand. The patrols had not passed by according to their usual pattern. The still hush of the night was suddenly sinister. No friendly voices carried on the cool air. Far in the distance, echoed against the wild woods, came the anguished cry of an animal. A patrol hound?

Instantly the Maji crossed the room and shook his Tyro's shoulder. "Awake, Amestoy! Trouble!"

"Mmmmm." Amestoy pulled the blanket over his head and Rune yanked it away. The green eyes blinked open. "What?"

Rune placed a hand over Amestoy's mouth. "Danger, Tyro!"

Amestoy rubbed his face, coming quickly to alert awareness. The urgency of his Mentor's warnings was enough to arouse his inborn defenses.

Without warning something crashed through the window toward Amestoy. Rune's reflexes were quicker and the Mentor sent the hurling fireball back through the window and into the night with a sweeping wave of touch-stone Majiq. It must have struck their attacker, for there was a scream that trailed off in the distance. The next instant Rune was sailing through the window, Amestoy somersaulting right behind him. They landed softly in the dirt and came up instantly into fighting positions. Almost in the same breath, enchanted-darts exploded the dirt around them.

There were five attackers. In a short, fierce skirmish the Maji deflected darts back to the attackers with touch-stone Majiq shields. The flashing shots blistered the night with singeing death. Moments later only Maji were standing.

Still on guard, both felt the imminent presence of Darkness and raced around the corner of the house. In the common square were huddled, frightened, unarmed townspeople who had been dragged from their beds. A handful of vicious bandit-dragons with swords and daggers guarded the hapless hostages. No longer in their bright harlequin garb, they were dirty, disheveled and lethal-looking. The Maji approached cautiously.

Rune could call upon the reserves of the realm to aid him in his fight. A lush province, the elements of wood and rich iron in the soil could fortify his Majiq. But what if an even greater battle lies ahead? If he summoned the particles now they would not be there to aid them later. "We were waiting for the magnificent Maji to join us." The old woman stepped forward. Just behind her was the young man with the orange tattoos. "I have decided I wish a Maji touch-stone as my own." She leveled a glowing wand at Rune. "Yours, Maji Mentor. And that of your student."

Amestoy drew closer to stand next to his Teacher. Neither killed the energy sizzling blue-silver from their amulets and rings.

The woman laughed. "I didn't expect you to surrender it, but I will have your wand from you. Alive, or, preferably, dead. Then I shall have your enchanted jewelry, too." She gave a nod. Her cohort stepped aside to reveal the shivering form of the Praetor on the ground. The smoke-grey blade tip touched her shoulder and she yelped in pain. "Shall my student take her head? Or your touch-stone as a prize? Your choice Maji."

Rune's voice was even, calm. "Then we shall surrender our weapons to your pupil."

"Without enchantment," the woman ordered. "And first, of course, must be your touch-stones."

"Of course."

Amestoy did not have to look at his Mentor to know it was a ruse. The Tyro had been commanded to never surrender his amulet under any circumstances. Rune would not break that important rule. So there was another game afoot. Both Maji stepped forward and removed the wooden hilts from their belts.

"Whatever you wish."

As Rune spoke the deceptively placid words, Amestoy tensed, coiled to spring into action. The Majiq-bond prepared him. Amestoy didn't even have time to feign shock at his Mentor's choice of surrender because the younger opponent stepped forward -- too eager to claim the prize of a Maji wand for his sinister master. The impetuousness of youth! Amestoy condemned loftily as the boy walked in front of him toward Rune.

Blocked from the sight of the old woman for just an instant, it was enough for Amestoy to spin and instantly ignite his touch-stone ring, leaping forward to smash the wand from the woman's hand. Her accomplice saw the trick too late and swung around to attack Amestoy. That left Rune free to charge the old woman, shove the Praetor out of the way, and offensively drive the dragon leader and her band away from the townspeople.

Assured, through the Bond, that Rune had his battle well in hand, Amestoy concentrated on defeating his opponent. The boy was good; lithe, fast and aggressive in Dark Majiq. As far as Amestoy was concerned, however, there could be no real equality to the match. He was empowered with two distinct advantages: skill and Majiq. The charm of Light gave him a centered strength that could not be rivaled by the Darkness of his adversary.

Linked through their training unity, Rune guided Amestoy to stay psychically connected, locked into a pattern of customary military exercises of defense, alternating with offensive moves. As they had drilled, the days of study and practice melded into seamless combat techniques. Pre-set methods flashed through his mind as the most common defensive stance, but within seconds of the aggression by the criminals, Amestoy's Maji senses kicked into his own unique style. This conflict was for real, the stakes – his life and the life of his Mentor -- along with innocent bystanders. That made this the most important moment of his life. Every element of Maji history, philosophy and skill combined in this singleness of purpose.

Amestoy tried his mind reading abilities, but it was hard to utilize that un-tested gift during a full-on battle. He needed to perfect that talent. It would be invaluable in a fight. For now, he thrived within the Warrior Bond that linked him to his Mentor.

Rolling to the dirt, Amestoy drew his wand through the air and nipped a sleeve of the orange-dragon boy who yelped out a cry, attracting all attention to their fight. Occasionally, Amestoy cast glances at his Mentor. In the faint glow of moonlight streaming through the trees, Rune's face reflected the intensity of concern, then relief as he realized imminent jeopardy was not upon his Tyro. Instantly his attention was back on his own tactics, somber intent reflected in the sharp eyes, the hard-angled planes of the strong face, the tight jaw.

They had practiced these exercises in training, but this time Amestoy could feel the difference. An insidious undercurrent of Darkness touched him. Like a wave of Blackness, the depravity could have overwhelmed him, but he drew strength from the Bond enchantment emanating from his partner-Maji. Together they could defeat this malfeasance.

The raw savagery of the brutal techniques was countered by Amestoy's adept gymnastic feats and grace. Both possessed speed and talent with the sabres, but soon Amestoy was driving the teen, channeling the fight away from the others, isolating his enemy. Stab, feign, dive, sweep; the battle was joined, raging as each participant tenaciously grappled for their life and their prize – the ultimate victory of their side. The orange-dragon opponent was good, but he did not have the discipline and patience of the Maji training, nor the years and years of practice and Majiq discipline that hallmarked any member of the Order.

The most distinct advantage belonged to the Maji warriors. The Majiq-link between Mentor and Tyro assured Amestoy that his partner had his side of the fight well in hand. Even though Rune was outnumbered, the Tyro knew only a few marauders remained to challenge the Maji Mentor.

Feigning to the right, flashes of fore-tell spun in his mind and Amestoy saw his foe's next moves before he made them. Lunging to try and catch Amestoy on the side, the teen's chest collided squarely with the shimmering silver-blue blade of the wand. With a horrifying gasp the boy cried out, clutching his chest. The smoke-grey bladed sabre dropped, the flame dying to a charred shaft of burned metal seconds before he folded to the ground.

Behind Amestoy, the old woman screamed out an anguished cry while she furiously threw Dark Majiq sprays of deadly powder at Rune. Screeching in anger, she dropped the wand and whipped out the small crossbow from a capacious pocket, firing scatter darts that whipped through the air, slicing toward Rune and beyond. The Maji deflected the tiny arrows with his blue-silver touch-stone light, whipping the deadly needles into the ground or spinning them around. Some of the cluster darts struck home to their owner. The woman froze and for an instant could not make another move. With a final look of horror on her face, she fell to the ground with a thud.

Amestoy had witnessed the final moments of the duel and ran toward the downed enemy, feeling flushed with the residual adrenaline of battle. The woman and her evil Novitiate were dead. The townspeople, meanwhile, had turned on the few remaining bandits, who were trapped by the enraged citizenry.

Catching his breath, Amestoy stared at his Mentor, profoundly respectful of the great Maji in action. The battle, the talent, the connection to Majiq was amazing. Secondarily, Amestoy had engaged in his first bouts of serious fighting. He had killed another being. Nerves still pounding with the surge of adrenalin, Amestoy knew the gravity of what had just occurred would hit him later.

Both Maji were disturbed to see the townsfolk had not taken prisoners. Fighting for their lives and families and homes, the people had massacred the remaining dragons. When Amestoy walked over to join his Mentor, he offered the older Wizard the hilt of the burned, smoke-grey staff.

"For you, Mentor."

Amestoy glanced over to stare at the body of the old woman. She was killed quite literally by her own evil. There was something poetic and just about it all except for the tragedy of lives lost so meaninglessly. He could summon no pity for her, the boy she trained, or her band of brigands.

'Darts!'

Just then the still woman's hand twitched and snaked toward him. Amestoy threw out a splash of touch-stone sparks, but too late! Shoved to the ground, the Tyro flattened as tiny needles shot through the air. He felt some of them prick his tunic. Then the singing of a Majiq sabre swept near his head and he looked up in time to see his Mentor's blade plunge into the old woman's chest. She released a final gasp, and then collapsed to the dirt.

"Mentor!" Amestoy sprang to his feet to join his Teacher.

"Are you hurt?" Rune asked, using his wand to shine illumination onto his Tyro's sleeve. "Did the darts scratch your skin?"

Amestoy removed his outer shirt and studied his arm. "No, I'm fine." He glanced at the scene of carnage -- the triumphant townspeople who were hugging each other -- weeping in joy and anguish that they had suffered, but had emerged victorious from the threat of the bandits. "I suppose it's over now."

"Yes. Are you all right? About killing, I mean."

"Not that I'm sorry, but with he and his twisted master gone we'll never know the secrets of their Majiq."

Rune reached for the woman's wand. "Any --"

"Mentor! Your arm!"

In the glowing silver light Rune saw two thin darts protruding from his tunic sleeve. Drawing the sleeve up, he winced as the material caught on the imbedded needles. Through Majiq-bond Amestoy could feel dizziness, disorientation from Rune.

"I felt the – the Dark Majiq, Tyro. The same . . . . In death she got her wish," the tall Maji sighed, his eyes rolled back.

Amestoy caught him as he fell and eased him to the ground. Trying not to panic he called others to help. The Praetor, now recovered, calmly assured they were familiar with the poison used by the bandits. Known as dragon venom, it was a toxin extracted from local, poisonous plants. Ordering Rune to be taken to her house, she promised the antidote would spare his life.

**

It was well past dawn before Amestoy moved from beside the bed, and then only to pace a few steps away before returning to sit at his Teacher's side. All night Rune had lain still, sweating and distressed in constant pain. The cure -- a potent extract using the local brew for a base -- he was never going to touch that stuff again! -- seemed to be slow and ineffective so far. Wizard potions and spells had been tried, but Amestoy knew only the bare basics of such Majiq and was inadequate at the talent. He wanted to believe he had helped, but the time crept by without any obvious improvement and he grew more and more alarmed. He could not lose his Mentor! Rune was too good to be killed -- especially by someone as hateful as the old crone who had already murdered some unknown Maji.

Was there any latent Ameden skill he could use to cure his Teacher? He knew of none. What good was telepathy of fore-tell! What he needed was healing Majiq!

During the skirmish, clothing was torn and Rune's shirt was ripped open to reveal the dragon crystal lying dormant on his chest. Was the clouded gem some kind of sign that Rune would die? Amestoy knew crystals were not the source of Maji enchantment, but the receptacles and channeling tools for Majiq. The jewels reflected and enhanced the natural gifts endowed by Majiq. Amestoy had never seen one completely devoid of light.

A pouch hung just below Rune's dragon talisman, and Amestoy sensed it was more than just another pocket for powders and such. Tempted to check the contents, he felt that would be too much of an invasion of privacy. Whatever it was would be very important to Rune. If he thought Amestoy needed to know about it, he would tell him.

Not to rely completely on foreign means, Amestoy concocted a salve of Majiqal dust and herbs that he pasted onto the ugly dart wounds. That potion was also slow to kick into the damaged system. Rune still burned with fever and sweat. As a last resort the Tyro placed his hand against the injured arm and pushed Majiq through his own dragon crystal onto Rune. Meridians – neural pathways – energy streams through the body – were linked to nerves. Amestoy pressed his palms on Rune's forehead, his heart, his neck. He willed his own life force to aid strength to his Teacher.

"You promised you would train me, Mentor," he whispered. "You have never broken a promise I am sure. Don't let this evil ancient defeat you. Don't leave me. There is so much left for you to teach. And we have not established our Warrior Bond. It is there between us, Mentor. All we need do is accept it and Majiq will bind us."

The silent litany pummeled Rune's subconscious. Unendingly, Amestoy pushed for a Majiq-bond link to assail his Mentor with pleading entreaties, demands, even accusations and finally threats. How had he missed this! Where was his province's gift of fore-tell? He should have anticipated the attack! He was a disgrace to his realm. To his order. To his Mentor! He had failed to save Rune!

"If you leave me you will never solve the mystery of the murdered Maji. I will torment and haunt you forever if you don't come back!"

"A true threat since I know your persistence, my Tyro."

"Mentor!" The eyelids had not flickered, nor the face shone any hint of consciousness, but Rune was alive and awake! "You can hear me! You -- I can feel your strength returning!"

The dragon crystal was glowing with a faint shimmer over Rune's heart. The pouch was glowing, too! A crystal was inside there as well? Two amulets? He had never heard of that! Against his chest, Amestoy could feel the pulse of his own corresponding dragon crystal. Was that a connection, too? He had not noticed it during the battle, but could they be linked not only through their Maji bond, but through matching dragon gems? Was that not something akin to the Warrior Bond?

"You are going to be all right!"

"I wouldn't dare do otherwise, Amestoy. Not with such threats from my fiery Tyro."

"You were so still –"

Rune's eyes opened a slit. "A Maji healing state, my young friend."

"Oh. Yes. Of course. I've never seen one before."

Rune frowned. "My memory is slightly foggy. Did you feel a . . . ." He shook his head. "I thought, as I was hit by the darts, that there was Diaboliq . . . ."

Amestoy placed a hand on Rune's arm. "You killed her, Mentor."

He shook his head, confused. "A familiar Darkness."

"She was evil. And please don't risk your life to save me like that again, Mentor! I can take care of myself."

"I'll try to remember that." He grinned tiredly and opened his eyes wide. "Was that your way of thanking me, Tyro?"

"Yes. Thank you, Mentor, I am happy to be alive." Fatigued, he leaned his head on Rune's shoulder. "And grateful you are alive, too."

**

News of the small town's triumph over the worst of the malicious bandit gangs spread quickly throughout the countryside. Rune was fit enough to travel the next day and the Maji made a hasty escape for the port city. The local folk were heroes and that included the Paladins. Refusing various and sundry rewards offered by nearly everyone they met, Rune got them out of the area as quickly as possible. Even a discreet exit was denied the celebrated warriors. Some of the farmers created a little caravan across the hills to the sea so the Maji could journey in style, comfort and safety. Not that there was much risk anymore. In the last few days and nights the good citizens of the shire had taken courage from the small town's battle and gone out to hunt down and defeat the pirate dragons in the wilderness. In the future, it would be a safe province where the people could live in peace.

As they walked through the crowded and busy port city toward the ship's dock, Amestoy studied Rune. "You are unsettled about something," he asserted with a teasing grin. "Celebrity does not suit you? Nor being a revolutionary hero?"

"Not as much as you it seems," came the dry response. "No. It was altogether a disconcerting experience."

"The Dark force you felt that seemed familiar?"

After a moment's consideration, Rune shook his head. "I might have felt that at the time, but I can't be sure. Something I felt not long ago in Spania. Maybe. The poison made things a little hazy."

Amestoy's voice dropped to a whisper. "The Gadion-Obscura?"

"No. I am certain of that. But perhaps . . . a familiar . . . signature." He sighed, provisionally admitting his dilemma. "I did not want you to engage in battle so soon away from the Castle. Nor did I wish," he stopped for a moment, as though lost in thought, then continued, "Killing is a deep and lasting wound even when it is justified, Tyro. I am sorry it came to you so quickly. While it was warranted, even necessary, it is the part of growing as a Maji that I hoped you could avoid for a while." He shook his head. "In these dangerous times that was wishful thinking."

"There was no choice," Amestoy defended. "I know we were doing what was right, but I'm glad it did not cost your life."

"So am I." Rune warmly agreed. "It would be a shame to miss out on all I must teach you."

Amestoy nodded. "The order's way is spirituality first, but the bandits chose the way of the sword. And it is the right for every being to live in peace. Sometimes that means fighting and defending what you value."

"As when Maji must act as warriors."

"Exactly."

Rune patted him on the shoulder. "Spoken as if reading a textbook. Quite accurate."

"Thank you, Mentor. I take Majiq's creed to heart. I believe in it from the depths of my soul."

"Very sage words, my Tyro. You have been taught well."

Amestoy laughed at the unusual show of ego from the humble Rune.

As they reached the terminal, the large man with lumber loaded on his shoulder – the one they had met before their adventure -- halted them. It was the same local who had offered his protective services days ago.

"Well, didn't expect to see you two simpletons again."

"It seems a season for surprises," Amestoy quipped back with biting sarcasm.

The man snarled. "Thought the dragons would get you."

"As you can see," Rune politely countered, "we have emerged intact from the country."

"Heard the bandits are being overwhelmed by farmers! I'll be out of a job. Did you see any battles? Who is winning?"

"Good always triumphs over evil," Amestoy boldly answered with a certainty born of idealistic faith and trust.

"May it always be so," Rune agreed.

They moved on to board their cargo ship. As they settled into their cabin, Amestoy had a few last thoughts. "Too bad they weren't real dragons, though."

"Maybe, if you are lucky, you will meet the real version one day."

"What are they like? Do they have scales that sting? I've heard –"

"Enough! Give your old Teacher a chance to rest! We have plenty of time for lessons later."

"Really? No lecture?" Amestoy's smile was delightful. "As you wish, my Master."

**

This sailing ship was smaller and faster than their first vessel. It was weathered, the wood and masts creaking, the sails whipping against the stiff winds of the ocean. It was sturdy though, and cut smoothly through the waves with surprising efficiency. Rune expected to sleep soundly after the unexpected dragon encounter and the illness that could have been fatal. His sleep, however, was troubled. Not from the lingering pain of the poisoned darts, but from an inner disturbance; he had led his fresh Tyro into battle. It was a deep gnawing of spirit that came in whispers and shadows to his mind and heart.

Too restless for slumber, he rose early and meditated on his cot, careful that his motions did not disturb the deep sleep of his Learner in the upper bunk. Amestoy had performed brilliantly under extreme pressure; cool, controlled, lethal. Everything that would be expected of an older, more experienced Maji. Few fifteen year olds could have defeated the sinister dragons with such competence. The performance of this lad of twelve was nothing short of amazing!

Unable to sink into a meditative state of mind, Rune stared at his Tyro in the dim light of their small cabin. There was little room for much movement for training on this leg of the journey. It suited them both since this initial mission was as much about an assignment as it was about the two new partners growing accustomed to each other.

A pattern of teaching, learning and questioning had been established even before they were yoked together. It had continued in that vein on this passage. What disturbed Rune, though, was the incessant belief that Amestoy still held about the Warrior Bond. It was brought up constantly and in the least likely moments but Rune had refused to discuss it further.

Then, in his healing trance after the darts, Rune could feel the Majiq-touch of his Tyro by his side; cajoling, supporting, lending strength. In that silent sphere of the mystic Maji trance, Warrior Bond had surfaced again and again in Amestoy's words. Perhaps even his thoughts. There were hazy moments when Rune was certain they were communicating on a non-verbal level somewhere between this realm and the insubstantial sphere of shared thoughts, reinforcing the message until it was indelibly imprinted on his mind. That was not possible, of course. Not even Merlin-Maj could read minds!

In the privacy of his own contemplation he strayed back to the myths, back to the comforting legends that some strongly linked Maji could rise above the evils of Darkness and triumph for Light. Why did he fight such a benevolent philosophy? Wasn't that just what was needed in these times of the emerging Gadion-Obscura?

Because Bond Warriors of necessity must be one entity. Unified completely. They must be as close as sister to sister, brother and brother, father and son. Rune was not ready for that. He had lost a brother and could not bear to feel that grief again if he lost Amestoy. Even this early in the relationship Amestoy was engaging, clever and fun. How could Rune survive if he became so close they shared thoughts and bonded in spirit? These dark days of unrest were too dangerous to commit so closely to another person. He could not allow himself to feel that deeply again.

His heart skipped a beat at the remembered fear when he thought Amestoy had been hit by the poison darts. How could he live with himself if he lost this bright young man? The answer was not in believing in the Warrior Bond, but in conducting himself as a diligent Mentor and remaining aloof and distant from emotions. Teach, but not care too deeply. That was his only salvation.

A tickle in his conscience tweaked his mind and his eyes shot open. Foregoing all transitional steps out of deep meditation should have been disorienting, but his thoughts were instantly stabilized by a bastion of mental energy. He did not need more than the dim light to know his Tyro was awake, sitting up, staring at him. He could feel it clearly in his mind, as if the youth was standing next to him in the blinding light of the sun.

"You are troubled," came Amestoy's whisper.

His inner turmoil had been transmitted to his apprentice! Had the Warrior Bond been established? In the stress of side-by-side battle, in the desperation of his near-death-sickness, had their Majiq-link solidified to a refined Bond? Did the faith of his Tyro cinch together the errant whispers of legend to overcome a hesitant Mentor's reluctance to believe?

Rune felt a mental nudge from the boy and imagined seeing his lip curl.

"Yes, Mentor. Did you know, in your illness, you spoke to me, very clearly? It was the Bond."

Was that a sound or a thought? Was he asleep, dreaming?

Voice rough, he replied firmly, "There is no Bond, Tyro!"

The hurt resounding from Amestoy stabbed him like the tip of a javelin. The blade of disappointment was something Rune experienced rarely in his life. It sliced straight to his soul as he felt an emotional door close from his apprentice.

Amestoy grabbed his tunic and boots, jumped to the deck, and flung himself toward the door. "As you wish, Mentor," was his cutting remark. Then he flew out of the cabin.

In a un-Maji like fit of anger, Rune used his touch-stone charm to hurl his pillow across the tiny room, sending singed feathers flying. "Good job, Soren," he rebuked in the echoing emptiness. "Your Tyro performed brilliantly in life and death battles. He stayed up all night helping your healing trance. His minor flaw is a hopeless wish for a long-dead myth to be true. And in your subtle and elegant manner you thank him by crushing his faith. Good lesson, Mentor Maji."

For good measure he Majiq-threw his rucksack across the room, then slammed a fist into a very real bulkhead! And that hurt! The fit of impulsive pique and sarcasm did nothing to dull his irritation at himself. So Merlin thought it was a good idea for him to train a Tyro? It seemed the whole realm had a very twisted sense of humor.

PART THREE
SECRETS

A bland and stoically masked Amestoy returned a few hours later with news that delegates of Ionia wished to communicate with the Maji Mentor. Nothing was said of the uncomfortable, earlier rift, and Rune told his Tyro they would forego companion meditation and training this morning to deal with their mission. Amestoy seemed as relieved as Rune.

Months before a Maji team had been sent to deal with Ionia and they had failed to resolve the issues. Since then the conflict had only widened the gap between clans. It would take Rune's considerable skills in patience, tact and negotiations to make any progress. A strange first mission for him with a new Tyro.

"I have been reading about Ionia, Mentor. Did you know they have more delegates to public commissions, and more committees, than they have farms? And did you know the clan officials are paid not by the day, but for tasks performed, not even completed? In history we learned many a province's downfall came from such practices. It leads to slothfulness and a sense of dependence on a government instead of individual achievement."

Amestoy was bright and attentive, focused on the mission and not the past, not the type to hold grudges or nurse hurt feelings. A wonderful trait much appreciated by Rune who had not been sure what to say to Amestoy after their abrupt encounter earlier this morning.

"Enlighten me more, Tyro."

"Are you mocking me, Mentor?"

A sardonic question, met with a matching response. "Never, my pupil. The more you discover about our mission the better. It can only be of value to our ends."

The senior Maji only partially listened as Amestoy gave out more details, and several unsolicited opinions. The isle of Ionia, its tribal people and their disputations with neighboring shires, was rich in a sordid history common to many realms. Greed and power motivated the leaders. Into that mix Merlin suspected Faeries had infiltrated. How could Maji change those kinds of social conflicts?

"Then there is the prejudice factor," Amestoy added.

Rune had warned his Pupil of an element of danger on this first mission that was difficult for Maji to deal with, but seemed to be a rising problem in the kingdom. For centuries Maji were respected as the spiritual leaders of the known realm. Since the murder of the queen hundreds of years ago, faith in the Divine had been slipping. As the kingdoms expanded and more continents and realms populated, cultures vastly different from the core Dragonshire influenced the other dominions. Faeries, ghosts, were-creatures and Vampyres sought passage through the Thresholds. The Diaboliq had released a flood of treachery from the various supernatural beings held in check by the rulers of Dragonshire. Dark Arts were supported by the paranormal creatures, which made for more erosion of Majiq religion.

Worse than that, many began to feel jealousy that Maji were blood-related, tracing their lineage back for eons. Their Majiq was inherited and anyone with the Maji heart could develop their gift and use it for good. Some beings felt slighted that they did not have this ability and resented the Maji. They distrusted the advantages of others, such as the power wielded by Sorcerers. At first the rebellion was subtle, but when the Gadion-Obscura rose, many followers joined because it offered an alternative to a government with Majiq guidelines instead of chaos.

Rune thought back to his encounter with the bounty hunter at Spania. Then there was the most recent death of a Maji. There was an advancing mood of dissatisfaction sweeping their time. If they did not stem the murders and deceit the Maji and all good beings in the kingdoms were at risk.

"As you learned in Cumbri, sadly, there are those within the kingdom who don't like us or our religious symbolism. And the Gaels, well they don't like anyone."

The acrid complaint elicited a spurt of laughter. "It's so ridiculous!" Amestoy insisted with the passion of idealistic purity. "We're all part of the Dragonshire kingdom. We want our lives to be good!"

Under his breath, Rune grumbled. "I know, but it is the way of the realms in these uncertain times. Instead of assisting our efforts just as a matter of principle, they allow their prejudice to dictate and view us as intruders."

The untenable situation bonded them together and Rune was grateful their mild rift was smoothed over before the mission started. Whatever personality snags they needed to fix, they were still Mentor and Tyro and worked together in the same direction for a common purpose.

**

Debarking from the ship, they were met with a wild wind whipping up from the north. The dark sea churned at the coastal rocks, and the ship rocked against the wharf, ropes tied to the posts stretched and strained under the pressure. Cold spray of mist and drizzle slashed at their skin and Rune, then Amestoy, pulled their pointed hoods over their heads to shelter them from the elements.

A grim-faced Praetor bundled in a fur vestment and broad-brimmed hat met them as they stepped onto the main street. He introduced himself as the clan mediator. His cool, dark eyes assessed them warily, a matching sentiment of the icy weather. He led them along the paved, cobblestone street to a set of small cottages at the outskirts of the village.

In the command hut Rune felt a wave of Darkness as the Ionia representative talked. He felt Amestoy's eyes on him for he too had picked up on the negative energy. The session was brief and tense, with very little cooperation from the Ionian. It was reluctantly decided the Maji would be allowed to continue on their mission and arrive at Ionia within the day.

As they were about to leave the cabin, an army commander stopped them. A tall, lean man, his long face was serious as he told them, "We have just received a packet from Britania. Another one of your Majiq Templars has been killed in battle with Dark forces in Londonderry."

Beside him, Amestoy gasped. Rune felt the twinge of loss deep in his chest, but did not allow the bad news to break the surface of his cold expression. Taking the paper from the man, the Maji read the name of the fallen Maji. His Tyro peered over his arm.

"Salazar Tru! He's been a Tyro for two years!" Amestoy breathed out in shock.

Rune read on, the grim news drying his throat. Tru's Mentor . . . murdered also. He didn't know either Maji, but felt the distress from his Pupil as well as his own hurt from the loss.

"Too bad," the soldier said. "Happens a lot these days. Better watch your backs here on Ionia, Templars."

Walking away in the lush green grass of the misty harbor garrison, Rune asked no questions of his shocked Tyro. There were no words he could find to offer comfort. There was widespread turmoil on a dangerous and alarming scale and it was escalating. The death of these Maji might spawn additional attacks against other Sorcerers and increase chaos in the provinces. On a personal level, it brought a dire reality to their situation. What a time to give him a Learner! What was Merlin thinking? HE should be out there pursuing the Gadion-Obscura, not babysitting! He was a hunter! His Legion needed him! This latest murder must be avenged if they were to stop this avalanche of peril to their order!

**

Walking along the sea cliffs at sunset, Amestoy was momentarily distracted by the raw beauty of the island. There was green everywhere, in the grass covered hills, the thick blanket of forests, the moss covered rocks leading down to the ocean. Fog shrouded the paths, clouds covered the sky. Everything was damp and grey. It was also mysterious and exotic. It was similar to Avelon, but huge in comparison to what he had been able to explore in the open country behind the Castle.

"Are you listening?" Rune asked quietly, but sharply.

"Yes, Mentor," he responded automatically. "We are nearing the Threshold. We have come at dusk because the supernaturals travel in the cusp of time through the cavities between worlds where Majiq from both sides has sway."

Veering off the trail, they stepped into the deep woods that edged the lanes between villages. Almost instantly they were swallowed into the misty green region of tall, thick trees and matted shrubs. Keeping a pace parallel to the coastal paths, they traveled until they hit a steep slope.

Rune held up his hand to indicate they stop. Next to them was a deep, dark ravine where rainwater washed down from the mountains and into the sea. Next to the raging tributary, at the side of the narrow gorge, was a black hole as the backdrop of a marshy patch on a ledge above the river.

"That is exactly what we are looking for," Rune whispered as they crouched in the grass.

Amestoy could feel the surge of power emanating from the cavern. "A Threshold!" He had seen them in illustrated books, read about them in history and science, but was not prepared for the solid wave of enchantment radiating from the cave. "Amazing!"

"At any moment some creatures will emerge, coming from Dragonshire into this land. I suspect it will be Faeries, but there's no telling. Ionia is a popular dominion. Old Majiq and all kinds of supernaturals feel at home here in the dank, misty forests and green hills. And the people here are simple and superstitious. They allow the visitors, but don't trust them, and generally fear them."

A shape separated itself from the darkness of the cavern and Rune placed a hand on Amestoy's shoulder in a sign of steady warning. The delicate figure seemed to shimmer with an inner light. Feathery wings at the back faded and when the creature stood at the edge of the river she looked like a human maid in a white dress. Following, were other Faerie folk. Five, all told, male and female, dressed in light-toned country clothes. Taking flight, they vaulted over the ravine and skipped and floated along the edge of the trees before heading for a small village near the beach.

"Shouldn't we push them back into the Threshold?"

"Not yet. I want to know what they're up to."

"Are we going to regret this?"

Rune glared at him.

The younger man shook his head. "It would have been easier to just shove them back to the other realm and shut the door, Mentor."

Motioning for him to follow, Rune, then Amestoy, wrapped themselves in their cloaks, sprinkled iridescent dust over the Majiq cloth, and blended into the night as they trailed the Faeries. The band of intruders transitioned into more solid beings and stepped onto the roadway then followed a narrow foot trail to a hut nestled in a meadow just at the entrance to the forest, and within sight of the rocky shore.

Ducking under the straw-draped window in the front, Rune padded around to the back. Touching the reed wall with one hand, he held his right palm out, dragon ring up, and closed his eyes. A shimmery vision illuminated his crystal.

"Touch your ring to mine," he barely whispered to his Tyro.

Amestoy did so, and jumped when an apparition of what must be a collaboration of Faeries and humans inside the little cottage appeared within the bubble of combined crystals. The Majiqal beings spoke in high voices, while the man and woman inside were lower-toned. Clearly they were conspiring to overthrow the Ionian prefect and take over the shire for their own. Much of the pixie language was beyond his understanding, but from the grim set of his Mentor's thin mouth, he knew the news was not good.

"We must stop them!" Amestoy whispered.

Rune shook his head. "Forbearance," he admonished. "We will see what happens next."

They watched the exchange inside the hut until the quick plots were detailed. The Faeries were tricky, but not tactical planners by nature. Their ploy was to surround the Ionian leadership and vex them with tricks and Majiq until the Gael soldiers arrived to subdue the region. Then Faeries would help maintain control of the coastal province.

"Stay here and seal this window with Majiq," Rune whispered to his companion. "I will take care of them inside the cottage."

Irritated at being left out, Amestoy countered. "Their powers indoors are diminished, but still, Mentor, don't you think you will need me with you?"

"Just guard against anyone trying to escape."

Within a few heartbeats Rune was inside. At the moment he entered, Amestoy threw a charge from his wand, enhanced with mineral dust that closed the window so only a Paladin could open it. Having obeyed, he raced around to join his Mentor inside.

The Faeries had already recovered from the surprise of a Maji. Before he could order them to go back through the Threshold, they turned invisible and popped exploding pixie dust high in the air. The human man and woman were blinded, but the Maji were not. Using their amulet-talisman-ring crystals, both Mentor and Tyro shot blue streams of light in an arc from the ceiling to the walls to the floor.

The door slammed shut and all were sealed within a dome of sparkling energy. The creatures fought with all their might; flying, buzzing, snapping their wings and scratching with clawed fingers. The Wizards countered with intense beams of touch-stone energy. With focused drive the Majiq gradually squelched the Faerie power and reduced them into non-Majiqal creatures, compressing to the size of small dogs; their wings drooping and useless.

Rune swirled off his cloak and wrapped three of the Faeries into a glittering bag. Amestoy copied the maneuver, holding tight to the two captured creatures he held in his arms.

"Let's get them back where they belong."

Racing with Sorcerer speed, the Templars reached the Threshold within a moment. The cave no longer rippled with Majiq. It was just a small cavern next to a stream. Waving his ring-crystal, Rune opened a fissure and dancing, glistening light blasted through.

"Throw them in!" Rune shouted.

He pushed his bundle into the crack and whipped back the cloak with a flick of his wrist. Amestoy did the same, but without quite the panache of his Teacher. Then they stepped back and watched the slit close again into a black void.

"Whoa! That was amazing!" Amestoy breathed in a gasp as he fell to the ground. Battling captive Faeries had expended a lot of energy! Not to mention the quick, but intense battle with their crystals. "How did we do that?"

"Majiq," Rune shot back quickly. With a smile he explained, "It is beyond dusk. The Threshold was closed. Luckily, our powers will overcome that enough to return what was not wanted in this realm. But only for a short period between time-cusps, such as twilight, or midnight, or dawn."

Amestoy laughed. "That was incredible! We won against Faeries!"

"Not entirely. The Faeries have already put their plan into action."

Amestoy admitted he had not followed the rapid, chitter of the creatures.

"There are Faeries gathering in a Seelie grove not far from here."

Seelie – the ancient name for Faerie-folk. "A Threshold?"

"No, a Majiq grove. They have planned to ambush one of the Ionian military leaders. That is set for tonight at the witching hour. The Faeries are also massing for a sweep of some coastal villages. We have to undo what they have done and hope we can manage it in time. Let's move."

**

"One of us must warn the Ionians in the seaside cottages, Mentor. The Faeries are fixed on disrupting this region."

"I know."

"Then who will protect the Praetor?"

Not for the first time Soren Rune was required in more than one place at the same time. Turning to the colleague at his side as they jogged along the night trail, he confirmed that the need to perform multiple tasks was why the Maji made Tyros. Amestoy's raising of an eyebrow was accompanied by a smile. They were thinking the same thing. How did the boy manage to instill irony in an eyebrow, an expression? He didn't have to say anything. The sarcasm was in the very air around the adolescent.

From the beginning of the mission on Ionia, Amestoy had asserted his opinions that the province suffered from too much protocol. In a territorial dispute, the regulations had been more of a hindrance than the actual squabble. More than one lecture had been delivered quietly, reminding him the Maji was there to help stabilize the factions, not rewrite governmental protocol or provoke a revolution.

They came to a stop at a crossroads. Placing a firm hand on the Tyro's shoulder, Rune's warning was deep, somber, and intent. "I am afraid, to accomplish our purposes, we must separate, Amestoy. This is not something I want do."

"I know. I will be fine." He bounced with excitement at the anticipation of a solo adventure!

"I think the better job for you is to protect the Praetor. Keep him safe. Remember, he does not approve of our Order interfering on their island. He feels threatened that we are usurping his authority. We are here to help. Pay attention to your Majiq instincts."

An oft-repeated lesson. "Yes, Mentor," had been the ever-quick, but subtly disappointed, response.

In this week together the Maji Mentor and Tyro had achieved an acceptable, even efficient and solid, relationship. The youth was quick to learn, quick to obey and eager to attain excellence. His training skills were first rate and his enthusiasm unparalleled. His religious studies were sincere and pious without being sanctimonious. Occasionally his zealous nature translated into stubbornness, but rarely with anything beyond his obsession with mythical fantasies. Rune had very few complaints about his Tyro and trusted him completely. He was ready to take a next step in giving the lad more responsibility.

Amestoy had more than enough self-possession for both of them and Rune refused to encourage the high level of self-esteem. He felt the boy was always walking the invisible, tenuous, and sometimes perilous line between confidence and pride. Amestoy never seemed to slip into the darker emotions or perceptions of arrogance and conceit, perhaps because Rune was always there with a cold dash of reality to jolt him away from the ultimate danger zone of negative traits.

The great danger was Dark Majiq -- Diaboliq. He imagined he had felt it on Cumbri. Was that just a fevered dream from the poisoned darts? He had pondered that question in his meditations and could come to no conclusive answer. Were his second thoughts about this mission an intuitive dread that there was a Dark influence at work on Ionia? Or was he just worried about sending his Tyro out on his own at so early a stage in their relationship? Rumors flew around about Ionia, quickly attributing their disrespect of Maji to mean they were sympathetic to Diaboliq. Was it Rune's propensity to see Gadion-Obscura everywhere that urged him to sense Darkness? Or was it the reality that his fellow Order members were being murdered and he was unable to set off on a trail of justice because he was stuck here in province diplomacy?

The Templar path was not an easy trail to follow and no step should be taken for granted. These were desperate times. With the Gadion-Obscura now rising from the abyss they could not be too careful. He trusted Amestoy completely as a centered Maji Tyro. It was the rest of the realms he suspected. He could not protect his protégé forever, though, and knew there was no choice but to follow through with this necessary assignment.

His voice was as cool as his expression. "Just be aware of everything around you."

"I shall be on my best behavior."

Scowling at the twinkle-eyed sarcasm, Rune warned "Pay attention to your instincts, Tyro."

"I will," the boy promised too eagerly.

"The political situation is precarious."

"I know."

A twinge of regret persisted in the back of Rune's mind. This would be their first separation. Not as confident as the Tyro, Rune could still think of no other solutions. Uneasiness did not qualify. It was his idea to allow

Amestoy some room, and freedom, to grow into responsibility. Amestoy could handle it without problem. And the sooner they were away from here the sooner Rune could pursue the investigation of the latest Maji murder. Perhaps make contact with other members of the Legion and go after the Gadion-Obscura instead of wasting time with Faeries!

If they were more connected on a mental and emotional level, his misgivings would be eased considerably. Some Maji Mentors had incredibly deep links with their Tyros. Could theirs ever evolve to telepathy since Amestoy was from Amed? The Tyro had picked up mental anguish when Rune was poisoned. Thought transference had been imagined, surely. Or was it perhaps the Warrior Bond, came the unbidden aside. No, he had to protect himself against getting too close. It kept him sharp.

"And going out on your own can be dangerous."

"Yes, Mentor."

The lone mission sounded like an adventure to the boy. Excitement exuded from every pore. The chance to be on his own and prove his excellent skills was thrilling to the twelve-year-old. Even the stern lessons from a strict Mentor could do little to dampen the joyful spirit.

As solemnly as possible under the circumstances, Amestoy gave a quick bow. "I promise I will not disappoint you, Mentor."

The Tyro was remarkable. Rune hadn't decided if that was good or bad. Here was a composed, confident, steady young man holding the peace of an island province in his hands, and yet his biggest dread was failure in his Mentor's eyes. He was as close to fearless as it was possible to be, even for a Wizard. In their short relationship, Rune had not observed Amestoy shrink from any challenge. While Maji were taught to control and subdue trepidation, it was a basic instinct in all beings and not so easily ignored. In the few sword battles and dangerous moments they had shared in this last, fast week, Amestoy had distinguished himself with certainty and skill. Normally the elder Maji would count unswerving devotion as a positive trait. Why did he find it so uncomfortable in Amestoy? Because he wanted to distance himself, and despite his best efforts, the kid managed to circumvent everything and replace it with affection and trust.

Rune's sharp concern translated his final admonition into a harsh warning. "The Praetor of this clan is mistrustful and guarded against Maji, or anyone else not of Ionia, Tyro. Be -- be tactful -- and alert." Almost slipping into something more personal, he looked away from the sparking green eyes. Amestoy wouldn't have noticed the hesitation since his whole focus was on the adventure.

"Always, Mentor."

With a quick bow he was gone, dashing down the softly worn trail and into the nearby hills. Again, Rune wondered if he had procrastinated too long in training more diligently with touch-stone enchantment. They should have made a deeper Majiq connection, and the possibility of separation should have been foreseen. But so soon? He, better than most Maji, should understand how instantly – on the edge of a singing blade – life and death could change in the wilds of the realm. He had a duty to protect his Tyro, who was not experienced enough to protect himself in some cases. Kicking a small stone with the toe of his boot, he was irritated at himself for his limitations, still not entirely convinced he had any business being a Mentor. Nonetheless, the memory of the sparkling eyes, the bright face, and the bubbling personality made him almost grateful of his position, just not secure in it. What would Amestoy think about a Tyro being more confident than his Mentor?

**

As with most of the Ionia beings, Praetor Coloth was large, broad shouldered and rough-looking with his beard and shaggy hair. The Praetor's rude, demeaning remarks so far had not won him any personality prizes in Amestoy's mind. Disrespectful of Maji in general and young people particularly, Coloth was insulted a boy Maji came on a man's errand. Deciding diplomacy was more important than petty vindictiveness, Amestoy practiced some familiar mental exercises in patience and control. Drills Rune demanded from him on a daily basis. Now he understood why.

Their first week together had been a time of mutual adjustment. Rune was a little too stern and cool, and Amestoy a little too enthusiastic and boisterous, but eventually they had managed to find a comfortable middle-ground. As the Tyro, acquiescence was generally on Amestoy's part. Rune did occasionally give a little as well as he became more comfortable as a Mentor, more accepting of having a teen around. He also became more fun.

Occasionally there was even the stray word of affection or a quick hug of comfort or accolade when Rune's usually controlled emotions bubbled into something warmer than a Mentor's example. Those were some of the best moments of his life, Amestoy decided. And he did everything he could think of to repeat his achievements so his Mentor would shower him with more of the emotional rewards.

Never having a family, Amestoy had grown up believing a familial relationship would be part of the package of Mentor and Tyro. He anticipated that his whole life, enhanced by his belief in the Warrior Bond. When Rune became his Mentor, Amestoy expected the older Sorcerer to be the closest thing he would ever have to a father. He didn't really know what that should mean, but in those private moments of joy, the unguarded, secret flashes of affection, he knew he was closer to his Mentor than he had ever been -- than he would ever be -- to anyone else.

Those emotions stemmed from his years of hope that he would one day be included inside a Warrior Bond. When he met Rune in the library, Majiq had testified that it had led him to the right – the perfect – Mentor for him. It was a Bond match, he was certain. Since Rune was reluctant to interpret Majiq in those terms, it was up to Amestoy to convince him. Through diligence, obedience, and constant nibbling away at the mighty Rune reserves, he hoped the stubborn Mentor would eventually accept that they were Warrior Bond linked.

Amestoy kept as close as possible to the Praetor, but it was difficult as the large man insisted on blazing the trail out in front. Through the thick trees they wound along the paths that kept within sight of the coastline when possible. Sometimes they jagged into the woods where the pale sun filtered through the grey fog, becoming darker in the matted branches. Trying to stay focused on the trek, alert for danger in the close forest, Amestoy found his mind drifting as the mundane task seemed devoid of interest.

Getting ahead of himself, Amestoy was anticipating the end of the mission and once again let his thoughts wander. The first time he met Rune he had been researching the intriguing Maji. Rune's birthday, it turned out, was only a month ago, just a few weeks after Amestoy's twelfth birthday. Anniversaries and birthdays were not met with much celebration in Maji society, but as children, the initiates did have subdued merriment and commemoration along with either a special treat at dinner or even, occasionally, a token of recognition.

The most notable present was, of course, when a Novitiate turned twelve and was allowed to advance to a Tyro. That remarkable and wonderful event had just happened and if Amestoy never got another present or received another celebration in his life that would be enough for him. Being a Tyro -- to the greatest Maji Templar alive – to his Warrior Bond Mentor -- was a dream come true. Everything he'd imagined. Almost. The only exception was that Rune still believed the Bond a myth. Well, that faith would come with time and persistence on the part of the tenacious trainee.

Sharply he shut down that line of thought. Rune had ordered him to stop mentioning the legend of the Majiq Warrior Bond. Amestoy couldn't understand why Rune so vehemently disapproved of something supernatural that connected their pairing as Mentor and Tyro. Why did Rune refute the Warrior Bond? Was it perhaps his own Amed ancestry that allowed him to so easily accept the mystical within a Maji bond? Castle gossip, still prevalent about the controversial Rune, rumored that he might have taken a new Tyro sooner, but his heart would never accept anyone close to him again after his first Tyro died.

Countermanding that hearsay was the real evidence of Rune's developing warmth. After the bandit dragon attacks, they had grown closer. So Amestoy was not going to let his Mentor's lack of faith worry him. Rune wouldn't talk of the Bond, but he couldn't stop Amestoy from dreaming about the possibilities. Amestoy had Majiq on his side, and deep in his heart he still felt they were meant to be together within the tremendous connection of a Warrior Bond. Nothing would shake Amestoy's faith on that hope.

Amestoy had spent hours copying interesting scatterings of history -- Maji history -- in a leather-bound book just for his Mentor, to be given as a belated birthday gift. Not to be put off by Rune's warnings, the boy had even included some writings on the Warrior Bond. Rune would be reminded about the important myth even if he had forbidden Amestoy to speak of it. Not exactly in the spirit of obedience, but Amestoy could not stop himself. Majiq instincts pressured him to build a Warrior Bond even if it was only on one side for now.

He allowed his mind to once again drift to the Warrior Bond concept. The more he studied the legend, the more convinced he became that he and Rune could share it. Rune was blessed with profound and famous depths of Majiq ability. The noble Mentor certainly had the deserved reputation and all the qualities of a great Sorcerer. There was something else -- an elusive, mystical spark that was needed for a Warrior Bond -- and Amestoy hoped he was that spark, that he was the instrument to nudge Rune to this next fantastic level of Sorcerer ability.

Just penetrating the edge of a thick knot of trees, Majiq prickled his skin. Amestoy touched his wand-stick just as a flash of light sprang from a dense cluster of bushes. Pushing the Praetor to the dirt, Amestoy's amulet and ring crystals ignited with fire and shimmered energy through the wand in his hand.

The ball of light arcing toward him exploded as his own power cancelled out the threat. Grabbing the Praetor by the back of the collar, he scrambled down, off the trail, into a grouping of boulders.

"What --"

"We are under attack! Quiet!"

Sensing the threat on each side, Amestoy shot out Majiq in one direction, then the other. Whipping back and forth, he pushed the Praetor farther down the hill. The rocks were good cover, but he had lost the high ground. Moving as fast as possible, he pushed and ordered the big man to run with him. They maneuvered down the hill and across a stream, trying to reach the woods atop the ridge.

Fighting to steer clear of the impassable sections of the swampy forest, Amestoy felt the Darkness an instant before a tree shattered in an explosion of wood and fire right in front of them. Both Tyro and Praetor dived into the undergrowth, tumbling down the slope into muddy, marshy thickets.

**

A pervasive feeling of ill content had started at some point during Rune's speedy trek across the lowlands. Just before reaching the Seelie – Faerie -- grove, inside the heavy woods overlooking the grey sea, he slid to a stop. Now the oppressive foreboding was practically smothering him and he was surprised to see his hands were shaking. What was that? He was never nervous! Except when Majiq instincts were at work.

Trying to focus in preparation for his own battle, he could not concentrate! His heart told him he should not have separated from his Tyro. It was a mistake. The apprehension was defined. Dragon's breath! Too late he understood. Amestoy was in crisis. He could feel it through the amulet and ring crystals that linked his Majiq to that of his Pupil.

Was the empty, hollow ache inside his chest a message that Amestoy had died? How could he know what had gone wrong? Stubbornly rejecting a solid Majiq connection with the boy, how could he know if the promising student was gone?

Feeling sick, Rune gave himself a moment to clear his mind. He could not. All he heard within was rebuke of his obstinate pride. Decrying his foolish trepidation, he hoped he would have a chance to make up for the stupid fear, the personal cowardice, that prevented him from getting too close to his student.

A wash of alert swept over him. Three male Faeries appeared at the other end of the grove. Nearly transparent, their wings were visible, and they floated above the ground. Glittering gold pouches in their hands proved they were waiting for the Ionia Praetor who would never come.

Torn between his chance to rid the shire of these dangerous pixies, or go help his Pupil, the decision was made for him when he was spotted by the lead creature. Before they could use their enchantment, Rune employed his. Fire and light shot from his touch-stone, smashing into the first of the beings. The other two zipped away, one in each direction, but not quickly enough to go unscathed. Rune's Majiq sizzled them both, one falling to the ground, the other flying off into the woods.

"Dragon's tails," Rune viciously muttered as he took off in pursuit of the injured Faerie.

On the way he sprinkled charmed mineral powder over the recumbent creatures to keep them from leaving. The cover of the shrubbery and trees did not deter his Majiq, and Rune zapped the last one, bringing him down into the dirt. Carrying the unconscious Faerie back to the grove. He bound all of them up in his cloak and, using a sealing spell, trapped them in the hollow of a dead tree trunk. He had no time to search out a Threshold.

**

Dazed, he had blacked out briefly, and then Amestoy felt a subconscious force prod him awake. Thankful he had trained well to keep Majiq close to him, he was aware of the danger before he could clearly function on any level. Instinctively letting Majiq sway him, he popped his head above water, gasping for air! He would have drowned in the mucky swamp if not for his Wizard instincts!

Aching and trembling from the pain and shock of the tumble Amestoy calmed his nerves, centered, took control, and took stock of his situation. Pieces of trees and matted vines were wrapped around him, the muddy swamp sucking him under even as he fought to keep his head above the muck.

Desperately kicking out with his feet, he cleared a hole big enough to swim through and moved quickly. His leg snagged on more tangled debris and sharp wood, trapping his foot and ripping flesh as he sank under the mud. Grabbing for his wand, he gulped in a startled gasp! His weapon was gone! Mind going black, he refocused. Using Majiq to subdue the pain and expand his lungs, he struggled to free his bleeding limb.

Dragon crystals calmed and added confidence as practiced maneuvers and correct choices guided him on an intrinsic level. Groping for one of his potions, his heart sank when his hand felt only dissipated particles in his waist pouch. The tincture had dissolved in the water! So much for enhanced power! And his wand was gone!

Summoning an inner calm, he closed his mouth and used Sorcery to once again expand his lungs and reuse the air within. Panic at drowning caused him to lose focus several times, but mental discipline – and the fear of death – prevailed. It was a temporary fix. Not having the strength or concentration to sustain this kind of mind-over-physics enchantment for long, he had to get above water quickly. Knowing it was wrong, and possibly suicidal, he had no choice but to abandon the wand in exchange for survival.

Slowing his blood flow so he would not bleed to death, he twisted and shifted, agonizingly tearing up his leg, but was finally able to sidle out of the spiky, underwater tree spears. More tense moments followed as he groped his way through a forest of water plants thick enough to choke him. Murky growths and churned mud obscured vision anywhere past his nose, so again he called on his instincts to guide him. When his head was pounding and sight turning grey with the onset of unconsciousness, he finally broke the surface!

Taking in gasps of air, he glanced at his surroundings. The marsh was overrun with long- branched trees and smelled awful. Like death. Surveying the area, he was prepared to go back down for the Praetor, and then spotted a charcoal-shaded form near some rocks. The unnatural color belonged to the Praetor's uniform.

"Praetor!" he cried out. No response. "Great. First mission and I kill my assignment," Amestoy muttered and swam to the muddy edge of the swamp.

Except for a ringing in his head and some disorienting vision, he seemed okay, but the slowed blood flow was affecting his energy level. When he realized he was not swimming a straight course toward the high-priority victim, but veering off instead, he thought the conk on the head might be more serious than at first reckoned. However, this was no time to think about himself. First take care of the dead Praetor he was supposed to protect! Focus! Focus! The head injury was making him muzzy and it was so hard to concentrate. Blood loss was weakening and he had expended a great deal of energy to stay alive underwater. This was not going to be easy.

Crawling up on shore, Amestoy edged along the rocks. Reaching out to detect any threats, he felt no Dark Majiq or any immediate danger. Next duty – care for the Praetor. Stumbling over fallen tree branches and living mollusks that did not move out of his way, he reached the large man. Labored movement of the chest and the harsh trembling made it obvious the person he had been entrusted with was hurt, but what should he do?

Amestoy held his breath as if waiting for something to happen. When nothing did, he gave a few pushes to the Praetor's chest. He surged Majiq-sage through his hands, but his ring did not glow! What was wrong? His hand whipped to his chest. No amulet! His dragon crystal was gone! No! Idiot! Why didn't he check when he was underwater! What was he to do? His potions were gone! Wand lost! He was a Tyro! There was no meaningful training or charms in using Majiq without his touch- stone! How could he save the Praetor?

A wave of despair swept over him. First mission, first responsibility with another being and he had failed! The Praetor was dead! He couldn't accept that! He could not let down his Order or Rune!

Pushing harder on the Praetor he pumped at the chest and back. As he had when Rune was wounded, he pushed Sorcery through his hands to heal, to energize. Finally bubbles dribbled from the wide mouth, followed by gagging coughs. One muck-encrusted eye opened and roved around before fixing on Amestoy.

There was an almost immediate gasp. "Attack."

"We were attacked. Yes. There is no one here now." Who had sent the Majiq to destroy them? Where were the foes now when the Wizard and the Praetor were so vulnerable? He had so little experience in this area. If only he could talk – or somehow communicate – with his Mentor!

"Maji – to – save – us . . . ."

Was it a plea? A question? An accusation? All of the above as far as Amestoy was concerned. Rune and he were supposed to take care of the problems here and he had failed!

The Praetor's eye closed and he went limp. He was still breathing, though, so that was a good sign, Amestoy decided. Moving across the marshy ground he wedged the dignitary into the rocks. Exhausted, the pain in his leg throbbing and vying for attention, he closed down the input for his own damages and set his mind on control and problem solving.

Leaning his back against the rock to rest, he rubbed the crystal on his dragon ring. There was a faint energy spark, but it would never work without the touch-stone at his chest. He needed to go back and find his amulet and wand. To lose them – well – that was worse than failing the mission! But was it safe to leave the Praetor alone? Wasn't saving another person's life more important than saving himself from embarrassment?

Swaying, Amestoy felt dazed and slow. He leaned his head on the rock to think. Reaching out with his mind, his Majiq, his mental powers bounced back from nothing. There was no connection. Rune and he had never established a Majiq link on even an elemental level.

Should he go back down to the bottom of the swamp? Was there any hope of finding the crystal or wand? His thoughts spilled into a silent plea, calling for his Mentor to help him. Alone and hurting in a hostile environment, he needed the aid and comfort that only his Mentor could provide. If only the Warrior Bond was connecting them!

Frustrated with himself and his Teacher, he refocused. No help would be coming any time soon. Rune was on his own vital mission in the Seelie grove. Amestoy had to solve this problem alone. How? Staggering to his feet, he steadied himself against a slimy tree. With a wave of his hand, commanding Majiq, he unleashed all the enchantment he could summon from his Maji heart.

A line of light sang out from his ring. The physical expansion of his faith and desperation startled him, but he readjusted instantly. Was this part of Majiq or from his own heritage? He didn't know and didn't care. It was a personal emergency beacon! It just might save him and the Praetor. The light engulfed him and he could feel the energy emanate from his very soul to expand beyond his body, into the swamp and hopefully to his wand and touch-stone!

**

Sucking in a shuddered breath, Amestoy froze in near-paralyzing trepidation as the being – with red eyes glowing from beneath the dark hood – stared right at him – right through him. As if gliding on the foggy marshland, the Warlock approached, the advancing threat resurrecting the fear he had felt during his vision while meditating at the Castle. Different setting, but the same cloaked figure, the same visceral reaction of terror.

Instinctively, unsteadily, Amestoy came to his feet. He was completely defenseless. The red eyes seared into him and emanated a heat of pure Diaboliq. He had no doubt about the identity or the Wickedness; it spoke against his spirituality as clearly as if it had been shouted aloud. Darkness swept into Amestoy's soul. He had to flee! Backing away, he stumbled to the refuge of the swamp. Leave the Praetor? He had no choice! The evil was sapping his remaining strength. His life was forfeit without his touch-stone and he would not give up without a fight! He became a honed weapon with only one purpose: to find his talisman.

Hand, then arm, then body throbbing with power, a spark jolted him at the tip of his fingers, giving him the fortitude to re-enter the cloying swamp. Using his crystal ring he pointed ahead. Opening his eyes, through the murk he saw a dull glow reaching out to him from where it was nearly buried in the slimy goo. Guided as if with a tangible rope, he reached through twisted reeds and rotting stumps and grabbed onto his amulet. Tugging it securely around his neck, it fell naturally in place over his heart.

Act. Don't think. Don't feel anything but Majiq. Your Light comes from inside. While there has been no instruction on touch-stone combat, you know how to fight. Your training has prepared you for this.

Repeating the encouragement over and over, he broke the oily surface and watched as the cloaked figure slid across the swamp toward him. Feeling drained and sick, Amestoy summoned every bit of energy he could salvage and held his ground, keeping himself between the threat and the helpless Praetor. When the Dark spectre's arm whisked from beneath a coat, the gloved hand held the pommel of a sabre. Closing in on his prey, the Warlock threw black dust into the air and sliced it with his glowing blade! The action ignited a wall of fire that surged ahead and threw Amestoy completely free of the water and against the slimy trunk of a tree.

The Diaboliq then moved toward the Praetor. Before the evil reached the downed official, Amestoy launched himself to his feet and threw out a hand with all the Majiq he could muster at the threatening form. The crouching aggressor wavered, and then slowly turned to face the young Maji. As the Diaboliq once more threw up a hand, Amestoy countered with Majiq searing from his palm. The Warlock stumbled back into the mud, but the victory was only momentary. His next trick was to throw enchantment knots – small energy balls – toward the Maji.

Amestoy cupped his thumb and forefinger around the dragon amulet at his chest to achieve maximum power from his touch-stone. Then, raising his left hand which was now engulfed in blue, then teal-silver energy, deflected the tiny spheres that shot toward him. Majiq instinct guided him. The blue/teal, blade-like wave hummed in the gray, marsh mist as the glowing knots shattered and sparked to nothingness, the Majiq striking true every time.

In a blur, the Dark Wicken threw a small dagger. Amestoy leaped out of the way, stumbling as his injured leg missed one of the slick rocks and his foot dug into the muddy bank. Sweeping his arm, carving the air with glowing Wizard-dust, the Tyro blocked the deadly bolts exploding around him. Energy sizzled the swampy mist, the hair on his arms singed from the heat and fire. Deflecting the projectiles was rapidly depleting his already waning strength and the purely defensive actions were not lost on his foe. Closing in for the kill, the red-eyed creature advanced, shooting rapid fire, close range bolts from a crossbow until one dart blazed into the left forearm of the faltering Maji.

His touch-stone and ring sputtered. Amestoy dropped to the mud and slid behind the shelter of a rock. He was spent. What more could he do? Another agonizing bolt sliced through his arm! Crying out in pain, Amestoy scrambled back, fighting to salvage the sorcery. He needed enough energy to tear the weapons from the hands of the Diaboliq, but he was too unfocused, too consumed with pain and failure. How could he fight? How could he not? How could he fail his Mentor and himself?

Stumbling into the swamp, he abandoned his ragged strategy and concentrated on running. Working his way back around to stay close to the Praetor, he forced his dwindling senses to track the Dark Wicken. Making no effort to conceal itself, the Warlock was moving away. Retreating! Why? Then he heard a sound. A horse crashing through the brush.

Mentor!

The dragon crystal at his throat burned.

A shimmery ray of fine, blue-silver materialized out of the cloudy gray. Rune's tall form atop an advancing brown steed raced into his focus as the glow of the touch-stone pushed away the grim shadows. Like a dream, the Mentor Maji charged to the rescue! Hallucination? Vision! No! Just as in his dream-scape --- Rune was in danger!

No energy left, what could he do to help his Mentor? Clutching the heated talisman in his fist, Amestoy closed his eyes and, with all the drive left in his body, mind and spirit, shot out a warning to Rune.

'Drop! Now!'

The horse sailed through the mist just as a shattering blast turned everything a fiery orange and red. Against the incandescent rain of sparks and energy a Maji flipped through the air, landing in the concealing darkness.

'Mentor! Safe!'

Smiling, weariness turned his laughter into a sob as Amestoy grabbed onto the nearest object and fell against it.

The wounds from the Diaboliq shots were even more painful than he thought possible. His first such injuries. They hurt! He never wanted to feel any more wounds. Already sick and disoriented, he could barely keep his balance against the supporting tree stump.

Rune skidded to a halt in the depths of the swamp. Momentarily obsessed with retaliation and pursuit of the Dark Majiq, he instead chose his top priority. Running to his suffering Tyro, he barely restrained his consuming anguish. Crossing to the mud where the boy trembled, Rune wrapped his large cloak around him, folding the slighter form in his arms.

"You're hurt. Badly?"

Amestoy shivered first a negative shake, then a confused nod. "Your timing," he chattered, sinking his face into Rune's tunic. "Is perfect, my Mentor. Almost as good as your theatrical entrance!"

"Thank you, Amestoy." His voice was tight and harsh from livid emotions. "Can you walk?"

"I think so." It was on the edge of a sob.

"It is permitted to cry," Rune softly admonished. "It is not a sign of weakness."

"I am NOT crying," came the insulted, adamant defense.

"Of course not," Rune whispered gently.

If Rune had his way, he would have carried his Tyro and offered more comfort. Amestoy's pride, however, demanded subtle assistance, so Rune held onto the boy's arm and lent Wizardry strength as they shuffled toward the waiting horse. Just a little too late, a mounted patrol of soldiers arrived to help. Amestoy stopped when the Ionia team reached the Praetor. Covertly, the Mentor leaned against him, offering better support. When the Praetor was declared alive, Amestoy sagged back, the last of his energy spent.

Rune's resolve crumbled and he would not allow the brave young man to suffer any more just to preserve the Maji image of indestructibility and strength. "I have you now."

"I -- can – walk –"

The bravery humbled the great Rune. "You CAN. But there is no need, my Tyro. You are in my care now."

Rune easily lifted Amestoy in his arms and held him snugly as he strode swiftly to their mount. Neither needed to say anything, their mutual relief and affection transmitted through their impenetrable embrace. Looking down on the suffering face so close to his, Rune was jolted by the near-reenactment of the anguished moment of Ion-Gawain's death. He had not been there to hold his dying brother, but had imagined it a million times, wishing he could have healed the mortal wound. And if not that, at least share a last moment with his closest friend. How remarkable that there was such a physical similarity between Amestoy and Tor – the fine hair, the lean nose, the usual twinkle of mischief in the green eyes. He had never noticed it before!

Deeply shaken, Rune was consumed with a never-absent wave of renewed grief, and a new pain at his Tyro's suffering. He gripped tighter to his burden.

"Diaboliq," Amestoy whispered.

The boy was shaking and cold and hallucinating. Rune could see various wounds even through the filthy muck caked to the tan shirt and the exposed flesh. The young Wizard's green eyes, though, were bright with resolution. Rune laid a hand on his forehead to pour Majiq comfort and healing into him.

"Shhh. Be calm. You are safe. It is time to heal."

Amestoy adamantly shook his head. "Gadion-Obscura!" he repeated, this time fervent and agitated.

Rune ground his teeth in frustration. Composing his voice, he calmly related, "The creature escaped, Amestoy. Do not trouble yourself. We do not know if he was Gadion-Obscura." But even as he spoke the gentle rebuke, he knew differently. The Diaboliq was sharp as a blade and black as a pit. An assassin was the description that sprang to mind. That could wait until later.

"Diaboliq," came the quavering pronouncement with conviction. The boy's trembling increased and his eyes closed despite the fight to stay awake. "Beware – the red . . . ."

PART FOUR

THE LONG WAY BACK

Sweat poured in steamy rivulets down Amestoy's face, the salty liquid mercilessly stinging his eyes as he wiped them clear. Blinking, trying to focus, the grimy heat allowed him to see very little beyond the sweltering red dust that caked the inside of his throat, clung to his clothes and eyelashes and imprisoned him in a small cocoon of isolation.

It seemed as if he had been wandering the shrouded landscape for -- forever. No reference points, no sound, no bearings. Only the inner compass of the Warrior Bond kept the young Maji on his feet, kept him moving toward -- toward what, he didn't know.

Warrior Bond? Yes. He was certain of it. The Bond was like an invisible stream of touch-stone energy. He held one end and somewhere up ahead the Warrior Bond told him his Mentor was waiting for him, holding the other side of the blue-silver line that connected them. The image was figurative, but symbolically understandable. The Bond had been established!

Reason edged into his thoughts and doubt crept in on the wind of hesitation. How could the Bond be possible? Mentor Rune did not believe in the reality of a higher level of Maji enchantment. He considered Warrior legends to be myths. Amestoy stood perfectly still, controlled his breathing, closed his eyes, and allowed Majiq to feel and think for him. No, there was no doubt; this was a Warrior Bond link. He could feel his Mentor's presence somewhere ahead. They were connected on a deeper, more subliminal level than Majiq had touched Paladins in eons. How was it possible? He did not know. He only felt it and knew it to be true.

'So where are we, Mentor?'

There was no response. The mental and spiritual silence was troubling, but Amestoy could FEEL his Leader's presence. Instinct told him to press on, keep walking. He did. It was so confusing! Where was he? This was not the muddy, clinging dirt and vines in the moors of Ionia. Hadn't he recently been on the isle of Ionia? Yes, but he wasn't sure when.

Instead of the marshy jungle this was a desert void. Parched, hot, nasty plains with densely matted thickets of prickly trees and thorny bushes. Dry, dead overgrowths that snagged his tunic and scratched against his face. What was this province? The heat made it hard for even his fit lungs to breathe. Virtually blind, he thrashed through the brush, sensing his Mentor close, so very close, frustrated that he had no answers or direction save the subtle Bond. He had only heard stories of lands like this; Spania, Indies, Afrik.

Calling, his voice died before it reached his lips. The very air was closing in on him, drying his mouth and tongue. Stumbling, he freed himself of the burdensome vines to emerge at the lip of a chasm. The fault-line was so deep it disappeared into inky nothingness within a short distance of the rim. So wide was the rift that even his youthful strength and Majiq energy could not help him leap the divide.

It hurt to move, to think, to breathe in the thick atmosphere. The soft sand was deep and sucking, dragging his feet down with every labored step. How could he go on? He had to. His Mentor was waiting for him and he would endure any hardship rather than disappoint Rune. Never would he want Rune to think he was weak or unworthy. No matter how painful, he would grapple through this morass and find his Teacher.

His dragon amulet glowed warm under his sweaty shirt. The intensity signified a connection to his Master. Rune was close? Or in trouble? With effort, Amestoy struggled out of the sand that had somehow turned to mud, amazed to see Rune standing on the far side of the ravine! The Mentor was similarly worn, grubby and dirty. A gash along the side of Rune's head attested to an injury. Wincing, Amestoy saw a vision:

Fight. A lush, tropical province where giant trees stretched interwoven canopies into the sky. The flared colors of touch-stone beams and Majiq powders flashed tiny explosions against the red and copper of a fiery sunset. Then the landscape altered to a desert motif – raw heat, baked sands, towering cliffs of rust and tan. Maji were riding huge dragons and fighting black-cloaked Sinister Wickens who were murdering the Sorcerers! Explosions! Fires! Rune was there.

Valiant and fearless. He fought with bravery and power, his blue-silver blade slicing the foe with ruthless skill.

Behind Rune came a bronzed, red-eyed dragon controlled by a Gadion-Obscura.

'Mentor! Behind you!'

Rune could not hear him!

'Mentor! Dragon! Sinister! Behind you!'

With a gasp the vision ended. Amestoy opened his eyes. His Mentor was on the other side of the chasm still. Blood was dripping from a gash underneath the thick, tawny hair.

'Mentor, you're hurt!'

'So are you, my Tyro.'

Glancing down at his tunic, Amestoy realized the tan material was covered with splashes of red. Not just toffee-hued smears of mud and dust, but evidence of wounds. Touching his face his hand came away stained in crimson.

Now Amestoy felt the distant echo of pain in his head. No wonder it was hard to breathe, to talk -- he had been hurt. Not seriously, thankfully. And Rune seemed generally all right, too.

'We are speaking within our minds again!   A whole conversation this time!'

The astonishment of the teacher was more subdued than that of the learner. *'Yes, Tyro. Interesting. Maji normally do not have that advanced ability!'*

Amestoy grinned so wide his face ached. A laugh escaped. *'You can in the Warrior Bond, Mentor.'*

'Amestoy! Enough!' The exasperation was more a habitual reaction than a reprimand, and Rune's face soon smoothed in placid thought. *'I will have to consider that later.'*

There was a sense of urgency that communicated to both of them with surging alarm.   *'There is danger, Mentor. Or was – a battle. The Gadion-Obscura has dragons!'*

Rune gave a chuckle of indulgence. *'There are no dragons that I cannot handle, Amestoy. And you need not worry about the Gadion-Obscura. I will take care of them.'*

Such arrogance! But it was not without precedence. Ayelsborne was the home realm of dragons and dragon wizards. And Rune. This was not the time to argue, so

Amestoy did not voice – or think – his objections to his Teacher.

'I will come to you --'

'There is no way to cross.'

'I can try --'

'Not in your condition, Tyro. It's too dangerous.'

Amestoy touched his head – yes it hurt and so did his chest, but looking across the wide chasm at his injured Mentor, the danger to Rune was even more painful. There was no visible threat, no immediate identification of menace, but he knew from his vision of the future that peril was close and pressing. He was a fore-teller. It was in his blood. Or had what he seen been the past? Was that how they were injured? On this forsaken realm did they join in a massive battle of Majiq and Dark? No, not this province. And not the past. Rune did not believe in red- eyed demons and undefeatable dragons.

Something was not right.

With all his might he put his Wizardry, his heritage certainty, and his belief in the Warrior Bond into his thoughts. *'I have seen the future, Mentor. A fore-tell vision. You confront dragons and Gadion-Obscura and it is not good.'*

'Maji cannot see the future, Amestoy. Not even Merlin-Maj.'

'We are not supposed to communicate through telepathy either, my wise Mentor.'

'Don't get cheeky, Pupil. You worry too much. Let Majiq guide you.'

Not in the mood for more lectures, the Learner gave in. *'What shall we do?'*

'Continue on our journey. Perhaps the paths will converge up ahead.'

On the strange sojourn they walked side by side yet separated by the seemingly infinite gulf. Few words were exchanged, except through the Bond. Amestoy felt attached to his Teacher and as close as if they were walking astride, touching shoulders. Occasionally a huge bending tree with thick, spiny, tan branches and brittle leaves would block Rune's path. The Mentor would have to step away from the edge and skirt the obstruction. During the absence, Amestoy strained their Bond link to assure that all was well. In those moments of invisibility, the faint connection was his only source of confidence. Rune was injured. What if something happened to him while he was out of sight? What would he do? In those anxious moments Amestoy searched desperately for a means to cross the fathomless gulch.

Waiting on the edge of the precipice, Amestoy nearly held his breath as he watched for Rune to reappear. Clutching his amulet, Amestoy scanned his side of the ravine but no trees grew here. If they did, he could use one of the long, stringy branches to swing across. Where was Rune? Why did he disappear so often into the grey mist that shrouded the banks? Were the injuries slowing him down? The head injury seemed serious, but it hadn't restricted him during their rigorous march through the wilderness.

What if they were magically ensconced within the magnificent bounty of life within the Warrior Bond? How had it happened? Some Sorcery on this desert province? Where was Rune? There was a sense, just beyond Amestoy's perception, of terrible danger.

Like a cloud on the distant horizon, he could fore-see shadows – *strange, distorted images – of Maji battling wicked foes. Wizards collapsing in the dust, slain by the red-eyed monsters and fearsome dragons! Rune was among them, his blue-silver touch-stone slashing in the clogged air. Amestoy was there, with Paladin Artemis in a defensive circle. The Warlocks pushed in on them. Then the red-eyed Gadion-Obscura covered them in black death.*

They had discovered the Bond when Amestoy was near death. It had saved them in the past. So his vision of disaster was a fore-tell, no question! The Bond was something they could utilize in their favor, a gift, a treasure between Mentor and Pupil. Amestoy was grateful for its cohesive enchantments. Pacing, Amestoy grasped out with his mind, mentally punching through the thick murkiness and reaching the safe haven of his Mentor's thoughts.

'Mentor!'

'Amestoy, I am here.'

'Mentor, I cannot see you. There is death ahead. Maji will die!'

'Everything is fine.' The epitome of calm. Like cool water on burning skin. Tranquility shrouded Amestoy's mind. *'I am here.'* A moment later Rune emerged from the trees, his face a study in sobriety. *'All is well.'*

'No, Mentor, it is not. The future is terrible! I need to join you on the other side.'

'No. You stay there. I have a mission, Tyro.'

'I don't want you to leave!'

With a nod, Rune continued walking. *'I do not wish to leave, either.'*

Amestoy matched his pace on his side of the chasm. The path grew rocky. Each step became harder, more arduous and Amestoy was panting trying to keep up with his long-legged, stronger, less injured Mentor. Not wanting to seem weak or incapable, Amestoy forced himself to push harder. Rune's side of the gulf was clearing, without trees, and more level. Soon the rocks on Amestoy's side grew larger as the path traveled upward into the darkening mist. Rune stopped and stared across at the obstacles in his young Pupil's path.

'We will wait here and let you catch your breath.'

Amestoy felt the Bond between them strengthen.

'This journey is not without merit, Tyro. We should take the opportunity to learn what we can from the quest.'

'A teaching moment from being lost in the wilderness? Mentor, you are something else.'

Laughter rippled through the Bond. *'Dragon's breath. I will take that sarcastic remark as a compliment, my cheeky friend.'*

'So it is, Mentor. Hmm, dragon's breath. Is that a curse?'

'Yes. If you ever meet a dragon make sure he doesn't breathe on you. As I was saying before I was so rudely interrupted,' Rune continued with a mental smirk, *'this path we are on can be viewed as a metaphor of life, Amestoy. The future.'* He canted his head and gave a contemplative smile. *'Except when you believe you have seen the future. For the rest of us, what is to come, the past, even occasionally the details in the present, are obscured from our view.'*

'Sometimes we are on the journey just for the sake of the journey, is that what you're saying?'

'No, but that's a good lesson, too. Reminds me about that time when we --'

'Mentor!'

'All right.' He smiled, clearly appreciating the wit of his captive audience. *'What can we trust?'*

'Only each other. Only the Bond and Majiq.'

Rune shot him a stern look, and then sighed, his broad shoulders heaving. *'All right, I will grant you that you are correct.'* Trickles of pride floated through their link. *'It was a glorious day when I abandoned my stubborn arrogance and accepted you as my Tyro.'*

'Then you believe in the Bond?'

'That is a discussion for later.'

Amestoy decided not to push his luck right then. There would be time for debate later. *'It was the fulfillment of my greatest dream, when you became my Mentor. I am gratified you do not regret your choice.'*

Amestoy shivered suddenly. A chill, moist wind brushed against him. An inexplicable mist was thickening, descending from the higher planes, dampening the heat and dust. The blistering sun melted into gray. It was so cold and wet he felt as if a dank cloak had closed around him. The overwhelming sense of foreboding returned with the change in weather and he trembled.

'We must push on, Amestoy. Climb the rocks. I believe there to be easier terrain on the other side.'

Amestoy stumbled to his feet, pushing down the anxiety as he tried to lean on the Majiq and to find stability within the enchantment of the Bond. He reached for Majiq powder in his pouch and his hands came away empty! What? No potions, no herbs or dust to melt the rocks or give him strength? How was he to continue? How could he defeat the obstacles ahead? The mist was starting to cover Rune. He couldn't be separated from his Mentor!

'Mentor, throw me a branch, I will swing across.'

'Too dangerous.'

Amestoy edged to the rim of the chasm until pebbles crumbled under his feet, falling into the black, bottomless pit below. Again he urged the elder Maji to throw him a line and Rune refused, reproving the youth for his impulsive penchant for danger. Judging the gulf that separated them, feeling the darkness pressing against him, Amestoy reasoned any risk was worth taking to be with Rune on the other side. Anything was better than being swallowed by the bitter blackness here.

Amestoy took a running leap and used Majiq to push him with all the energy he had left. Soaring in the air he didn't look down, didn't think of the deepening shroud closing in behind.

'Trust in the Bond, Amestoy.'

While the encouragement was comforting, the acknowledgement of the Bond amazed him, but only for an instant. He was focused on survival, on reaching his Mentor. He looked ahead, to Rune on the other side; to the Maji holding out his arms in welcome, to the Bond gripping him in its power and warmth and pulling him to safety. Eternal moments crept by as the ensuing darkness and shimmering Bond fought for possession of the Tyro who seemed suspended above the abyss. Then Majiq from Rune surged in strength and Amestoy flew into the waiting arms of his Mentor.

**

Soren Rune blinked against the bright light streaming through the small port hole of the rocking ship. Had he dozed? What was that strange dream? A desert province? Amestoy was lost? Just vestiges of a memory . . . Amestoy! Subliminally he felt the presence of his Tyro before he turned to look to the side of the room. Amestoy was resting on a nearby bunk. Alive.

Rune's fists tightened. Alive, but within the grips of a Majiq so intense he feared the strength of its grasp. This Wizard trance WAS too deep, too long. He felt no sense of anything from Amestoy. The slight mumblings were all self-contained wrestling. As his Mentor, Rune should be able to read the feelings, sense the healing process. There was none of that here. Was it because Rune had failed to make a strong connection with his Learner? It seemed all the mistakes of this wretched mission stemmed from him being the one who was distant and impersonal. He was the one without the feelings necessary to reach out to his Tyro on an emotional level.

What he did understand was that because of Amestoy's inexperience with deep trances and mental links, there was a danger the youth could be lost in his own mind. Typically, Maji healers shepherded priests through the tricky mode of self-healing. It was his responsibility to guide Amestoy now. Such a task would require him to dissolve all his inhibitions at a close relationship with his Tyro. It would demand Rune be honest, open and completely trusting to another being. Something he had done only once. Not with his first Pupil, but with his sorely-missed friend, Tor.

Would his reluctance inhibit the depth required to safely navigate Amestoy out of the depths of his trance? If there was a danger of that, then Rune had to make sure he swept aside his prejudices and shortcomings to help his charge.

First, Rune assessed Amestoy's condition. Using Majiq to drop into a near focused-daze, he held his hands above the center point of Amestoy's forehead. There the inner-eye energy culminated to its most powerful point for Humans. He concentrated on the unconscious boy's physical condition: the injuries, the bad reaction to the swampy water on the jungle province, the venomous darts.

Flashes of errant emotions and fears splintered his thoughts. Rune's hands shook. Amestoy could have been killed. The incredible promise, the barely touched talent, could have ceased to exist. The loss would have been a grief to Majiq, to the Order – but to him personally, it would have been unbearable. It seemed impossible to feel so close to someone after such a short time, least of all a Pupil Rune had done everything to avoid. Now the Mentor wanted only for another chance to make things right with this brilliant Tyro.

There was no way to change the mistakes of his past, but Rune could change the future. As soon as Amestoy was well, Rune was going to work on establishing a bond. It may not be a Warrior Bond, but he would not fail his Tyro again. They had so much ahead of them if only he would open himself to the joy, and rewards, of teaching.

A bitter, self-castigating laugh escaped. Rune's brave and impulsive Student was not afraid of much, except displeasing him. And the Mentor he so admired was the one to fail first in their mission – both in decisions and relationships.

Again it begged the question as to his qualifications of being a Mentor. Sorcery had thrown them together and he had to trust that it was the right thing to do. In his heart he would not change it for anything, because in this short space of time he had learned to laugh and feel and hope again. What a priceless gift. Even if he never taught a thing to Amestoy, the Novitiate had already taught him more than he ever thought possible.

Rune stared at his charge. The pale, very still form of his pupil did not flinch a muscle. Leaning forward, the seasoned Maji reached out a hand and touched the cool skin of Amestoy's hand. If only there was already in place that fabled, mystical link Amestoy so wanted to believe was true. How he wished the Warrior Bond existed. Then Rune could know what was happening inside the quick mind and spirited soul of his Pupil.

'If only the Bond linked us, my Tyro. Even in a trance. Even death? Then I would thank the Warrior Bond. It would be worth it all to journey through any frightful realm, even the nether-realm of death, if we had that Bond in life.'

A wondrous and reassuring river of warmth suddenly flooded through Rune. His talisman glowed bright and stung even over his shirt.

'I agree, Mentor.'

Starting, Rune gasped, then looked to the pale face. It remained still, eyes closed. There was no question Rune was awake, so this was no dream!

'You can read my thoughts!'

It was Amestoy's sardonic and thrilled voice! In his head! *'That is correct, Mentor.'*

Through their link he knew Amestoy was conscious. Relaxing, allowing their Bond to provide the contact, Rune leaned back in his chair and studied his Tyro. Hesitantly, he released of the hold he had maintained of Amestoy's hand. Silence. He placed his hand back on that of his Tyro.

'You saved me, Mentor. Thank you.'

Beginning to speak, Rune shut his mouth and thought his reply. *'I cannot take credit. As I remember, it was you who stubbornly would not give up.'*

'And you who returned to help me in that frightful realm, Mentor. It was you who saved me.'

Humbled at the Majiq they possessed within their secret connection, FEELING the emotions in his heart, hearing more than words in his mind, Rune shivered. *'We are linked!'*

'We are!'

Was that a mental giggle?

'How?'

The thought-chide was sarcasm itself. *'The Bond, Mentor! You must believe it now!'*

Grateful his student was alive to argue with him; Rune smiled and closed his eyes, basking in the comfort of their alliance. How could he deny the power and solace coursing through him? This was amazing! Intrusive, yes. Scary, yes. Incredible – absolutely!

The warmth gradually withdrew and he knew somehow that their attachment was diminished. When he checked Amestoy, he seemed to be in a normal sleep, even quietly snoring. Was it all a dream? He knew it was not. Would that amazing Bond return? Remarkably, he hoped so.

Meditating, Rune pondered the stunning experience. Amestoy had placed himself into a healing trance. The young Maji had never dropped into such a powerful mental state before. Certainly not with sickness and wounds and the trauma of a life-threatening event. What had happened to produce the telepathic conduit between them? Amestoy's dual heritage undoubtedly. The Maji healing methods must have mingled and mixed with the Ameden vision-gifts. But those were mythical were they not? Just like the Warrior Bond? Was it all a hallucination? If so, then how could his Tyro's fevered delusions affect him? They were not linked in any deep sense for mental or emotional advantage. Not until now.

Rubbing his face, confounded and awed, Rune occasionally gave a reassuring touch of his hand on the now peaceful face. Consolation for whom, he wasn't sure. Both of them, he supposed. What should he do now?

He had to come to terms with the Bond -- this strange connection between them. Whether from Amestoy's racial heritage or from some supernatural tie to the ancient legends of the Maji past, he did not know, but he could not deny that it was, in fact, real. If ever there had been something resembling a Warrior Bond it had been the friendship, the brotherhood, with Tor. Now circumstances, Fate, Majiq, whatever, demanded such a commitment with Amestoy.

**

Lightly, in a non-intrusive brush of mental energy, Rune guided Amestoy through the last vestiges of the healing trance. The boy knew the basics, but had never needed something concentrated enough to mend his own wounds or serious illness. As their psyches melded, Rune shared the pain, the confusion. Beyond that he felt the extraordinary desire to be a perfect Maji -- more -- Rune's perfect Warrior Bond Tyro.

Startled, Soren removed his touch a little too abruptly. It jarred Amestoy awake and the green eyes flashed open, revealing the startled inner thoughts: the insecurity deep inside -- the fear of failing -- the willingness to do anything to prove his worth in Rune's eyes. As awareness filtered into the Mentor's mind, he perceived unguarded imaginings of unworthiness. Layered within and atop the negative emotions were awed senses of respect, regard and feelings of incredible love. Everything, negative and positive, was targeted at Rune.

Reluctant to interrupt the deep quiet with words, Rune edged his mind toward Amestoy's, but the earlier link was gone. Emotions were still easily read, but not thoughts anymore. He was disappointed. At first the strong tie seemed an intrusion. Now, there was a kind of emptiness being alone within his mind.

"How are you?" The whisper seemed loud.

"Better. You are an awesome warrior, Mentor."

Feeling a blush rise from his cheeks, Rune gruffed away the praise. "You are not so bad yourself, Amestoy. You handled a very rough life-and-death situation with courage and creativity."

"The praetor?"

"Alive. Thanks to you."

"Good." He gave a slow nod, still fatigued from the ordeal. He closed his eyes again. "I was afraid I'd failed."

"You did brilliantly. Now rest. We are on our way back to Avelon."

A dark shadow pierced Rune and he sensed they both felt it. Yes, Amestoy's green eyes whipped open, startled. Both their dragon-crystal rings sparked with a dull glow.

"What was that?"

Slowly shaking his head in wonder, Rune stared at the rings, feeling a corresponding heat from his matching amulet. Amestoy felt the same reaction from his own talisman, evidenced by him pulling the dragon-crystal from under his shirt. Without looking, the Mentor knew his own Majiq amulet would show an ember of blue.

"A Maji warning?"

Rune turned back to stare at his pupil. He saw and sensed Amestoy's understanding of this significant event. Unprecedented! There seemed untold depths to Amestoy's abilities in Majiq, but there was no time to address that now.

"Yes." Rune moved to his traveling cloak, hooked on a peg near the door, and reached into one of the deep pockets. He pulled out a small, palm-sized crystal ball. Hefting it in his hand, he returned to sit on the edge of the bed. "This is something rarely used, and only within the possession of Templars. A divining crystal. Those with strong enough Majiq can send messages through these crystals."

He concentrated on the opaque, smoky circle. Slowly the hue changed to a tint of ice blue. Then an image formed. Merlin.

"Wizards," the great Majiq leader called. "The dread we have been expecting has come upon us. Gadion-Obscura has moved to overtake our home realm."

Rune's blood chilled. At last! Diaboliq evil had made its move! Now was the time to be joined in battle against those who had taken Tor's life! Energized by the heat of vengeance, Rune clenched his fists in eager anticipation of the fight ahead.

Merlin admonished, "Go with all speed to Ayelsborne! Beware of the dragons! They have turned against their Wizards!"

The image of the great Maji faded, the crystal returning to its cloudy grey. Rune crossed the cabin in a few quick strides and replaced the orb. Practically tossing items from his capacious pockets, stuffing other tools and pouches into his tunic or tucked inside his tall boots, he was already focused on the mission.

"How do we get to Ayelsborne?" Amestoy asked.

The voice startled him. He stopped in mid-motion. He had forgotten Amestoy was even in the cabin with him. Drawing in a deep breath, the enormity of the predicament sank in with a crushing weight. He was not alone anymore. He was responsible for this young man. Revenge could not be his master now, for he was a Mentor to a Pupil with such mettle it defied understanding. His world could no longer revolve around vengeance and lust for Diaboliq blood.

Rune knew what must be done before he turned to see the reaction of his Tyro. The determined expression on the wan face carried no hint of surprise. Instead of making the Mentor's job easier, the willingness to charge into another battle while still recovering from the last, made it that much harder.

In the space of a few short days they had been called upon to face the worst circumstances. Perhaps it was the way of the realm now, the desperate times they lived in, that escalated the danger to degrees never seen before. All he knew was that he was on the front lines – exactly where he was needed. But now it was with a brave lad who would do anything he asked – even more.

Rune kept his tone terse, his emotions tightly controlled. "Rest while you can, Amestoy. You may not get much chance in the next few days. I will handle all the arrangements."

PART FIVE
HERE THERE BE DRAGONS

After speaking to the captain of the ship, Rune returned to find Amestoy already packing gear into their travel bags. With sharp, quick efficiency, the Mentor tossed the kits into a corner, explaining the belongings would be shipped back to Avelon. He had paid handsomely for the transport, so he was confident their meager goods would reach home. If not, those few affects could be easily replaced.

Stuffed into pockets, pouches, boot-tops and belts were the true necessities carried by Wizards. Potions, powders and wands were part of a Wizard, almost as important as their crystals.

Rune was watchful of his Tyro as they prepared to leave, but was careful not to interfere. Although still recovering, this was part of the process of battle; arming, mentally priming mind and body for Majiq, for opposition, for being the vessel of intense energy. There were also the emotional considerations, calming and settling the nerves for quick thinking, combat, injury, and the taking of life. To Rune, the worst, the trauma that could never be fully prepared for, was the hurt and possible death of fellow Templars.

Flinching, he buried his trepidation and double-checked Amestoy's gear. With a nod, he swept out the door, jogging through the candle-lit, narrow corridor of the rocking ship, trotting up the steep steps and into the cool, drizzly night of the North Channel. Limited visibility provided no sight of land, of course. Clouds draped the sky and sea, blanketing the ship in hushed isolation. Nonetheless, trusting the navigation, and Majiq, Rune knew they were close to landfall.

With a last word to the captain, Rune took Amestoy by the arm. "We will swim to shore. Our destination is near the beach. Just keep in touch with my Majiq and this will be a quick trip."

Amestoy gave a tight nod.

Assuring the skeptical captain he was obligated only to see their kitbags to an Avelon trading vessel, Rune strode back, knowing the crew thought this curious, suspicious, even downright strange, Maji were never entirely trusted by Mankind. There was an element of respect, yet circumspect distance. Earth-kind tolerated Majiq when it fit their purposes, but remained skeptical, thinking it could turn on them in an instant. It was a natural inclination to fear something more powerful. Little did they know there was good reason for their caution. Majiq, in the wrong hands, could destroy this world. Fortunately, Templars stood at the ready to protect that unseen barrier between good and evil.

The water was icy cold when Amestoy dove into the ocean, but he had prepared for it by dusting himself with a crushed-gem powder that melded with the skin to resist physical distress. Infused with Majiq, the fine, silty particles insulated against the worst of the shock, allowing his recuperating system and recent injuries, to withstand the freezing water.

Aware of Rune swimming beside him, they propelled through the sea swells with supernatural speed. Within only moments they touched the rocks along the choppy tideline. Trudging to shore, Amestoy followed his Mentor to the grassy rise at the crest of the coastal road.

Reaching their destination, Rune put a hand on Amestoy's shoulder and, using Majiq, determined that he was all right. Neither spoke. A tug at the sleeve and quick nod was the only communication needed as they abandoned the knoll and ran a short distance along the road. When the path dipped into a ravine that cut along the edge of a deep forest, they trotted down, then off-trail alongside a rocky stream. At a hollow where rocks, water and woods met amid the spongy underbrush, Rune stopped. He held out his dragon-crystal and a pale blue glow illuminated a wedge between large boulders set into the slope.

"In case you didn't recognize it, Tyro, this is a Threshold."

The doorway between realms was always a cusp of land where worlds, elements and geographical sinks met. Here, the natural components combined to create an entrance for Majiqal beings. For their purposes, it would also be the exit from this kingdom to the next.

Rune's ring pulsed and the hue inside the faceted gem shifted to deeper blue. Feeling the heat of his own dragon-crystals, Amestoy realized his ring and amulet were also strobes; in his case, with a turquoise tint.

"There is nothing to it, Amestoy. The crystals act as our keys. They will open the Threshold and we will step through. Ready?"

This was another new experience for him, and Amestoy was more than prepared. Reading, studying, hearing tales within the Castle for all of his life, intellectually, he knew the ways of Wizards. Now, as reality reflected back on those childhood imaginings, he found eagerness, not anxiety, pushing him to leap into the next new adventure.

"Ready, Mentor."

"Good lad." Rune smiled, taking hold of his arm. "Follow me."

Dragon-crystal lighting the way, they held their rings in front and Rune, then Amestoy, stepped into the void where the rocks had been melted by Majiq. An instantaneous shift of blackness, to bright, blue-green light washed over and through them. Then they stepped into the other side of the dimension.

**

"Whoa! That was amazing!"

Rune's chuckle was soft and swallowed up in the strange, new atmosphere.

Ayelsborne's rocky plains were even more barren and inhospitable than anything in Britania. Rust-red brown, dusty and forbidding. An amazing array of craters, mounds and volcanic cones, scorched under the huge amber sun, peppered the landscape. No greenery appeared to mitigate the terrain or break up the desolation. How depressing. This was so unlike Amestoy's own beautiful province, the lush land of his clans, of which he carried a vague visual and soul-imprint memory. The starkly bright contrast of night to harsh day should have hurt his eyes, but Majiq had transitioned them well and tempered the change in conditions.

"It is desolate, Mentor." His voice was as scratchy as the surroundings. He had to salivate to moisten his tongue. "I have never seen anything so – so – dry!" He cleared his suddenly parched throat. "No offense, Mentor."

Rune smiled. "None taken. This is the arid side of the province. Harsh conditions here. The wyvern dragons that make this home are gnarly and tough. They are not domesticated, but wild beasts. Most formidable. That they are being used as pawns for Diaboliq is disgusting."

When they were readying to leave the ship, the senior Maji had railed about the disrespect, the horror of his home province being attacked. Rune's family, long dead, were not a concern as much as the population of the world that was a contradiction in itself. One quarter of the province, the side that orbited closest to the sun, was hot, mostly uninhabitable, and a barren, danger-filled wilderness. The untamable plains wyverns, covered with hard, rust-colored scales, were vicious and hungry, attacking anything that moved across the desert. Fortunately, the wyvern could not survive for long in anything but an arid landscape, so they remained behind the massive mountains that isolated the treacherous wasteland.

The side of the province where the humanoids and other sentient beings lived, protected from the worst of the sun's rays, was legendarily beautiful. Waterways bordered verdant gardens while lush, forest-covered mountains bordered the sea. There, tamed dragons provided not only part of the cultural history, but practical commerce of the realm as well. Dragon Lords – one of the most popular and colorful occupations in the provinces, were heroes across all the Majiq kingdoms.

"Will you teach me to ride a dragon while we are here, Mentor?"

"I doubt there will be time for that, Amestoy."

"A pity." Came the disappointed sigh, "You are a legend."

"Tyro, you listen to way too much gossip at the Castle."

Hardly a beat went by before the next line of questioning. "Why would the Gadion-Obscura attack here?"

Rune had been wondering that the whole trip. While it had been long years since he had returned to his home, he felt a tugging of heartstrings for his realm. "Greed. The desert lands of Ayelsborne are rich in minerals. Those who are audacious enough to set up subterranean mines can make a quick profit then move on to another site. If the terrain and the wyverns don't kill them, that is. Arid dragons, if subdued by Majiq, can claw their way through rock and mountain given the time and motivation. Those fortunate enough to successfully mine here will be rewarded with copper, gold, silver, and rich veins of many other metals and gems."

"So the Gadion-Obscura seeks wealth."

"They need lucre to fund their war machine. They also need the minerals for their alchemy. Without the potions they would lose most of their power."

Amestoy shivered. "It's the blood-drinking that scares me," he admitted.

"Then we will make sure no Diaboliq gets close enough to you for any of that." He surveyed the landscape, and then nodded toward the west, toward the crevices of the towering, rust-colored mountains. "We need to move. There is an unusual amount of dust over those ridges. We are needed there."

Setting a sharp run, Rune zigged and zagged over and around boulders, sand-pits and thick, needle-pointed shrubbery that tore at their trousers. When they ascended the steep, but flat hillside, their pace evened out.

Rune concentrated on the trail as well as the impression of fighting over the rise, but glancing back over his shoulder, continued Ayelsborne is the ruling home of our Queen Garraden, most of our Wizards colonized here only briefly. Remember, the line of Avelon left long ago to live on Earth. House of Garraden is dominant, but smaller, and not as strong."

"Is that clan pride talking?" Amestoy teased, now starting to breathe a little heavy at their brisk pace.

"When I left home as a youth, this whole region had been taken over by career merchants intent on capitalizing on the dragons."

"But how can that be? I thought you had to be a Maji to control the dragons."

"Dragonshire Wizards are of the Avelon heredity. Dragon Lords and trainers are talented – uh – soldiers – I suppose you can call them, of the domesticated beasts. They are not Maji, but possess an inherent aptitude for dragon wrangling and talking."

"They talk to dragons?"

"After a fashion."

"Can you talk to dragons, Mentor? I want to! And you'll take me for a ride, won't you?"

"We are here as warriors, Tyro. Let's keep focused."

When they reached the rim of the hill they saw what could only be described as an enormous caldera. Dust billowed from the cavity and huge blurs buzzed above like angry insects. Dragons. Below, barely visible through the blowing sand, were two Mentor and Tyro teams and one single Paladin engaged in fighting. A band of Gadion-Obscura warriors were scrambling down the opposite side of the slope, barely controlling the wild, ginger-hued dragons. All the dragon riders of Ayelsborne were enlisted to assist, circling and diving above them. But they possessed no Majiq abilities and were of little practical help, except to use their own forest dragons to fight the desert creatures. Frighteningly, the intense and confusing situation was causing some of the blue-green dragons to turn on their masters!

Rune paused only for a moment. "Stay here and recuperate, Amestoy."

They had debated this point in the ship's cabin and still had not settled on an agreeable conclusion. Rune demanded and Amestoy objected. It was time to lay down the law. Soren disliked being a dictator. He was more comfortable with the gentle give and take they had established, but his Pupil could be so stubborn!

"You said we would not be separated –"

"It can't be helped." The stony expression, the bitter tone could have been from either regret or anger – hard to tell. "You will be providing vital intelligence by observing from this high ground!" He paused, anxious to leave, but needing to part with something more satisfying to both. "Just take care of yourself, Tyro. All will be well."

Rune raced down the hill at a run. Irritated, hurt at being left out and left behind, Amestoy slumped onto a rock. The Majiq rippled within, warning that there was danger and Dark power around him. Angst from the energy of battle and death hovered in the very air. Not to mention mean dragons! Pain greater than his physical inabilities rankled within. If only he was well enough to help his Mentor! Why did he have to be injured at Ionia? In this crucial moment his Teacher was out risking his life, and the useless Learner was forgotten.

"All will be well," he repeated in a grim whisper. "That's what you said in the dream-vision."

Should he disobey his Mentor and go join the fight? As much as he longed to do so, he knew to be disobedient was wrong. What if Rune needed him up here to relay necessary tactical input? Besides, the Teacher was right. A wounded Tyro who had barely tasted conflict – what good could he do? What if something happened to Rune? He would never forgive himself, but what could he do?

The Warrior Bond. It came to him in a flash of nearly metaphysical clarity. Of course! The Bond could help them both! They had connected during what had started as a healing trance and had now become so much more. Yes!

Not knowing what to do exactly, but pleased he had a goal, Amestoy relaxed. Eyes open, seeing both the exterior ground combat and the inside of his being, he settled into a mental calm. Ignoring the heat, the dust, the cries of pain, the screeching of the dragons overhead, he centered himself in Majiq until he felt the familiar and comforting, singular essence-stamp that was his Mentor. Thoughts, emotions, senses, Majiq were all bundled together in a psych-signature to every being. To Maji the impression was unique with each member of the Order. Now that they had a deeper Bond, it was almost effortless to scan the nebulous and myriad impressions of other Maji imprints, and connect with his Mentor.

Rune was in the midst of a violent clash; the classic spirit of Light against Evil. Dark-cloaked figures with no faces against the Maji. No fear, just pure Majiq guiding Rune through spells, wand-energy and explosions. Almost as if Amestoy were peering through a cloudy veil, he observed the approaching onslaught of auburn dragons! Rune slashed with the blue-silver touch-stone light, vanquishing the enemy with every sweep, black-cloaked men and rust-colored wyverns falling before the mighty power! He had read about, but never seen, such valor.

Regardless of their bravery, the Maji were outnumbered! Amestoy shot to his feet in terror. They would all be slaughtered! A sound came first to his ears, then to the senses that were so focused on the desperate survivors. The buzzing sound of flying wyverns? Glancing around he watched dozens of black-cloaked troops swooping into the crater, followed almost immediately by popping explosions.

A trap! A trap to gather many Wizards in one place! But collective Maji power could defeat anything! Almost anything. Was it enough to overcome dozens of Diaboliq Sinisters? For that was what they had to be – the Dark Arts assassins! Wyvern with sweeping bronze wings swooped down from the sky under the control of the evil Warlocks.

Without thinking, Amestoy started down the slope. His instinct was to help, to be a warrior for good took over any other thought. He had not taken more than a few steps when a slender dragon raced by nearly taking his head off! With it came a wave of Diaboliq so strong he could taste it! Red eyes bore into him as the rider passed. The same Sinister he had felt on Ionia!

There was no thought to his actions, no plan. The same Diaboliq he had felt before was here! The wicked Assassin may have escaped the last time, but Amestoy would not allow him to leave this battle! He ran ahead. The air above the pit glittered with Majiq powders and sparking wands. Space was cluttered with diving wyverns and sleek, huge, blue-green dragons swooping to kill the desert beasts! A wounded wyvern faltered, its tail slicing through the sky, sweeping wings and gnarled claws flailing as it spiraled to the ground. Amestoy dove under a rock, just barely escaping the doomed monster.

Potent balls of energy suddenly began smashing into the ground! The Diaboliq and wounded beasts were coming back around again! Dust and smoke roiled around him as he crawled low and scampered to better cover. Sick with nausea and choked from fumes and filth, Amestoy managed to stumble behind another boulder before the last one was obliterated into a thousand fiery shards of lethal rain. Using Majiq to shield himself from the cascade of hot ash and rubble, he turned just in time to see a wyvern and black-cloaked rider clambering toward him, emitting shrieks of impending doom –

hunters who had cornered their prey. Monsters of mindless commitment.

The terrain was filled with dragons as the rust-colored, untamed beasts from the desert were pitted against the woefully outnumbered blue, teal-green scaled dragons from beyond the mountains. Sinisters in black robes flew high, sprinkling out a grey fog. Diaboliq was driving the beasts, easily subduing their unguarded wills, to attack Wizards. Amestoy saw Dragon Wizards fall as the magnificent creatures turned on them, or were killed by the overwhelming army of wyverns.

Only seven Maji were here on Ayelsborne, and one of them was Rune! Amestoy had to reach his Mentor. With the army of Diaboliq and the Dark Majiq aiding the dragons, they were lost unless they could combine their power!

Before the lumbering beast-of-death could come closer, Amestoy poured on his Majiq energy and zipped past the brown, scaly creature edging toward his position. Huge machines of dumb instinct, they knew only what their brains were forced to think from Dark enchantment. He had never imagined facing this on his first excursion from the Castle! Far from Avelon and the safety of his Order, his first mission had turned into several nightmares.

Through the smoke and dust, Amestoy spotted two Sorcerers battling more of the desert dragons. Taking heart that there was a way to fight these monsters, maybe even beat them, he took a deep breath for courage. As one behemoth scrambled toward him, Amestoy leveled his left hand and slashed at its legs with his touch-stone power. The beast screamed and shook, twisting convulsively before collapsing in the sand. Another turned its attention his way. Dashing forward, Amestoy used Majiq with one hand to push the wyvern back long enough to whip the wings, then chest, into pieces before the deadly, spiked tail could strike him.

Fear fled in the heat of battle and rush of adrenalin. As it had aided in his brief engagements before, the energy of Majiq, combined with skill and optimism, melded into a blur of fatal expertise. The wyverns came at him in an army of Darkness, but he severed and impaled his way through countless creatures. Fatigued and weak, through Majiq he struggled beyond his own abilities to attain a greater, more pure level of energy reserved strictly for combat. He staggered across the burning sand and rocks, barely able to stay on his feet as he took down dragon after dragon. Racing into the valley to meet his compatriots, Amestoy was aware of the other two Maji nearby, and was energized by proximity. Surrounding them there was also an atmosphere of staunch determination. Some Wizards had fallen and their fellow Templars were working to bring the Sinister to justice, but on a sub-level of awareness, he knew Rune was still alive.

A hot blast of flame flashed across his shoulder and he fell to the dirt, rolling back down part of the slope. Aware he was sliding into grave danger, he twisted and fired out his crystal touch-power just in time to eliminate a fire-breathing wyvern that was right on top of him! Stay focused! He had heard the warning echoed in the halls of the Castle thousands of times. Now it rang in his head with the voice of his Mentor.

'*Focus!*'

This was the country of his fore-tell vision! The realm where Rune had been lost to him! The desert void had separated them! Was it an analogy for death? Had Rune been killed?

Seeking refuge behind a large boulder, he glanced around. No more Maji in sight. Was he the only one left? They were being massacred by wyvern! By a Diaboliq army! No! No! This was no way for Maji to die! This was no way for him to die! And he vowed he wouldn't! He had to live! He was a Wizard! He was half of a Warrior Bond. Even though his Mentor steadfastly denied it, they were linked by Majiq.

Amestoy could sense the oppressive approach of a throng of dragons, but even if he was the only one left standing, he would make this a good fight. He would not go down without taking many of these monsters with him. He took a deep breath to steady his nerves and strengthen his weary muscles and aching injuries. A long exhale followed to gird his resolve.

Then he felt it – a ripple of strength. Rune! His Mentor was still alive! Others were still alive as well and at the edges of his senses he could feel the gathering of their collective power! Summoning all the energy he could muster, he inhaled deeply and leaped from his sand pit, running up the mountain, firing his blue-silver touch-power at any beast that moved.

Slash, strike, burn, and tear. Amestoy whirled through the advancing, beating-wing monsters with no thought of anything beyond the moment. Focus was complete as his reality became himself as a machine, slicing, stabbing and flying into the midst of the foe. Stings and smolders were ignored, sweat and blood disregarded. Unheeded was any thought of safety or self-preservation. His objective was to eliminate the enemy and every move, every breath, focused on triumph and survival.

All at once, he felt it again. Strength like a wave, somewhere beyond him, coming from other Wizards. It was drawing on the formidable might of this rich province; iron, rock, waterfalls, elements and minerals intrinsic to Ayelsborne. The energy rose from the earth and air to coalesce around the Sorcerers.

When an explosive bolt from a Diaboliq struck his foot he stumbled, tumbling, then clambered back to come to his knees. Resources nearly spent, he refused to give in to mortal weakness. They would have to fight and die to finish him off. He dropped behind a rock and came up almost instantly to surprise the nearest wyvern, but the Sinister astride item him with a level stare. The red-eyed evil might influence weaker beings, but it was no match for a Maji. Amestoy deflected the scarlet light with his blue/teal touch-power, the wickedness bouncing back to strike the Sinister who instantly dissolved in flames!

Exhausted, he folded into the hot sand. He had nothing left. When another wyvern swung toward him he knew his time was up. Use Majiq to overpower the dragons and turn them on their masters! came the thought. How? Only one way. He could not do it alone. He must have help from the Warrior Bond. With everything he had left he pushed his strength, his Majiq, his essence into a Bond connection. He needed Rune's help.

Suddenly the last dragon screeched in pain, then collapsed. It crashed to the dirt and there, behind the smoke and silty powder, was the best sight Amestoy had ever seen. Rune gave him a nod, and then slashed the wyvern once more with his wand. Dead. Amestoy rose unsteadily to his feet and, with as much dignity as he could manage, rose to meet his Mentor.

The noise of a screaming dragon came from behind and Amestoy spun, nearly losing his footing. The cloaked figure with the red eyes! The menace was heading straight for him! It was the same Diaboliq signature he had felt at Ionia. Strange how evil had such a distinct imprint that it could be felt and recognized by Maji.

Racing to reach his Tyro, Rune watched the Diaboliq, who leaped from the wyvern and stood on the rise like a monument to all that was malevolent. The maliciousness surrounding the spectre was so profound it was more than an impression on his spirit, but even going so far as to leave a bitter taste in Rune's mouth. He had touched this foulness before. On Spania, on Ionia, and now here. The Diaboliq was potent in its power, and the Sinister agent strong in wickedness.

The black- cloaked figure was between him and Amestoy. When the Sinister threw a potion-charged dart toward him, it was as if time stopped. Waves of energy radiated around the creature. Rune's right hand was already aimed at the figure, his touch-power surging toward the threat before he realized what was happening. A blue/ teal/silver force from behind the Sinister was freezing any aggression from the enemy! Amestoy! Rune could feel the unique stamp of touch-stone might, weak, but recognizable! Amazing! Calling upon the last of his strength, the Tyro was protecting him!

The twin beams of touch-stone searing converged on the Sinister. The cloak suddenly collapsed as the Diaboliq body imploded, then shriveled, sending the head rolling away in one direction and the body smashing into a rock at the opposite angle! Hand shaking, there stood Rune, grim and deadly. Hardly able to stand, Amestoy beamed with pride across the short expanse of sand. They had done it! What a magnificent battle!

"Dragon's breath!" Amestoy whispered.

Rushing to close the few meters between them, the Mentor smiled, and then offered a slow nod accompanied by a strong grip on the arm. "Well done, Amestoy. Your fighting was brilliant." Sensing his Pupil's weakness, Rune supported Amestoy to the nearest boulder where he knelt down next to him. "You were superb today."

Amestoy was almost giddy with delight at the amazing praise. Was it the Bond that had softened his Mentor's heart? Was it their connection, that he could still feel, that forged them tighter than he imagined was possible? He could FEEL the pride his Mentor held for him. Sense it and share it in an inexplicable way. Not inexplicable. Easily explained within the Bond.

"It was the Bond, Mentor."

A wave of irritation flashed instantly from Rune, but it vanished almost before it was felt. A slow smile and a shake of the head preceded a deep chuckle. "I can only hope you are so persistent in everything you undertake, my Tyro," he grumbled, but the emotion in his eyes proved how touched he was by the experience.

"That Diaboliq Sinister. It was the one from Ionia."

Rune's eyebrows rose almost to the sweat-soaked tawny hair that had tumbled across his forehead. "You felt that?"

"Very clearly."

"You are spooky sometimes, Tyro." The easy smile accompanying the accusation preceded a deep chuckle that seemed cracked with emotion. "Amazing." He paused for a moment, as if contemplating what to say. "That Sinister has been tracking me for some time," he finally confessed. "He was on Spania, also, when I was attacked by a bounty hunter."

Amestoy's green eyes narrowed. "You do lead an adventurous life, Mentor." He took a few breaths. "What does it mean? Are they coming after specific Maji?"

As soon as the words were uttered, Rune's spine tingled with mystic confirmation. "Perhaps," he countered, but was already certain of the hypothesis. They would have to be very careful, constantly on guard, all Wizards. The Diaboliq Sinisters were on a mission. To gain control of the kingdoms they first had to eliminate the Maji. "We will worry about that later. You have fought valiantly, Tyro. Beyond what any Mentor would have expected. Or asked."

"Did you see my touch-stone, Mentor? It has changed color! It changed at Ionia, and now it is staying blue. The same as yours. Why do you think that is?"

"I had noticed," Rune admitted, perplexed. "We will have to figure that out at some point, I suppose. For now, it only matters that you are so adept at using it."

A shout from the hill preceded Maji Artemis trotting down the crumbly slope. Amestoy didn't realize she was the other Paladin who had been fighting beside Rune. The lithe woman knelt down in the gritty soil beside Amestoy.

"Young ones like you, Amestoy, must face battles now. The Gadion-Obscura has risen. Initiates will have to grow up fast and take their places as battle Tyro's. This is war."

"War." He had been on the front lines when the opening shots were fired! The first war in centuries for the realms! "Mentor?"

With a hand of support on Amestoy's shoulder, Rune gave a squeeze of support. "There is much to explain, Amestoy. We will take it in measured stride. First, you are to be taken to my shire and get some rest. I'll help Artemis and the others with finishing off any more Diaboliq and controlling the wyvern."

"The other Maji? Who else is here?"

Rune patted his shoulder for a moment and looked away. He shook his head.

Artemis filled in with a solemn voice. "We lost a Tyro here today. But the others are safe."

Rune helped him to his feet. "Come along. You will be in good hands, I promise. This order you must obey." There was no quarter for denial.

"Yes, sir."

Before they reached the next rise Amestoy felt his knees go out from under him. A cushion of gentle arms stopped him from hitting the ground.

**

Resting at the crest of a gently sloping hill was a modest manor where thick trees, stooped with age, shaded it from the heat of the day. The lush forests and towering waterfalls of surrounding mountains could be glimpsed from the spacious turret bedroom. In and out of consciousness for the last few hours, Amestoy had learned he was in the family home of Rune. It was kept as a refuge for the Wizard who seldom returned. Amestoy shifted on the lounge to glance at his Mentor, who had just re-entered the room.

"You are still not asleep."

"I'm unsettled, Mentor. There is so much to think about. I can't focus."

"Not surprising"

There was a comfortable understanding between them. The challenging and stinging debates were past. Behind were the turbulent oppositions and arguments. They had faced life and death side-by-side, sometimes wounded, sometimes near a mortal end, and had triumphed together.

Sitting on the edge of his Tyro's bed, Rune brushed the back of his hand against Amestoy's cheek and then held both the smaller hands within his large fists. "I will help you achieve a healing trance which will promote recovery. A normal trance." He leaned forward and whispered, "I will react negatively if you drop into the kind of near-death coma you were in before." He leaned back and in a normal tone said, "You must wipe away all thoughts now to clear your mind."

"Yes, Mentor. But there is so much --"

"Later. There will be plenty of time for us to talk when you are stronger." The hands within the strong fists were squeezed firmly. "You turned the tide for us out there, Tyro. Your bravery was incredible."

"Fear," he confessed. "I was afraid you were lost –"

"Then there is no need for that fear anymore. We are safe. Now you must rest. Understood? All questions will be answered later. Patience."

"One of my weakest traits." The boy meekly conceded.

Chuckling, Rune gave a nod. "Something we share in common. Now we must both strive to do better at patience. And save more discussion for later. Yes?" he finished firmly.

"Yes, Mentor."

The commonplace orders were said with deep conviction. All who instruct and all who learn need patience, which was not the strongest virtue for either teacher or pupil.

Rune didn't know how to communicate the contrition and tenderness in his heart, so he allowed the sensitivity of affection to speak for him.

"Then you will take me on a dragon ride?"

Rune chuckled. "You are incorrigible."

"Is that a yes?"

"Rest now! We will talk later."

With a gentle hand he wiped the boy's eyes closed, a sense of calm endearment settled between them, filling in the gaps his words could never reach. Both leveled off in a serene plane of mutual appreciation. The first step to a deeper Mentor and Tyro Bond.

**

This time he knew it was not a dream or a fore-tell. Not knowing why, but immediately recognizing it through some deep instinct from his heritage, Amestoy was aware the vision playing out in his mind was of the past.

Diaboliq. Murder. Crying. Terror. Amestoy was protected and removed from it all under a glimmering umbrella of a Majiq-dusted spell. The scene glistened with unreality, but the feelings and sounds and heart wrenching, tangible terror in the air was real.

Though he had never met the renowned Wizard, he knew Tor Ion-Gawain when he saw him in this dream set on Amed. He was there to protect the Amed people. A new threat was upon them. Like a shimmering mirage, Ion-Gawain was weeping when he knelt down and waved his hand in the air.

The scene cleared. Chilled, Amestoy realized this was from his own point of view! He had been watching murder and attacks from under a protective Majiq shield. Ion-Gawain removed a dragon ring on a chain from around the neck of the baby -- Amestoy. That had been the talisman that protected the child from murder – Tor's own amulet! Merlin was there, too. The two Wizards took Amestoy away.

The ring he now wore on his left hand was that same ring. A dragon Iolite that had spared him from the Diaboliq assassins that had killed his parents – no – killed his mother

and her family. Tears streamed down his face as the impact
of the attack drove terror and grief through him – inside and
out. But the mourning was tempered. There was a
background of warmth and love, of protection and healing
woven into the threads of his memory of the horror, and the
ensuing days of nurturing. Ion-Gawain had rescued him.

When Amestoy rose from the grips of slumber, his
cheeks was still wet from tears. Wiping them against the
pillow, he was surprised the lingering of panic from the
nightmarish recollection was not there to haunt him. Instead,
he felt a placid rise to consciousness, an easy climb from
sleep to clarity. Before he opened his eyes he could feel the
presence of his Mentor. Rune was here with him in the room.
The psychic mark was so clear it was as if Amestoy was
watching him. It was an inclusive attendance of all senses
except sight. He could smell the faint scent of the oil
Rune used to wipe down his boots. He could hear the
subsurface breathing of a Maji at rest, either in meditation or
completely calm. He could sense the familiarity of the person
that had now come to be as much a part of him as his
own shadow. The be-all of his universe. His past, present
and future. His entire being was wrapped around his Mentor,
not only as a wise councilor, but as his teacher, friend, second
father, and at last, his fellow Bond Warrior.
　　　"Are you ever going to open your eyes?"
　　　It was a whisper so soft it penetrated his ears as faintly
as it did his mind. They were connected on a subliminal level
that was even deeper than anything he could have imagined.
Not as intense as during a crisis, but as an extra layer to his
soul at all times.
　　　He tried to speak telepathically only, but was not
successful in relaying words, only impressions. Little more
than any Maji could do with influence power. He would have
to work on that. He was confident they could communicate
with minds only. It had been as such in his dream-vision.
Probably because of his Ameden heritage.
　　　"I felt that," Rune whispered in amusement. Leaning
close, the Mentor told him, "I don't think it works all the time.

We can't slip in and out of this – this – Bond – at will. I don't think."

The Pupil's eyes flashed open. "That is the first time you've admitted there is such a thing –"

"I know, Amestoy. Give me a little time. I have argued against it for so long, it will take this stubborn old Wizard a bit to accept what has happened in the last several days."

Of the many ways he could have responded, he stayed focused on the most important. "You believe in the Bond."

"I believe in you," the older man countered. "Time will tell what this link between us means. How we can use it to our advantage. Or even what we label it."

The gentle compromise was good enough for now. Amestoy looked around the room, a large, pleasant turret chamber. Books lined one wall and a giant tapestry of dragons adorned the wall opposite the comfortable bed.

Emblazoned above the tapestry:

R

At first Amestoy thought it was the initial for the family Rune. Looking at it more critically, he decided it could just as well be the runic symbol for travel -- quest, adventure. Was the family named for the ancient symbols? Fitting. He realized there was a great deal he had to learn about Rune. And Ion-Gawain.

Numerous windows welcomed bright sunlight. Sofas were angled toward double glass doors that opened to a landing. Beyond he could see a beautiful province with trees and meadows. A village and farms stretched across the rolling hills.

"For now, Amestoy, you are ordered to rest. We will discuss this at length later.

"Certainly. "

"I knew you wouldn't let me just ignore it." The tone was light.

Amestoy knew how to win graciously. "Of course. Are you going to teach me how to ride dragons?"

"With your penchant for danger? That doesn't sound safe at all!"

Against his better judgment, Rune knew it was impossible to reject this request. First things first for the hungry Pupil, though. After a hearty meal, Amestoy seemed strong and fit and too energetic to confine. A tour of the ancient manor followed. Family portraits and artifacts lined the walls of a home more militaristic than socially styled. Ancestors atop dragons, horses, wearing battle-gear and Wizard capes were the predominate décor. It was all interesting, but Amestoy was restless. He was an adventure-anxious young man, after all! There was only one thing that could quell the anticipation.

Rune took him to the foothills behind the stately home. Rolling green fields stretched toward lush, emerald forests and, in the distance, a rippling stream spilled into a silver lake. White clouds that swirled far into the atmosphere drifted lazily across the peaceful land. At times like this the Wizard Mentor wondered why he did not come home more often. This was a wonderful place; enhanced now by the overpowering sense of awe emanating from Amestoy.

"Your home is incredible!"

"Thank you."

Rune couldn't resist the smile, nor the dramatic conclusion of the day. He whistled a shrill tone and held up his right hand. His touch-stone glowed a blue beam into the sky. First the sound, then the sight of a long, elegant, indigo-scaled dragon with a triangle-tipped tail swooped toward them. The lengthy, delicate wings beat a rhythmic pattern that sounded like thunder and stirred the grass and trees with a billowing wind.

Fierce looking, with a long nose and snarling roar accentuated by fangs that protruded from its jaws, it glided down and landed just meters from Rune. With a growling hiss it snorted and sniffed at the Wizards on the hill. Rune talked to it in native Ayelsborne. The dragon wiped its nostrils in the grass and approached. He bent his fore-legs and extended his stretchy neck so his jaw rested on the ground.

Smiling at the awestruck youth beside him, Rune encouraged Amestoy to approach.

He instructed that the dragon trusted Rune, and therefore trusted Daavv, with a wary element of shyness. To win over the beast, Amestoy must show that he was not a threat and that he completely honored the dragon he would command once they were in the air.

"How do I do that?"

"Give yourself over to his nature, just as we learn to work within the Bond," Rune advised.

"That's easy," Amestoy admitted.

With his left hand he reached over and petted the end of the damp, dragon nose. The skin was soft, and as his hand rubbed up the scales he was surprised they were pliable and tender to the touch. They glinted and glittered in the sun, much like Rune's Wizard cloak, or the fire from Rune's touch-stone. Blue/indigo/silver seemed the colors of this realm and the Wizard who hailed from here.

Running a hand along the neck, Rune lithely jumped atop the dragon's back and beckoned Amestoy to join him. Leaping up behind Rune and with a gentle kick to the sides of the beast, the dragon pushed off from the ground and they sailed into the heavens!

Amestoy laughed as they soared above the beautiful landscape, zooming over streams and lakes and deep forests. They glided around other dragons that were not nearly so fast, nor magnificent! The graceful creature took them over farms and roads where the cheering people waved and clapped. They angled close along the sea shore and tipped alongside craggy mountains. It was exhilarating to feel the wind on his face, his hair ruffling in the breeze while the smells and sights from the kingdom filled all his senses.

Most of all, Amestoy reveled in the freedom. Spreading his arms, he delighted in the speed and dizzying twirls so high above the ground! At his whim, their ride dipped down to skim along streams, or rustle stalks of grain with the majestic and mighty wings beating the air.

The orange sun was just touching the horizon when they returned to the hilltop behind Rune's home. Still breathless with elation from the journey, Amestoy was disappointed the magnificent ride was over, but Soren explained dragons returned to their caves to sleep at night.

"Besides, I believe that is enough thrills for one day."

Sliding off the beast, Amestoy hugged the wide neck as best he could, smiling as he felt the pride swelling within the older Wizard. He giggled when Rune patted the dragon, whispering something into its ear, causing it to twitch, as if tickled.

"Thank you, dragon," Amestoy told the creature to his face. "What is your name?"

The thought came to him as clearly as if the creature had spoken aloud. "Thank you for the ride, Pen. I hope we meet again."

Beside him, Rune sputtered. "How – what manner – how did you know his name?"

"He told me," Amestoy replied. Only then did he realize what an absurd comment that was!

Pen pushed into his shoulder with a wet nose, nearly knocking the trim youth off his feet. Amestoy rebalanced quickly to pat the beast on the nose again. Then Pen twirled around, swirled his wings and pushed off, sailing into the twilight, heading for the mountains.

Amestoy bounced with delight.

Rune halted him with a firm hand on his shoulder.

"You talked to my dragon!"

Trepidation gave him the jitters, but he looked up into Rune's face anyway. "I just thought it. I don't know how." He suspected through the talent of his mixed heritage. No telling what kind of crazy skills he would have as an Ayelsborne/Amed/Maji. Was that something he should confess to Rune? When he really didn't know himself? Best not. "It must have been the Bond. You must have thought it, Mentor and I picked it up."

A slow nod was offered, but Rune seemed unconvinced. "Must have been," he repeated uncertainly.

"So, shall we see Pen tomorrow?"

"I am afraid not, Amestoy. We will be leaving for Avelon. There is much to do now that the Gadion-Obscura has made their aggressions known."

"That is sad. How can you bear to leave this magnificent land?" He stared wistfully at the purple mountains ringed with misty clouds. "Pen pines when you go."

"What?"

Amestoy cleared his throat. He had to stop revealing his secrets. For now. "I said Pen must miss you when you go."

Rune's sigh was plaintive. "I suppose. I miss him. But Maji are needed in many places in the kingdoms. Usually not of our choosing, and sometimes rather unpleasant. There is no accommodation made for dragons, I'm afraid."

That was disappointing.

"It is the nature of our calling to leave our root homes, sometimes for a long time." His nostalgic gaze swept over the landscape. "Sometimes forever."

Amestoy knew he was thinking about Tor. He maintained a respectful silence so as not to mar his Mentor's reflective moment. Such restraint was difficult for someone with a great deal of energy and many questions. There was so much more Amestoy needed to find out about Rune and Ayelsborne.

And his cool dragon! Pen. Pen Dragon. Amestoy stopped and searched the sky for the beast, but the magnificent winged creature was already far beyond sight. Pendragon. The name of the legendary line of Arthur, the founding king of Camelot. Hmm. And Ion-Gawain – the end of his name that of the great knight of the Round Table. More pieces of the very intriguing and mysterious puzzle that was his Mentor. Did it mean nothing, or a great deal? He had much to ponder as they made their way back to the manor.

PART SIX
THE WARRIOR LEGION

In the huge dining hall where a long table was only occupied by a few guests, Amestoy arrived for early breakfast. Maji Izelt, along with priest Artemis and one of the other Maji involved in the battle of Ayelsborne were there. The newest arrival was Gwen, a tall, lean, red-headed Celt woman. She was the Mentor who lost her Tyro while fighting the Diaboliq and the wyverns. She reported the Dark Warlocks had been defeated; none remained on Ayelsborne. Rune and Amestoy had emerged as heroes, but the accolades were subdued, tempered with the loss of life and the sober reality of a war. Maji had arrived to help restore order and offer aid to the stricken province. The skirmish, while difficult on the inhabitants of Ayelsborne, had been limited in scope. The Gadion-Obscura had fled quickly, as if this was just a testing ground for future advances.

After the filling meal of local meats, fruits and grains, Izelt left for Avelon. Rune led his last guests to an expansive portico overlooking a green valley patch-worked with verdant farmland. As a rich backdrop, the emerald mountains – the dragon aerie -- loomed against the cobalt sky.

Amestoy hoped there would be time to explore his Mentor's home realm. So much of his past remained as Ion-Gawain's son was here, too. Amestoy vowed he would return here and cull the history of Ayelsborne's Templars from the old tomes lurking in the ancient libraries. He would meet those who knew Tor and Rune as boys and discover what kind of life they led before entering the Castle of the Maji. And his Mentor would teach him how to ride dragons!

While seated on cushioned benches, Rune gave a serious look to Artemis, and then to Gwen, whose short red hair matched her bright traveling cloak and complimented the deep blue hue of her large eyes.

"I have conferred with my colleagues." He nodded at the women, and then rested his gaze on Amestoy. "We have agreed that it is time you learn of a secret I've been keeping." Lest the young man mistake the opening words as a reference to the Bond, he quickly explained, "The three of us, and now you, are part of a secret group within the Maji Order. We call ourselves, for lack of a more creative label, the League. We are dedicated to seeking out and destroying the Gadion-Obscura wherever we find them."

The ancient evil had emerged from obscurity and come into the light years before. Amestoy knew the history. He had known also that Rune had held things back from him, such as the secrecy with Artemis. Now those intrigues were explained and it was a weight of relief off of Amestoy's heart. He had never been sure what caused the separation and coolness of his Mentor, but he thought he was to blame. To discover it was something else entirely – a noble and covert unit! – that was – fantastic!

Rune's deep hurt at the murder of Tor had to be at the root of this Legion. There were other factors, too. The natural heroic nature of the renowned Templar made it obvious he would align himself with any effort to fight for the good of their realm.

"I thought defeating the Diaboliq was the goal of all Maji."

"More or less," Artemis agreed. "We just go out of our way a little to investigate Diaboliq appearances. And eliminate the threat immediately." Her lithe frame stretched out, a hand brushing through her blond hair. "It is still the same. We are not breaking rules."

Glowing with pride that he was part of this select, hidden group of elite Maji, Amestoy strove for maturity. "Tell me more about the sect?"

Gwen explained, "You know Diaboliq are an ancient cult of assassins known to be the elite of the secret order of Gadion-Obscura. Practitioners of Dark Majiq, this sect of Black Wizards manipulated governments, provinces and commerce in the old days of the kingdom. It is rumored Merlin's ancient foe, Mordred, was said to be a member. That he learned his wicked Majiq from the demon twins years ago in the queen's purge when they killed the monarch and her court."

This much Amestoy knew from his history classes and books.

"Diaboliq assassins were said to be the ones who did the hands-on murders," Rune told him, his voice unsteady. "It was rumored they had red eyes and no faces. The perfect demon killer."

"They do," Amestoy affirmed. He would never forget the fight with the Warlock with the scarlet eyes. They haunted his past and fore-visions and he was certain of their reality and deadliness. "Is that the effect of Black Majiq? It eats away at the vessel?"

Rune thoughtfully rubbed his chin. After moments of contemplation, he considered, "Exactly. Kyre and Maksym wield power over the Diaboliq. And the Sinisters have risen again, in force," Rune concluded. "And they are targeting the Maji, of course, since we are the first line of defense against evil for the kingdoms."

"As we complete our missions for the Order," Artemis told Amestoy, "We investigate the trail of Gadion-Obscura. Where are they now, where is their hidden base of power? How can we defeat them? We are more focused in our investigations than Merlin has been in the past."

Nodding, Amestoy quietly defined, "The tip of the spear."

"Precisely," Artemis confirmed.

"The pertinent question is where Kyre and Maksym are hiding?" Gwen joined in.

"And where to hunt down the Diaboliq," Rune reminded.

Artemis scowled at him and offered, "It is slow work." Her voice was colored with frustration. Then she turned to Amestoy and smiled. "And now young man, you will be part of it."

A grin flitted on the Amed's lips. "I am – honored." His face adopted a familiar expression of mirth. "Do I need to take an oath? Or swear on some sacred object? Or sign my name in blood? And yes! I accept! Thank you!"

The women were more amused than the Mentor. "Tyro!" Rune glared as he realized his charge must have known something of this before. Through the Bond? He would have to find out later.

"What do we do now?"

"Eager, isn't he?" Artemis asked Rune.

"Very." To his Tyro he answered, "We do nothing overt, yet. We follow Merlin's commands. At the same time, we investigate the Gadion-Obscura that we defeated. Where they came from, what their origins are, their identities if possible. Elementary facts."

"If we find their path through Ayelsborne, and what Threshold they used we'll know more," Gwen added. "That will be our mission," she waved toward Artemis.

As much as he reveled in this new aspect of life as a Maji, Amestoy wondered if the League was necessary. Wouldn't Merlin and every other Maji be out to find the evil twins now? Wouldn't Maji take the fight to the Gadion-Obscura? Rune was skeptical that they would. Chaos was bubbling throughout the kingdoms. Maji were tied up in policing the realms. It was exactly what the twin demons wanted. They thrived on, and hid behind, disorder and strife. The League needed to slip through the factions and search out the leaders of the opposition.

"It doesn't sound very exciting," Amestoy admitted.

"Not every day in the life of a Maji is exciting, but I would think that in the last several days you've had enough thrills to tide you over for a while." The exuberant youth did not look like he agreed with the sage comment, but Rune was more than ready to have time to meditatively reflect on all that had happened to them.

**

For once, his Mentor was so wrong. Every day so far as a Tyro had been beyond exciting! And this day was starting out to be one of the best that he would ever have in his entire life. As he and Rune stood on the green plain behind the manor, Amestoy's heart raced as he watched the sky. Gradually two small dots grew larger, finally distinguishable as dragons! One, the large blue/green/teal, Pen. The other dragon, somewhat slighter, was a pale grey/white with light blue bands around the neck and wings. Both were graceful and majestic as they soared through the air with mighty speed. They swooped down in a semi-circle, before gliding to a halt just in front of the Wizards.

With healthy respect for the size and power of the beasts that were bigger than cottages, Amestoy reached over to the smaller dragon and petted the neck. The scales were more feathery and pliable than Pen's. The blue eyes, identical to the hue of the sky, watched him as he stroked the long wings. Like the larger dragon, this new one had a collar woven with gems that matched the shading of the skin.

"Her name is Agate. She is Pen's little sister."

Agate. A Majiq name for the mineral that was said to cure poison and stop storms. Those who were aligned with this gem were independent. And such a talisman could make its match victorious over foes. Those were certainly qualities they needed in their fight against Diaboliq!

Amestoy was puzzled by the actions of the lovely creature. "She seems like she's happy to see me."

"She is. She is your dragon."

The young man gulped, awed and thrilled at the prospect of his own dragon! Then he threw his arms around her neck, startling his Mentor. Leaning close to him, the dragon seemed to be returning his affection.

"Thank you, thank you, Mentor! So much!" He raced over and hugged Rune, then ran back and embraced his new dragon again. "I can't believe I have a dragon!"

"It was not my idea," Rune admitted. "It was Pen's. And Agate's."

Startled, Amestoy allowed his mind to be open to the thoughts and feelings surrounding him and surrendered a grin of understanding. "Yes! I have a dragon! Whoa, this is so amazing!"

Rune's sigh said a great deal about his mood. "Patience, Amestoy. Agate is a young dragon. She has never had a Dragon Lord. You will be her first."

His excitement could not be dampened by the stern Mentor. "Great! We'll be learning together!"

With a shake of his head, Rune gave another long sigh. "Just listen to me. And her, and she will listen to you also. It is a two-way communication between Dragon Lord and dragon."

Amestoy's thrill level heightened. "Like a Warrior Bond?"

Thoughtfully, the Mentor gave a small shrug. "I suppose so. Like the Bond that we share," he gestured to his Tyro, "the link with a dragon and rider is one of mutual respect, protection, and survival. In the olden days Dragon Lords and their mounts saved the kingdoms. It may come to that again in these perilous times."

Even as the words were spoken a chill passed through each Maji, their touch-rings sparked with a faint ember of light.

Rune sucked in a sharp gulp of air. "We must return to the house. There will be a message on the crystal ball."

With a bow of his head and a last, lingering pet on the neck of Pen, Rune dismissed the large dragon. Amestoy emulated the ceremony and Agate turned, following her older brother into the air. He had to run to catch up with Rune, who was trotting toward the manor. Once inside, they settled into the library where the walls were lined with books and the air smelled of leather, must and Majiq smoke. He would have loved to live here for weeks in this room of knowledge, but there were important matters to address.

Forcing his curious mind to not speculate, but be patient, Amestoy concentrated on the swirling red mist within the opaque ball atop a stand, as a vision of Merlin solidified.

"Grave news, Maji. The Gadion-Obscura is laying waste to Karpatia, on Earth. This time, they are not using wyverns against the people. They have enslaved Ayelsborne dragons as their weapons."

Amestoy felt Rune stiffen and take in a sharp breath. There was no time to comment. Merlin hurriedly concluded, "Get there with all haste!"

The crystal went dark, Merlin not waiting for a reply.

Rune was already on the move toward the grassy area where Pen and Agate, somehow knowing they were needed, had returned. "My apologies again, Tyro. I did not expect to plunge into another battle so soon. It is the curse or your generation, and all good people, I am afraid. Rising evil must be put down and we are on the front lines of this war." He reached his dragon and stopped, spinning around to face the younger man. "You are under no obligation to go wi –"

"I go where you go, Mentor. It is part of the Bond." The words were stern, almost ferocious.

A tight, quick smile was instantly replaced with a grim expression as he clapped a hand on Amestoy's shoulder. "Good lad. I thought as much. Mount your dragon. You and your beast will see battle today. Trust to your instincts, and those of Agate, who will take her lead from Pen. We will protect you as we can, but it sounds like the long-awaited Diaboliq conquest is at hand. We must fight to preserve Dragonshire and all we hold dear."

Amestoy agreed and rushed to gather his cloak, pouches and wand. Glancing back, he saw that the dragon collars were glowing with embers of color, indicating they were in tune with each other and their masters. A flush of excitement flowed through him and he quickly gathered all he would need to face their enemy. Returning as quickly as possible, he saw that Rune was already seated on Pen, and he wasted no time in settling in on the back of Agate. The beasts jumped into the air, their massive wings beating to lift into the sky. They banked, and then dove, flying low and fast into the forest and a moss-encrusted ravine. It seemed that Rune and Pen were about to crash into a jagged cliff when a cloud of Majiq dust and dragon fire spit into the air. A crevice appeared, then parted, the gaping maw seeming to reach out and swallow the pair from sight.

**

In ancient days the Threshold was protected by spells and Maji from Dragonshire – the keepers of order for the kingdoms. Faery trickery, however, allowed Elves and other Majiq creatures, including dragons to slip through the Threshold into Earth and other domains. Dragon Wizards were then called upon to bring them back. The borders between worlds were easily traversed by the enchanted. Thus, Earth was filled with tales of being threatened by dragons and all manner of supernaturals. Diaboliq, in the days when they murdered the queen, allowed enslaved dragons and Dark Majiq practitioners to seep through the Thresholds.

Plunging through the tunnel of light, mist and infinitesimal shards of matter, Rune and Pen broke through the filmy lip of the Threshold with a pop, followed seconds later by Amestoy and Agate.

Surrounding them was grey sky and dank drizzle. The rancorous odor of sulfur-scorch, was intermingled with by the smell of dragon fire and blood; and the stench of death. The world seemed engulfed in wavering shadow, punctuated by cries of pain and terror. They landed in the midst of a pillaging rampage where evil stormed through the simple villages of the Slavic moors and cut a swath of destruction along the looming mountains.

Swooping low from the craggy crevice of the Threshold, Pen dived close to the ground, stretching out his scaly neck and wings as he soared toward the enemy. Much like the Warrior Bond, Rune and his beast were attuned through Majiq, sharing common impulse and reflex, instinctively homing in on the heart of the foe. Knowing Amestoy was close behind, they were the tip of the spear as they converged on their prey.

Plunging down from the spires of looming, foreboding mountains, sharply scaled dragons with spiky wings attacked the villagers. Amestoy recognized the beasts as Tatzlwurm — Austrian mountain dragons – vicious and deadly. Gems gave them warmth and power, and it was said they guarded their hilltop crags with fatal, poison-laced blood that oozed from their teeth, claws and spikes!

Girding his courage, Amestoy gave a reassuring pat to Agate, mentally warning her to be careful!

Ahead, through the misty rain and beyond a snaking river, was a hamlet afire. Terror was one of the most effective of the Diaboliq tools. Simple farmers and merchants, the villagers of the Karpatia, all knew of the enchanted beings from other dimensions. Living so close to a Threshold, their nights were guarded against otherworldly beings, their days spent in watchful wariness for visitors from enchanted realms. Gypsies roamed the land with spells and incantations designed to ward off the worst of devilish invaders.

Folklore and nomad superstitions, however, were no match for the new horrors emerging from Dragonshire. Diaboliq had encroached this time. For some, rescue was too late. Rune would do his best to stave off the threat, even conquer if possible. But this time it would require more than a gypsy chant, a string of garlic, or a sprinkling of wolfs-bane to save the native population.

At the center of the hamlet a church and other buildings were aflame. Corpses ringed with scarlet were discarded like refuse on the avenues. As they swooped through the pathways their nostrils were assaulted by the acrid reek of blood, scorched flesh and pungent dragon venom. People cringed and ran when they saw the flying dragons, but Rune could not stop to reassure that he and his Tyro were on their side. Shifting and turning through the narrow lanes, he saw, in the cobbled center of the village square, the source of wickedness had taken a stand.

Two tall, thin Diaboliqs each held a chained, Tatzlwurm dragon. Fire dribbled from the beasts, all eyes glowed red. Minions of these controllers ran through the streets, burning, killing, terrorizing as they moved to destroy the town. The Diaboliq and their animals seemed to feed on the horror.

Targeting the easily identified leaders, Rune nudged with his knee to angle right into the square. Even more pronounced and scalding than the heat of the brimstone cinders, was the overhanging pall of suffocating evil. Pen flinched, but Rune urged him on. The two Diaboliq observed as shrouded minions dragged a metal chest out of the burning building. A church. Glistening in the reflected flames licking around it, the treasure trove shone with uncommon brightness. The Diaboliq pulling it into the square would not touch it; they used a cloak wrapped around the sides to bump it over the cobblestones. Of course. Gold was pure. Corrosive to evil. Inside must be holy relics. Things Diaboliq must destroy to survive in this proximity.

Amestoy drew in a sharp breath, clutching to Agate's neck as an unbidden picture filled his mind:

In the reflected glimmer of dragon breath, the gold of the chest nearly blinded Amestoy. As he blinked, fore-tell blackened all but the edges of his mind's eye. He saw a flaxen-haired, regal man burned by the dragons. His blood sizzled from the flames and poison corroded the skin. He was infected . . . .

The scream of an attacking beast jarred him from the mental scene... Confused at what it meant, disconcerted he had received this vision on the brink of battle, Amestoy concentrated on supporting Rune in the attack. He dared one last glance at the golden chest in the town square. There was something Majiqal about that treasure trove; an energy that called to him. But there was no time to sort it all out now!

More Tatzlwurm swarmed from above! These most feared, mountain crag-dwelling dragons, descended with glistening claws and fangs extended. Their razor-sharp, barbed scales saturated with seeping poison from their blood. As they turned in a wide circle a curtain of fire, seemingly shot out of nowhere, incinerated a cluster of the enemy beasts. A whoop of warrior excitement echoed in the confines of the close street. Rune turned, and over his shoulder saw a thrilling sight! Five mounted dragons wearing the livery of the Garraden Royal Army cascaded in from all sides, attacking the Tatzlwurm! Two lead dragons and their riders arched down and swiveled low, the men giving salutes, and then screaming onward to continue their offensive. Just behind them astride a sage green dragon, appeared Artemis, who gave them a cavalier wave as she flew past.

Rune returned their salute, then wheeled his mount around for another sweeping pass through the main street. Roaring out flames, Pen blazed a swath of fire along the pavement. It reached the two Diaboliq, but was warded off with a shower of black glitter thrown into the air. Rune stretched out his arm and a touch-stone beam seared into the circle of unearthly forms. Deadly potions were hurled at the Maji, but Rune's touch-stone shot through it all. Then the pair of demon-dragons leaped, striking out at him, but could not connect while bound with chains.

Through Bond-thought, Rune ordered Amestoy to distract the imprisoned beasts using Agate and Pen as his allies. Knowing he was protected by his shielding Tyro, Rune jumped from Pen's scaly back and landed on the other side of the Diaboliq.

Using his touch-stone sparks to strike at them, he wielded his wand to sweep away their black dust. Under the screeches of beasts and cries of terror, he heard the chilling chants of spell-cast from the Diaboliq. Aside from their pure evil, there was an unnerving aura about them that he had never felt before. No . . . he had! In their last battle with the Wyverns! And in the swampy mists of Ionia. He had felt this strain of black malevolence. It was as singular and identifiable as a dragon's face. No Dark Sorcerers were alike. Emanating from these two, he felt similar characteristics of Diaboliq, but one element was unmistakable. One was the Warlock who tried to kill them on several separate occasions.

Their faces turned to him and even experienced, battle-proven Rune was shocked. Not just their eyes, but their entire faces glowed red, their long teeth dripping with blood, their black cloaks soaked in human scarlet.

The Warlocks ultimately responsible for the death of Tor and so many others were before his very eyes! Rune understood the nature of that familiar wickedness – so pungent, so vile he could taste it! The Warlock encountered before was bent on destroying him! Well, so be it! They were now face-to-face. Let the fight be decided. And Rune had every intention of being the only one to walk away. The air had become thick with smoke, fumes and acidic rain. Clouds hugged close to the ground. The entire world was a colorless grey, punctuated by errant flares of flame and echoing with cries, snarls, shouts and thunder. Tatzlwurm seemed to spread out of the heavens, their deadly dragon shapes descending upon the earth, fire belching and claws extended. With a flap of his robe, one of the twins spurred the beasts on, laughing in sheer malevolence as he commanded the lethal creatures to attack. They came at Rune together, the Diaboliq Sorcerers crowding in to surround and overpower him with a haze of potion-silt.

Rune continued his touch-stone assault, with Amestoy following his lead. Knowing Pen and Agate would defend them from behind. He regretted the noble dragons might die in defense of the wizards. There was no choice. Gadion-Obscura could not gain the power of these prized relics, whatever they were. The cost of this brazen attack demonstrated how valued this treasure was by the wicked twins, and if it was that important, they must not obtain it!

An agonizing cry came from over his shoulder. Rune winced. Pen had been injured. He felt and heard it, but knew the trusted mount was still fighting. Even to the death they were bound to defeat evil.

They were making no progress. Rune had to change tactics or they might all die. Aware of the battle raging all around him, his Tyro and dragons weakening, he made his move. Boldly shutting down his touch-stone, he ran between Pen and a clawed Tatzlwurm, and then rolled to the side of another enemy dragon, throwing blinding Majiq dust into its eyes. As the beast screamed, he leaped over the slumped neck and came up to the side of the church.

At that moment, the Garraden riders descended, their dragons blowing flames across the cobblestones. Rune sparked white light into the air. His left hand stretched out toward heaven, and drew in the combined energies of sky, wind, rain and smoke. The searing glow from his touch-stone glinted with power. It sizzled and burned the particles, lighting the square, the entire atmosphere, with flame.

Other touch-stone streams also poured into the center battlefield. As the magnetic conflagration of crystal energy and Maji enchantment surged, it swept like a glowing wave across the dark sheets of pelting rain. As it touched the Diaboliq Sorcerers there were pops and flashes of fire as the power of good destroyed the evil.

The Diaboliq screamed as dazzling, alabaster combustion ignited from the very air, traveled along the blood-soaked cobbles, and incinerated their cloaks. The twins flared with an incandescent surge, consumed in the white, yellow, orange heat of Majiq fire! In their death throes, they charged at Rune. Simultaneously aiming their cinder wands, they shot out black dust heading right at him.

With a whoosh of sound, flame and wind, Agate, and Pen seared the square with fire. The blue/silver of Amestoy's touch-stone sparked and mingled with Rune's azure flash. The combined blaze swept onto the twin standing in front of the other.

Rune knelt, aimed, and shot off streaming blue light as clean as a burnished blade. The light struck the golden chest, glancing off the curved lid, and directly into the torso of the nearest Diaboliq Twin. The enraged scream was agony itself as Rune threw every ounce of energy into the crystal power. The second twin snarled, grabbing his brother's arm, but the touch was scalding and he jerked his hand back in fear and rage.

All at once, light, sound and matter exploded!

Rune reacted instantly, curling into a ball at the last split-second, repelling the heat and fire with his robe. When Rune regained his senses he was on the ground. The heavy air was rank with the coppery bite of blood, his hands and face sticky with bits of scales and flesh. A smoldering pit marred the cobblestoned square, black cinder scorching the ground for many steps. The carcasses of the Tatzlwurm were crumpled on the street. A clawed hand extending from a smoking cloak was all that remained of what was once a Diaboliq twin.

Anxious to check on his Tyro, Amestoy shook his head and leaned on Rune as he came to his feet. Thin strands of acrid smoke defied the splattering drizzle and rose in snaking trails into the sky while assorted mounds of ash marred the flagstones.

"Only one," Rune whispered.

"What?"

"There were two sorcerers . . . ."

"Where's the other one?"

Around him others came to their feet. Confident that Amestoy was fine, Rune moved to make sure that the dragons, the Garraden riders and Artemis and her mount were all well. Gripping his wand, he slowly approached the charred enemy, his nose wrinkling at the foul stench. Others crowded around him.

Amestoy wanted to stare at the destruction of evil, but was compelled to study the man beside him. It was the blond man of his fore-tell as they were going into battle. Beyond the man was Pen, who was still on the ground, a bleeding gash on the scaly neck, not coming to his feet as did the other dragons. Then the blond man, who was also injured, slapped a hand on his lacerated arm and cringed, falling to his knees. He was caught by the Cadre commander and gently eased to the ground.

The vision, the injuries, the solution came to Amestoy in the flash of an instant. He ran to Agate and commanded her in the language of the ancient dragons to expel fire! With a sweep of his touch-stone light he corralled the flame into a spinning ball of glowing sparks, then shot it to the open wound on Pen's neck. Forming another sphere in the air, he sent that one onto the blond man's arm.

With a final flash of bright white light, the wounds disappeared. The injuries were sealed, leaving only the stain of dried blood and the thin, scarlet line of a scar on both the dragon rider and the dragon.

Rune caught his breath, then reached out and hugged Amestoy. "You healed them!"

The Tyro nodded, but could not respond before he was slapped on the shoulders by the blond man. "You saved my life! I owe you, young Maji. Thank you!" He rubbed his forearm. "It stings like a dragon scratch, but it's better than dying."

"Or worse," the Cadre commander deeply intoned, grim as he checked out the injury.

Amestoy just shook his head. He didn't understand all that had transpired, obviously. He thought he had saved Pen and the warrior from poison. What was worse than death? He petted Agate's wet, tender nose, then slid his hand along the soft scales that rippled in subtle nuances of blue-silver. Into her ear he whispered his thanks for saving their friend, then reminded those around him that Agate was blessed to carry the namesake gemstone around her halter. It imbued her with the ability to cure poison.

The blond Garraden moved to stand over the burned corpse, taking the attention away from the incident. He whistled. "So this is what Diaboliq look like. And smell like."

The Cadre commander's dark, worried eyes still regarded the blond man with concern and deference. In counterpoint, his voice was sarcastic, as if to show he didn't care that his comrade had nearly died. "Hmph," he commented. "They stink on the inside as well as out. To be expected."

Artemis snorted. "At least he's dead. I can't believe the twins are – were – still alive."

Amestoy crouched down without getting too close to the skeleton.

The Cadre commander cautiously kicked at the corpse with the tip of his boot. "How do we know which one is which? Or does it even matter?"

Artemis touched the robe of the fallen Diaboliq with her wand. A singed, gem-encrusted pouch of enchanted leather slid from beneath the burnt bones. With the tip of her wand she split the material to reveal dark red rubies fused together in a Dark Majiq formation.

"It is said the twin born second by only moments did not possess quite the wickedness of the firstborn. He needed special symbols to aid his Black Majiq. His element was a blood ruby."

"Kyre," Rune breathed between clenched teeth. "The second devil escaped."

A taller, more weathered man with a dark scratch of beard on his swarthy face, and a scar between his brown eyes, gave a nod. "He won't give us the slip a second time, Soren."

"I know he won't." The escape of Maksym, the more dangerous of the two, was bitter, but soothed by the sweet taste of victory at the death of his brother. Kyre, he was certain, was the one who had killed Tor and now met his demise at Rune's hand. Fitting. The only justice he would ever have, he wagered. "I will find Maksym again," Rune vowed. "There will be no true satisfaction until he is dead, too, of course, but that will be another day. Dark Sorcery was given a telling blow today and we can all be happy with that," he told them. "And my old friends let me introduce you to my Tyro, Amestoy Daavv. Amestoy, this is Prince Brishen of the House of Garraden," he gestured to the blond. "And the commander of the Dragon Cadre of Ayelsborne, Alesser Keir."

Not sure what to do, the youth gave a waist-bow and stuttered something even he couldn't understand in his confused fluster. The prince and the leader of the dragon armies! He felt as awed as when he came face to face with Merlin the first time! And Rune! And dragons! Battles, devils, Wizards and royalty! And his own dragon! Life could not get any better! "I helped save a prince?"

"The prince," Brishen corrected. Then flashed a brilliant grin.

"You have a Tyro?" Alesser questioned with a laugh. "What is Merlin thinking these days?"

"Scraping the bottom of the barrel," Prince Brishen countered, snickering.

"All right, you two jesters. Get about your business. Help calm the people. Amestoy and I need to find out why the Diaboliq was looting a church."

The dragons gathered close. To the emerging townsfolk, Rune assured that these beasts, from Dragonshire, were safe. Brishen's regal demeanor, and Alesser's masterful nature aided in reassuring the populous. Maji and Dragon Lords were here to take command of the situation. There would be no more evil visitors in the near future. He could promise that with impunity, because he knew Merlin and other Maji were on their way to keep a guardian here at this Threshold.

Kneeling on the wet cobblestones next to the recovered church property, Rune carefully sparked a shot of power through his wand. The gold lock popped with a slow sizzle. Opening the lid with a sweep of a touch-stone wave Rune, with Amestoy at his side, jumped. Inside the chest was a treasure so profound it took the Mentor's breath away. A small, carved wood dragon with Amed markings. In the talons of the talisman, an indigo pearl was clutched by the claws. Aside from the beauty, the object seemed to throb with waves of energy! The touch-stone rings of the Maji glowed and Rune felt a flush of potent energy.

"What is it?" Brishen wondered.

"A rowan-wood dragon," Amestoy whispered. "It's inscribed in Amed tongue. It is called the Pure Link." His voice quavered as he looked at Rune. "Such a talisman has the power to bind elements that are genuine . . . ."

Alesser cleared his throat. "Why is it in the shape of a dragon? There is – was -- no Amed Dragon Cadre."

"Rowan-wood is splintered from Majiq," Brishen reminded.

"That has nothing to do with the shape," Alesser retorted.

Brishen nudged him with a kick to his boot. "Some respect is wanted here for royalty, commander!" he ordered with a smirk.

The officer merely shrugged.

Artemis recounted the legend of the rowan-wood. Said to spring from the branches of a Devonshire witch's tree.

Imbued with the spark of originality, it enhanced fore-tell talent, and shaped order. It was a force to ward off evil, and the enemy of Darkness. The pearl was a symbol and agent of virtue.

Order, fore-tell, goodness, protection against evil. The thoughts swirled around in Amestoy's mind like a whirlwind of myths, bits of legends, Amed instinct, and a growing sense of awe. Everything pointed to this as a completion and enhancement to the Warrior Bond. That it was connected to him he knew on a level as deep as his soul.

Knowing it was what he needed to do, Amestoy reached out and clasped the talisman in his hand. At the same instant, Rune's fist shot out to stop him, and their fingers knotted around the wooden dragon.

The vision was not a fore-tell, but a past-scene. It was the battle on Amed when he had been orphaned. No, he had been left without a mother, but his father had come to rescue him. His father was the great Wizard and Dragon Lord Tor Ion-Gawain. As they retreated from the field of death, Tor placed a Majiq dragon amulet around his son's neck.

Tor Ion-Gawain was Amestoy's father. And through the Warrior Bond, Soren Rune, Tor's closest friend, now knew the truth, too. The clues had been visible all along but he never put them together. The change in the touch-stone color, the choosing of the dragons and crystals that matched those of Ion-Gawain and Rune from Ayelsborne. Amestoy was the blend of two mightily enchanted species and he would bring strength and a future to Amed again, while taking depth from his father's Ayelsborne heritage. And Soren Rune, the brother/friend of the fallen Wizard, would be his Warrior Bond Mentor. As the past-vision came to an end, Amestoy and Rune shared a settled calm. They knew the past, their mission, and their future.

Knitting it all together – the Warrior Bond!!

Amestoy blinked, stepping slightly away, drawing in deep breaths, staring at his Mentor. Tears glistened on Rune's face. Instead of wiping them away, he moved over and drew Amestoy into a tight embrace. For long moments neither spoke, both too overcome by tender emotion to use any words. But the Bond translated the feelings; gratitude, awe, in this new revelation that clarified so much.

This was the reason they were fated to be together. Amestoy could not have a mother and father here to rear him. So the closest person his father had to a brother would fill in and take the place of Tor.

Holding him at arm's length, Rune smiled with a warmth that had never been in his expression before, a profound concern that deepened the richness of his blue eyes. Both the dragon rings and amulets came to life with an inner glow. Even the crystals in the dragon harness's – silver/blue agates on the little sister and blue/teal Aventurine on Pen's -- were alight.

"So much is explained," Rune whispered, his voice cracking. "So much." He shook his head and put an arm around Amestoy's shoulder. "The dragon ring and amulet, the ability to empathize with dragons. The color change in your touch-stone." He gently cupped Amestoy's talisman in his hand. "Your father left this for you." His voice cracking with emotion. "Majiq has guided your journey from him. To me."

"Through the Warrior Bond," Amestoy reminded. "Do you think that is what you shared with my father and never realized it?"

The theory was amazing. Tor had been like his brother. Perhaps that was what a Warrior Bond meant. Not sure that it mattered, he concluded with pleasure, "It all makes sense now."

The boy could only nod. When he felt his voice was steady enough, he recounted his dream-vision. It was easier to speak of it now that his relationship with his Mentor was not only explained, but cemented. Protected within the Warrior Bond and linked to a powerful Wizard and formidable dragons, the memory of the terrible slaughter was tolerable. His mother and her clan murdered, the heroic rescue by his father. Finally, heart-pain tempered with humility that he was part of two dynamic heritages, and an even more profound and legendary Majiq Bond.

Rune placed the talisman onto the clasp holding Amestoy's Dragon pendant and crystal. Double blessings of power. Added to the natural abilities of a child of Amed and Dragonshire, there was no telling how vital young Amestoy would be in their future. Rune only knew that for now, the Warrior Bond had solidified them as close as any blood-relation family.

**

On the outskirts of the small hamlet the Wizards and dragon riders sat with the prefect of the township. The woman was old and worn by a hard life of farming in the harsh and wintery climate. Descended from gypsies, Madame Turline gave them the background of why the devils Kyre and Maksym had plagued their small village.

While they drank their mead around the crackling embers of the fire in the hearth, they listened to the old woman's scratchy voice. Amestoy could envision the tale with such rich clarity it was as if he was reliving the old story. With the cold barely held back by the walls of the warm pub, he could understand that Karpatia was an ancient land with the tendrils of Majiq and lore still alive in society.

Back in the days of the Avelon kings and queens, Turline reminded them, Karpatia served as the main Threshold between worlds. As everyone knew, three sons – triplets – were born to the royals. The eldest was set to inherit all. The younger brothers – Maksym following his older sibling by only minutes, and Kyre born last – devised a plan to kill and rule in place of the rightful heir.

The foul deed was done in this very town. Maksym and Kyre pledged their souls to the Darkest powers of fire and earth, using an ancient and Black Majiq to change into creatures that would live forever by drinking the blood of the righteous. They succeeded in murdering their brother, and went on to murder the old king and queen. Their secret society of Gadion-Obscura – the dark and hidden – helped ravage Dragonshire and all the worlds connected through the Thresholds.

Merlin and his Maji countered, decimating the evil Sorcerers. The secret band dissolved, and Merlin thought they were gone forever. The damage, however, was lasting in

Dragonshire. The queen and her court murdered, a new line, the House of Garraden, became the ruling order. The Avelon line – Merlin's own heritage – was forced from power.

Alesser placed a hand on Prince Brishen's scarred arm. "This is why it was so deadly to have blood drawn by Kyre or Maksym's dragons. The Dark Sorcerers are -- were -- blood sucking creatures of Darkness. Brishen's arm is not healing." He was angry and desperate. "It is Dark Majiq. You must do something, Soren!"

Rune shook his head. "The Majiq is working, Alesser. It will be fine."

Brishen shrugged. "I've gotten worse injuries training dragons, friend Alesser. Don't be such an old mother dragon."

The ribbing did not alleviate the concern. Artemis leaned over and examined the wound. She withdrew some silver powder from a pouch and sprinkled it over the prince's skin, then rubbed it in with a crystal.

"It will heal, but it will take time," she advised. "Dark Majiq is potent against thin bloods like royals." She finished her tease with a wink.

Amestoy brought the focus back to what he really wanted to know. "They really drink blood?" he cringed.

"They thrive on it!" Alesser assured.

Despite Rune's scowl, Amestoy asked for more details. Turline revealed how the twin murderers became the vilest of the walking dead. Immortal to death by normal means, they could be killed only by dragon fire, beheading, dragon poison or pure crystal power. A blade made from the ash or rowan tree also worked. They could bring others into their cause, either willingly or unwillingly, through forcing the wicked to drink their blood.

Amestoy gulped, taking a long drink of mead to get the imagined, coppery, salty taste of blood from his thoughts. And throat. "Why don't you wizards teach this at our classes when we are at the Castle?"

"Too ghoulish for the likes of the young," Alesser supplied. "In this day and age you will learn soon enough, I'm afraid."

"We never thought the twins would resurface," Rune replied.

"Until recently," Artemis continued, "They were more legend and myth than real. At first Merlin felt the resurgence of the Gadion-Obscura and Diaboliq was just an attempt to mimic the twin's horrible exploits."

Everyone at the table was thoughtfully silent. Rune released a heavy sigh and broke the weighted silence. "To our loss, we learn too late that true evil is very real." Rune's sad countenance was a reminder that taking a stand against the Darkness rising came with a high cost.

PART SEVEN
BROTHERHOOD OF THE BOND

Rune stroked the long neck of Pen, who leaned appreciatively into his Master's touch as the crystals embedded in the harness sparkled in the sunlight. "You see, he is all healed. Thanks to your quick thinking, Amestoy."

"And Agate's restorative powers."

"That, too."

"Why didn't the prince heal as quickly?"

"I don't know." Rune was concerned about that also, but chose not to reveal that to the young hero of the day. They would relish their hard-won victory for now. And he would keep in touch with Alesser to make sure Brishen was all right after being exposed to the Diaboliq poison. "But I'm sure he will be fine."

Amestoy's brow furrowed in concern. "He won't turn evil, will he?"

Although still uneasy, the possibility seemed absurd. "No, he is the prince! Too much arrogant blood in his veins. Besides, Alesser would never allow it! He is a mighty protector of his liege." While he had lost his closest friend, he appreciated the loyalty of those who surrounded him now. The most solid of those allies being his Warrior Bond Tyro.

"Now, my courageous Tyro, it is time to leave for Avelon."

"Can't we return to Ayelsborne? I love it there."

Heartened, Rune smiled briefly. "We will be back there, I promise. It is part of you, as it was such a rich homeland for your father. But we must return to Avelon."

"Of course." Still coming to terms with the shocking revelations and powerful emotions, he knew that much more lay ahead. "What about Pen and Agate? I will miss them so much. I just barely earned a dragon and now she is being taken out of my life!"

Amused at the histrionics, Rune informed him that was how they were returning to the Castle.

"We'll be riding our own dragons? Dragon's breath! I have never seen dragons at the Castle!"

"They are usually not allowed. But Merlin is about to make an exception."

Here was some of Rune's legendary rogue attitude coming to the fore. Amestoy shook his head, more amused than concerned. "I am sure Merlin will make an exception for you."

The dragons lowered their wings and allowed the Wizards to give a Majiq leap and settle onto their backs. Then they launched from the soft earth and banked away from the manor, sliding into the sky and clouds. It was all Majiqal for Amestoy, who vowed he would never tire of this amazing form of travel!

Then they dipped down along the sea coast and turned slightly under a rock bridge arching over a cavern. The walls were barely wide enough for the wingspan of Pen, but they managed to fly inside without disaster. Unable to shout loud enough to be heard above the flapping of the mighty wings, Amestoy's curiosity was felt by Rune and the dragons.

One word returned into his mind: Threshold.

Dragon's breath! He was about to exit this doorway into Avelon's on the back of his own dragon! As if the forces of Majiq might tear him apart from his mount, he held tighter to the harness and took a deep breath as the walls and light around them started to pop and it felt, to his stomach, that he was falling down a deep, whirlpool pit!

In a few blinks of an eye he was in a damp, foggy tunnel, and then they flew out into the grey and familiar feel of their island home. Avelon. Through thick, soggy trees and drooping branches they swerved in and out of the woods, drifting along a coastline shrouded with vapors. Then they emerged into the cloudy sky above the Castle. The sight took Amestoy's breath away as they soared over the turrets and spires and Rune directed them to land within the enormous courtyard.

Wizards stopped and stared. People were hanging out of the windows gawking at the amazing sight. Keeping his composure, Amestoy slid down the neck of Agate as if it was the most natural thing in the world. Inside, he was bubbling with pride. He left here over a week ago as a callow and nervous Tyro, whom many of his peers believed to be unworthy of Rune. Now he returned as a Dragon Rider and a Legion member, partnered within a Warrior Bond! He would never brag of his honored experiences, or the sacred mantle he shared with his Mentor. But it felt so fantastic to return in such triumph!

"Humility," Rune whispered, then smiled, as he passed Amestoy and strode around the stable master. The large man with a flowing, grey beard stepped toward them slowly, his mouth open. Without batting an eye, the Wizard-Mentor ordered, "See to our dragons, please," and then tapped his Tyro on the shoulder, indicating he should follow.

Resisting the urge to look back or around, Amestoy was content to wear his smile on the inside. Never having a great desire to be famous, or infamous like his Mentor, he acknowledged that it felt very good anyway. He ground to a skidding stop, though, sliding into Rune's back, when Merlin blocked their way into the arched doorway of the Castle.

Cool and calm, Rune gave a respectful nod to the great Wizard-maj. "Merlin."

There was a twinkle in the eyes of the Majiq leader, who slowly smiled as he surveyed the dragons, then the two recent arrivals, then back to the dragons. Finally, his gaze settled on Amestoy. He raised an eyebrow, and looked to Rune.

Not intending to shower the great Merlin with questions just yet, the need to know burned within, and Rune confronted the great Wizard directly. "Merlin, you never told us about Tor." He gestured at Amestoy, and lifted the leather of the talisman around the boy's neck. "Amestoy is Tor's son! He left this amulet for Amestoy, didn't he?"

Merlin gave a slow nod. "I wondered when you would deduce the truth." Holding up his hands, he admitted, "We have much to discuss, my dear Maji. Know that you have been tested and deserve an explanation. It will be more certain, and satisfying, to savor the veracity of your – bond," he gave them a slight nod, "than if I had told you those long days ago when you first met."

Feeling somewhat irked that he had been misled, Rune could not deny the sagacious methods. Amestoy had earned his love and respect before he knew the boy was his best friend's child. He had acknowledged the Warrior Bond and accepted this boy into his life without knowing the deep connection. He sighed and shook his head at Merlin's quirky grin. Amestoy seemed pleased. Vowing there would be more discussion about this later, Rune changed the subject.

He pulled from his pack the rowen-wood dragon and handed it to Merlin. "You knew about the connection. Why was this left in a gold chest in Karpatia?"

A little taken aback, Merlin reverently took the figure in his hands. He actually trembled as he studied the carving. "Rowen-wood. Found in the gold chest in the Karpatia chapel. Do you not understand the chest was a dragon treasure? Guarded by a mighty creature born in those mystic mountains?" He stared at Soren Rune as it dawned on the Mentor. Merlin smiled knowingly.

Rune shook his head, and spoke in a heavy tone of emotion. "Rowen. Tor's dragon." Too shocked to speak, pale with wonder and grief, he patted Amestoy's shoulder.

Merlin explained to the boy, "When Tor, your father, was murdered, his dragon disappeared. Now we know he must have hidden away in the mountains from whence he came. Not Ayelsborne, but the ancient keep of the Draconian mountains. Did any other treasure survive?"

Stunned by the new revelations, Amestoy slowly nodded. "Yes. Gold in the chest. And the chest itself. We left it in the village."

"As it should be."

Rune realized with certainty, "The dragons there will take care of it and make sure it is hidden where no demon can find it."

Merlin's eyes twinkled. "Dragons. It has been ages since we have allowed them on Avelon." He cleared his throat and gestured around with his hand. The courtyard was ringed with spectators. "As you can see, dragons cause quite a stir."

Rune smiled in agreement. "Yes, they do attract a great deal of attention. That's only natural, Merlin. They are rather – uh – large."

Thoughtfully, Merlin twirled the end of his white beard. "And they are notoriously rowdy."

"These are my family dragons. They are remarkably well behaved."

Amestoy sputtered a giggle, quickly covering his mouth. Both of the other Wizards stared at him, then back at each other. Merlin had an inkling of a grin teasing at the end of his lips, barely visible around his grey beard. "Well, be that as it may, I trust these dragons will behave themselves better than their master." He gave a last, admiring look at the magnificent beasts. "Always something up your sleeve, Soren. Meet me in the tower chamber after supper, both of you. We must discuss your next venture. I am not at all sure you will be able to take those dragons but," he shrugged as he walked away. "We'll see."

Beaming a smile, Rune gave Amestoy a wink. "He's always liked dragons."

**

"It was AMAZING was it not, Mentor? I know I am not to desire battle or fame, but it was awesome! The prince is your friend! We killed one of the worst Diaboliq! And a dragon! And I am Tor's son! Our whole time together has been more than I dreamed!"

"And that is saying a lot." Rune was unusually somber. "Amestoy." The stern, but soft tone brought an abrupt end to the excited monolog. "You are experiencing the flush of Majiq syncopation." Voice suddenly deep from unexpectedly profound emotions, Rune cleared his throat. "You were valiant and skillful. Now, I command that you meditate. You are a very exceptional young man, but you need to rein in some of that enthusiasm and use it at the right times. Now is your season for recovery. To recharge and refocus. So when we leave on our next quest you will be ready."

Sitting across from each other in the guest quarters over the stables, Rune gathered his scattered thoughts as he gazed across the small space between himself and his Pupil. There was supreme triumph and joy bounding from the Tyro since Rune openly adopted the Warrior Bond as fact and Amestoy was admitted into the League. Not to mention the dragons. And discovering the heritage linking them.

"But it is so fantastic! Don't you understand, Mentor? I never felt so cared for. So integrally a part of – of – everything! Being your greatest friend's son, being a dragon rider, being a Maji!" His eyes glittering with awe and devotion he whispered conspiratorially, "And now a secret Legion! With my own dragon! When can we go riding again?"

"Patience!"

Amestoy giggled. "I thought that was one of our weaker traits!"

"Obviously, I was right. As usual." Giving up all pretenses of teaching and quiet, Rune breathed out a loud and dramatic sigh. "All right. You know my secrets." Rune drew a deep breath, sobering, without humor he admitted, "Here is one more. I am not perfect." The lilt at the end of the sentence showed it was a serious, but also self-effacing admission.

Amestoy grinned. "Really?" The irony was typical and droll.

Yes, the Tyro was still a master at sarcasm and would hold that title for some time. Together they had faced life and death. The experience had taken them beyond anything either could have imagined and Rune felt compelled to confess some deep thoughts to his Pupil. Besides, with that tricky Warrior Bond, his inner heart might be revealed soon enough anyway so best to come clean now.

"I struggled with accepting you as my Tyro. I did not want to believe in the Warrior Bond, as you know. I regret those early prejudices. You are so --" he searched for a description that could possibly fit. "-- so much more than I expected. You have given me back levels of myself that I had forgotten. They were buried deep, Amestoy. Very deep. Locked away ever since I lost Tor." For once his voice didn't crack when he spoke the name aloud. How many years had it been since he'd been able to do so? That, in itself, was a failure he was going to rectify. Tor had been a magnificent brother. How could he live on in the minds of others if Rune didn't share his greatness? "Or maybe those qualities never existed at all, and you have awakened these – noble – traits within me. I am honored, and humbled, to be able to teach the son of my dearest brother-in-arms. Thank you for being open to the Bond when I was not. When I would not, listen."

Was this what it was supposed to be like between Mentor and Tyro -- within families? Such caring emotions and protective devotion, from both sides, on a nearly equal level? It had never been such with other Maji. At least not that he had ever heard. The intensity and depth of dedication was profound. Natural instincts enhanced and amplified by the Warrior Bond? He couldn't be sure. He was now, though, more certain than ever that the Bond was real.

A spark flowed between them. The faith was absolute. The Warrior Bond. A powerful gift to aid in battle. A perfect sync. A family. Everything with Amestoy was different; more intense, more personal. The highs were joyous and frequent. The rare lows, with their deep emotional pain, were profound, but short-lived.

Rune also grudgingly acknowledged the waves of subliminal energy he had experienced since taking on Amestoy as his Pupil. To his surprise, it was almost a relief to accept Amestoy's mystical tie as reality. This was uncharted territory for a jaded Mentor and a new Tyro, but the responding energy eagerly acknowledged that the closeness was appreciated.

"It seems that Mentor and the Tyro learn from each other, don't we?"

"Really?" Some of the teasing humor returned around a yawn. "And I thought Mentors knew everything."

"We do." Rune winked. "And I hope you can keep my secret."

"Promise," he vowed, stretching. The busy week had finally caught up with him. "I have a few secrets of my own you know."

"I'll bet you do."

The Mentor studied his half-dozing protégé. To his amazement, their relationship had quickly transcended from teacher/pupil to parent/child. He now wondered what surprises his Tyro had in store for the future. Whatever they were, Rune looked forward to finding out, anticipating exciting adventures with his son at his side.

THE END

**

Georgina M Donovan's first career choice was secret agent. At age nine that was not a viable option. To bide her time she submersed herself in reading, and writing stories about surfing spies and other adventurers, that took her far from the desert to exotic locations, mostly Hawaii.

Years later, when Georgina announced she had written a mystery novel, everyone who knew her expected it to be set in Hawaii. And they were right. Former business owner of a shave ice shop, her connection with Hawaii goes back many years including frequent visits to family friends on Oahu. Long appreciation of the Islands has brought her a profound love of the aloha spirit and the magic that is unique to Hawaii.

Writing background includes: Sherlock Holmes societies, literacy coach, newsletters, plays, book clubs, creating amateur music videos and a role-play murder mystery. She is also the co-writer of a stage musical.

The culmination of the passions for writing and Hawaii have inspired her mystery novels READS LIKE MURDER IN HONOLULU, READS LIKE MURDER IN KAHALA and coming next: READS LIKE MURDER AT KILAUEA.

A Disneyland fan from childhood, castles, wizards and other worlds were never far from her mind. Forays into the realms of fantasy and science fiction also come from a classic base of fanzines in the days before computers. Her children's fantasy short stories have become a family tradition. As a lecturer at Summer School in Forks Symposium, her interest in supernatural swerved into a new line of enchanted thinking.

DRAGONSHIRE WIZARDS OF THE WARRIOR BOND is the first in a series exploring Merlin, his Order of wizards, and their heroic struggle to keep blood-drinking, Dark wizards from overtaking Earth, and the Majiqal realms where Faeries, Elves, and other supernaturals live.

www.ingramcontent.com/pod-product-compliance
Lightning Source LLC
Chambersburg PA
CBHW070815120626
46556CB00002B/514